RAVE REVIEWS FOR STACY DITTRICH'S CHILLING DEBUT, *THE DEVIL'S CLOSET*!

"Twists, turns and non-stop action."
—*The Mansfield News Journal*

"Dittrich explores every parent's nightmare in this chilling police procedural. The drama is intense and the plot terrifying as Dittrich's police detective heroine leads readers through an intricate maze set to entrap her. CeeCee Gallagher is a highly complex heroine whose private life is in shambles but whose dedication to the job is impeccable."
—*Romantic Times BOOKreviews*

"Stacy Dittrich is an absolute master at devising and then executing a story that is not only realistic but downright chilling. Dittrich's law enforcement background, coupled with her command of descriptive adjectives, made it nearly impossible for me to put *The Devil's Closet* down. She captured the ultimate fear and terrifying reality of a child sexual victim at the hands of a heinous predator."
—Robin Sax, Los Angeles County Deputy District Attorney—Sex Crimes Division, author of *Everything Parents Need to Know about Predators and Molesters*

"CeeCee Gallagher is the real McCoy—gritty and tough, but with smooth edges. She embodies what a true detective needs to be."
—Andrew Peterson, author of *First to Kill*

"A terrific thriller."

"*The Devil's Closet* is a v
speaks from experience."

STAKE OUT AT THE GRAVE

I wasn't in a position to see what she was looking at, but one of the girls with Danielle stopped walking and turned to the woods to her right. What followed was a scream that made my hair stand up on end. All the teens dropped their flashlights, leaving the cemetery in complete darkness, and started running in different directions. All of them were yelling and screaming.

Naomi was screaming, too, on the radio, telling us to move in. I went to grab Coop, but he was gone. I hadn't seen him leave. Over the sounds of the yelling I heard something I couldn't possibly believe. It began low and gradually got louder until it hurt my ears. It was a baby crying. I was spinning my flashlight around trying to see where it was coming from when I heard something behind me. In a flash, I saw a shadow move to my right....

MARY JANE'S GRAVE

STACY DITTRICH

LEISURE BOOKS NEW YORK CITY

Always for Rich, Brooke, and Jordyn

A LEISURE BOOK®

May 2009

Published by

Dorchester Publishing Co., Inc.
200 Madison Avenue
New York, NY 10016

ISBN 10: 0-8439-6160-0
ISBN 13: 978-0-8439-6160-7
E-ISBN: 978-1-4285-0670-1

The name "Leisure Books" and the stylized "L" with design are trademarks of Dorchester Publishing Co., Inc.

Printed in the United States of America.

10 9 8 7 6 5 4 3 2 1

Visit us on the web at www.dorchesterpub.com.

ACKNOWLEDGMENTS

I'd like to thank the usual suspects: my agent, Claire, editor, Don, and friends and family who supported me through these endeavors. Most importantly, to the residents of Richland County, Mansfield, Ohio for keeping the legend of Mary Jane alive and always giving us a good ghost story to tell outsiders.

MARY JANE'S GRAVE

"The first time I went to Mary Jane's Grave, I was young then, only eight years old, but went with sisters and friends. Four people urinated on her tree, and all four are dead today . . . That was 1973."
—graveaddiction.com

"When, however, one reads of a witch being ducked, of a woman possessed by devils, of a wise woman selling herbs, or even a very remarkable man who had a mother, then I think we are on the track of a lost novelist, a suppressed poet . . . "
—Virginia Woolf

"My mother says I must not pass, Too near that glass; She is afraid that I will see, A little witch that looks like me; With a red mouth to whisper low, The very thing I should not know."
—Sarah Morgan Bryant Piatt

"Thou shalt not suffer a witch to live."
—Exodus 22:18

PROLOGUE

March 3, 1898

She had been unconscious only a few moments, but that brief reprieve had been more than welcome. Now, as she opened her eyes and saw the men peering down at her, she prayed for the blackness to envelop her once again.

Her legs were broken, and she was unable to move away. The runt of the bunch and the one with the terrible skin had been responsible, their leader standing apart watching it all, laughing. Now the brightness of their torches was an assault upon her sight, and she closed her eyes to restore the bleak comfort of the dark, cold night.

She opened her swollen eyes and tried to focus on the small lifeless shape that lay ten feet away; it had once been her baby son, Ezra. They had killed him, just as they intended to kill her, and had forced her to watch. Never had she known such anguish, and a part of her had died along with the child. Only her body continued to endure, but for how long? And did it really matter?

She pulled herself up by her arms, feeling blood run into her eyes, blinding her. A sharp pain in her left side forced her to lie down on the ground again. Their kicking had finally begun to taper off. Could they be getting tired? She lay motionless, praying that Madeline had gotten away, if only to be spared witnessing the horrific acts taking place here in front of their home.

She knew the men blamed her for something she'd had no part in, and she rued the day the girl had pulled up in her horse and buggy asking for the medicine. If she'd only known then, she would have sent the girl away and told her never to return. But now it was too late. There was no escaping her nightmare. There was only "the blessing."

Ever since she was a small child, her mother had taught her that the blessing was only to be used for the good of others, not for their downfall. Her mother had had the blessing, as had her sister and her grandmother, and she suspected that Madeline had it, too, although they'd never discussed it. She had wanted to wait until Madeline was eighteen and a grown woman before telling her of the special gift God had blessed her with. But from this day forward, if Madeline escaped from these men, she would be on her own and would have to discover it for herself.

She smelled the sour alcohol on their breath as the men's rough hands reached out to grab her arms and drag her toward the large pine tree that dominated the land in front of her house. She suddenly flashed on an image of her husband, Joseph, who had died two months after Ezra was born. How proud he had been of his son! She hoped they were together now, and she told herself she would be seeing them soon, very soon. She stared at baby Ezra's body one last time as they pulled the rope around her neck, and as it tightened, finally a new emotion rose within her. Rage.

"Die, witch!" the men shouted in unison.

It was then that she made the decision. Putting aside all she had been taught, she cursed these men and vowed they would pay dearly for what they had done.

"Do it!" the leader yelled. And as she felt the rope begin to pull her upward, she used every ounce of her last breath to finish the curse she had begun. *"Ego vomica quisque vestrum, Ego vomica vos totus!"* she managed to croak as the noose grew tighter.

And then the darkness she had prayed for finally came.

CHAPTER ONE

Present Day

The healing rays of the sun shone down on me as I dug my toes into the warm, crystal white sand. Closing my eyes, I listened to the tranquil sound of the waves breaking ten feet away. Michael's hands lovingly caressed my shoulders, and I knew I was about as close as I could get to heaven on earth. . . .

And then the phone rang, and I was no longer on my fantasy beach, but here in bed, my body screaming that I had been asleep for only five minutes. After painfully forcing my eyes open, I focused on the clock next to me.

Wrong! I had been asleep for five hours. I closed my eyes again as Michael sleepily groped toward the phone, picked it up, and mumbled, "Hello?"

I prayed that the call was for him, not me, but I expected the worst. Michael was a supervising agent with the FBI, but rarely got phone calls in the middle of the night. I, on the other hand, received them at least once a week. Because I worked in the major crimes division for the Mansfield, Ohio, Richland Metropolitan Police Department, most calls came straight to me. Still, I prayed the call was for Michael. God, I needed more sleep.

"It's for you, Cee," he mumbled, handing me the phone and snuggling deeper beneath the covers.

Damn! As my dream of suntan lotion and a fabulous

massage ebbed away, I switched on the bedside lamp. "Detective Sergeant Gallagher," I said, trying to sound official.

"Sergeant Gallagher, it's Jan at the Communications Center. There's been a homicide at Mount Olive Cemetery at the end of Tucker Road, and we need you there as soon as possible."

"Are you talking about Mary Jane's Grave? Seriously?"

"Yes, ma'am, we were all talking about that, too. Captain Cooper is already on her way and told us to call you."

"All right, give me half an hour." I cradled the phone, threw on some clothes, and gulped down some O.J. There was no way that I wanted to leave my fiancé and my warm bed to examine a dead body at this ungodly hour. But Mary Jane's Grave added a new level of urgency to this summons.

First, though, let me explain my less-than-eager attitude to leave hearth and home. I've been looking at dead bodies since I was a kid. My father and his two brothers are also policemen with Metro. My uncle Matt, a third brother, had proudly joined them on the force and was building an impressive reputation when he was shot and forced to go on disability. That was almost thirty years ago.

Despite the family setback, Dad and his remaining brothers stayed on to share a combined ninety-five years' experience on the force, and bless them all, they're still going strong.

When I was about eleven, my family began the somewhat bizarre practice of keeping homicide photographs in albums to share with one another at family gatherings. Despite my tender years, I eagerly joined my cousins in poring over pictures of victims who had been brutally disemboweled. My reaction? Awe and wonderment.

Back in the day, I considered all this to be cool. At age fifteen, my dad invited me to ride in his police cruiser for an entire shift, keeping him company and getting a feel for what he did every day. That was the year I saw my first dead body up close, and that was even cooler.

When I was twelve, I shot my first gun. My father was going to the police department's pistol range to qualify the other officers on their weapons. I begged to go, and my mother, utterly horrified at the thought, finally relented when my father promised to closely supervise me. My older brother, Tony, who was sixteen at the time, tagged along, too.

That first gun had been a .38 revolver: a *wheel* gun. Even now I remember the mixture of fear and excitement that rose in my chest when it was time to pull the trigger. I applied the minimal two pounds of pressure and heard a loud *pop!* Jumping back against my father, I exclaimed, "Wow! That was cool." I proudly exchanged a grin with my father, who'd been watching me closely for signs of trauma.

But all he saw was a preteen wearing a wide grin with bullets sticking out of her ears. (When there wasn't enough ear protection to go around, bullets did the trick.)

In fact, I proved to be a damn good shot. After more practice, Dad winked at me and said, "Show 'em how it's done, baby!" I fired six shots from twenty-five yards directly into the center target. Bull's-eye. Of course, I look at guns differently nowadays.

My fascination for law enforcement goes back as far as I can remember. I read my first "adult" novel when I was eight years old. It was about Ted Bundy. The author's take on Ted's homicide spree kept me locked in my bedroom for two days straight until I finished the last page. I would look up from the book and gaze around my room, terrified that my parents could telepathically sense what I was reading. (I had swiped it from my father's bookshelf without his knowledge.)

Never without an escape route, I kept one of my favorite Judy Blume books within reaching distance. If someone knocked on my door, I'd quickly shove Ted Bundy under my blanket and launch into the middle pages of *Shelia the Great* or *Superfudge*.

Yes, law enforcement was all around me, and I was a willing captive audience. Now, after having been a cop for fifteen years, I no longer find it "cool" when I have to deal with victims' loved ones and surviving family members. In fact, it's thoroughly disheartening. Most cops get burned out around their twenty-year mark, but then again, I'm not like most cops.

Breaking into my reverie, Michael asked, "What was that all about? Who's Mary Jane?"

I laughed, a reprieve from my dismal thoughts. Michael had the grace and confidence of a scholar, but could sometimes be as cute as a toddler trying to pronounce "Pennsylvania." He'd grown up in Virginia, the son of a respected FBI agent and a local professor. His first experience in Mansfield came when we met on the Murder Mountain case. At the time, he was living in Cleveland with his first wife, which is why I sometimes have to update him on local history.

"Mary Jane's Grave has been a local haunt for as long as I can remember. Legend has it a witch, Mary Jane, was hanged from a pine tree in the middle of this old cemetery. Supposedly, a burnt cross formed in the tree because she was buried underneath it.

"People tell stories about weird things that happened to them at the grave site. My friends and I would go there when I was in high school, daring each other to stay there for a while."

"Are the stories true?" Michael asked.

"Nope. Obviously, local historians have looked into it. Mary Jane was nothing but an herbalist who cleaned houses, died of cancer, and was buried in a normal grave. There's a campground nearby, so the legend probably got started to scare campers. The cemetery *is* pretty creepy, though."

"Sounds like it. I'll go make you some coffee," Michael offered, now awake. What a guy, I marveled. But then I reminded myself that he'd probably jump back into bed the minute I kissed him good-bye and shut the door. Life wasn't fair.

If someone had told me two years ago that I'd be engaged to Michael Hagerman, I wouldn't have believed it. Two years ago, I'd said good-bye to him for what I thought would be the last time.

Michael and I had met and fallen in love while working a tough case together. I was married at the time to the father of my two children and chose to stay with him. Eric Schroeder, my ex-husband, is—what else—a uniformed officer at Richland Metro. Although I was in love with both men, I decided to save my marriage and said a tearful good-bye to Michael.

Then, last year, Fate brought us back together again while investigating a child's murder case. I tried desperately to fight my feelings for Michael, but they grew deeper and more intense, despite my honorable intentions.

In the end, it didn't matter. I found out that Eric had been having an affair with Jordan Miller, a rookie officer he subsequently got pregnant. That was the end of our marriage and the beginning for Michael and me.

Eric and I share custody of our two daughters, twelve-year-old Selina and five-year-old Isabelle. Without a doubt, these girls are the most miraculous creatures that ever entered my life. My daughters are the reason I wake up in the morning, my reason for living. I hadn't ever known the depth of my own emotions until the girls were born.

Emotion had been a foreign word to me until I became a mother. The expression of feelings had been absent in my house as a child, and I had never seen my father cry, react, or exhibit a shred of emotion. Clearly, this was how a law enforcer behaved.

As a child, if I fell down and skinned my knee, any initial cries were quickly aborted by my father's calm voice asking, "Are you bleeding? Do you need to go to the hospital?"

"No," I would say through quivering lips and blinding tears.

"Then there's no need to cry."

Crying or visible emotions were for the weak, I learned. Don't get me wrong, my father didn't choose to be the way he was. Vietnam and thirty years of policing unquestionably changes a person—and were most likely why he and my mother finally divorced.

I admit it. I have a real blind spot when it comes to my father, and the love and respect I have for the man is indescribable. When my mother moved back to Cleveland, I chose to stay behind with Dad. Tony was already in college, so it was me and Dad, an oddly compatible twosome.

As a single parent, a cop no less, raising a young daughter could be harried at times, but he took it all in stride. Never lecturing, he guided me in the right direction with his stern advice and kind words. He taught me to stand up for myself, become my own person and deal with whatever consequences followed.

Subsequently, by the time I was twelve, I scoffed at such minor occurrences as a bee sting or menstrual cramps. Of course, this proved to be quite an obstacle for me in high school, where I was dubbed the Ice Queen.

My daughters, and ultimately Michael, changed all that. Unfortunately, I was still the Ice Queen while married to Eric, at the helm of a marriage that was doomed from the beginning. My divorce from Eric had been finalized six months ago, and his son with Jordan was now five months old, so everything had worked out just fine. Even Michael's six-year-old son, Sean, got tossed into the mix, staying with us every other weekend. His ex-wife, Vanessa, now lives in Cleveland.

Michael makes the hour commute to the Cleveland FBI office every day and has never complained. It meant the world to him for us to be together; we'd been through a lot. I wore my engagement ring faithfully, but continued putting off a wedding date. I tried not to let my failed ten-year marriage to Eric make me bitter, but sometimes it got the better of me.

After the Murder Mountain case and the hunt for child murderer Carl James Malone, I had become somewhat of a celebrity for a while. I took a book deal and decided to write about my experiences.

The advance alone bought us a monstrous house on the south side of town, something Michael often complained about. He didn't think we needed a house with five bedrooms. But the girls and I loved it. Quite frankly, I could've probably bought the house without the advance. Eric and I always had money smarts, and I was financially better off (even after the divorce) than most cops I knew.

Looking into the mirror for a final inspection before I left, I paused. I saw what everyone else did. CeeCee Gallagher: long blonde hair, piercing green eyes, and a face that, for a brief time, graced the covers of news magazines.

On the outside, I was an attractive thirty-four-year-old woman admired by her coworkers, with a reputation for toughness beyond her years. But deep down, I heard the occasional whisper of insecurity as I found myself questioning my ability to continue pulling off law-enforcement miracles. The curse of high expectations—my own as well as those of my community—was a shadow that followed me everywhere. Sure, it made me a better cop, but I often wondered at what expense?

I sighed. It was time to get my butt out of here and find out why this latest victim was lying dead at Mary Jane's Grave.

Michael handed me my coffee as I was walking out the door.

"Do you want some garlic or something to take with you? I can't have my gorgeous, soon-to-be-wife getting hurt."

"Very cute. There's supposedly a witch buried there, not a vampire," I reminded him.

He grinned impishly as I gulped down my first coffee of the day, welcoming the warm burst of caffeine. "Sorry, I'll be home today brushing up on my creatures-of-the-night facts," he said.

"You'd better," I murmured, kissing him good-bye. "There'll be a quiz when I get home."

On my way to the homicide scene, I turned up the SUV's heater and admonished myself for not grabbing a jacket. Although the days were still warm, the fall nights could be bitter cold.

This murderer had a sick sense of humor. With Halloween just weeks away, the perp evidently thought law enforcement would get turned on by the location. But I was not amused. Although the grave is nothing but a myth, the childhood stories I'd heard about my clairvoyant relatives and bona fide exorcisms were enough to make me fear anything that lacked a pulse. Raised as a good Catholic girl, I don't believe in ghosts, but I do believe in something; I just don't know what that is—yet. Let's just say I respect the dead.

Turning onto Tucker Road brought back a flood of memories. The foothills of the Appalachian Mountains are beautiful terrain by daylight, but very different at night. I hadn't been on Tucker Road since high school. Even after I began working for the force, I wouldn't drive back here; there was no reason to, I told myself.

As the asphalt narrowed into a dirt road and then into something that resembled a hiking trail, I was careful to maneuver my SUV around the deep ruts in the ground. I parked behind the last car in a line of police vehicles, their lights spinning in the darkness like a Friday night disco.

As I walked between the line of cars, I passed two uniformed officers talking to four teenagers seated on the ground. All looked pale and grief stricken. One of the girls was crying hysterically, and I assumed they were the ones who had found the body.

"Excuse me, Officer, are they witnesses?" I asked Jack, the taller of the two men.

"They found the body, Sergeant. You need to talk to them, right?" he asked, knowing the answer.

"Of course. Have their parents been notified?"

"They're on the way."

"Just have them all go downtown and wait for me. There's no sense in them standing out here freezing. I'll probably be a while."

I continued toward the bright floodlights illuminating the cemetery. I felt bad for those kids. Unfortunately, what they had seen tonight was something they would never forget as long as they lived.

The crime laboratory had managed to get its vans

back into the cemetery so they could collect all the evidence and process the entire scene. Until they finished, no one could do a thing. I saw Captain Naomi Cooper, head of the major crimes division, and her husband, Jeff, also a detective, standing by the entrance to the cemetery.

Naomi and I have a shaky past. When we initially started working together after the Mansfield Police Department and the Richland County Sheriff's Department merged to become Richland Metro, things couldn't have been worse. Our personalities clashed in epic proportions. However, during the Murder Mountain case, Naomi ended up getting shot trying to protect me and saved my life. Then, last year, she almost died after getting captured by child murderer Carl James Malone, and our hatchet was forever buried. She married Jeff, "Coop," shortly afterward, and I was her maid of honor.

With all the crime lab equipment and vans, I couldn't see the body, and since I knew nothing about the murder, I promptly asked Naomi, "What happened?"

"Spooky, isn't it, CeeCee?" Coop whispered.

"Not hardly. Prank gone bad or what?"

"I don't think so." Naomi continued to look out over the vans. "It's not pretty. She was strangled, and apparently parts of her body were burned. Someone also cut her wrist."

Not your ordinary recitation of physical abuses. "Why?" I asked.

"Probably to paint the big bloody *M* that's on the tree above her," offered Naomi.

"You mean she's actually at *the* tree?"

"Yes, and wait until you hear what the kids who found her are saying."

"Was there any sexual assault?"

"We don't know yet," Coop put in. "As remote as this

place is, no one would hear anything if there had been."

I looked over at the vans and saw one of the crime lab technicians wave us over. They had finally completed the scene, and we were now free to poke about.

As I came around the side of the van to face the site where the body lay, I felt myself suck in a massive amount of air. The victim, a pretty young blonde, was sitting upright with her back against the tree. Her eyes were open and speckled with broken blood vessels from the strangulation. She was shirtless and braless, exposing odd triangular burn marks that went across her chest just below her neck.

Her arms were down at her sides with the palms facing upward; a large cut across her left wrist had poured blood into her palm. It was this blood that had likely been used to paint the large *M* on the tree directly above her. Like most homicide scenes, it was not for the faint of heart.

One disturbing reaction I tend to have at homicides that involve young girls is superimposing the image of my daughters' faces onto that of the victim. I wonder what it would be like to be a parent and have your child brutalized to the point of death. While just a split-second reaction, the idea always makes me feel momentarily light-headed.

"Good Lord," I muttered under my breath. I began to walk slowly around the body, observing it from a closer point of view. One of the crime lab technicians was standing a few feet away and sauntered over to compare notes.

"What do you make of this, Bob?" I asked. I was pleased to see him here—Bob was one of our better lab techs, and I respected his opinion.

Rubbing his chin thoughtfully, he offered: "Other than

the fact that the murderer was a very disturbed individual, I haven't made much, CeeCee. I took blood samples and photographed the burns. I couldn't find any shoe prints other than hers and those of the kids who walked up here. No trace of any weapon that could have cut her wrist. Her shirt and bra are nowhere to be found. I photographed the kids' shoe treads and took dirt samples from the area and from inside their car."

"What about the strangulation? If it was done manually, you should be able to swab her neck for DNA, no?"

"I don't see any ligature marks, so a manual strangulation would be my first guess, too. The coroner should be here any minute," Bob said, looking toward the road.

"Why don't you go ahead and swab her neck anyway, just in case," I suggested.

"No problem," he agreed. "Nothing else to do while we wait."

I watched as Bob took out a long cotton swab from the back of the van and put a couple of drops of sterile water on it. Wearing latex gloves, he carefully took the swab and rubbed it over the victim's neck. Most people don't realize that during a bare-hand strangulation, the friction between the killer's hand and the victim's neck loosens skin cells from the killer—and those skin cells, which differ from the victim's when tested, hang on tight to the victim's neck.

Our best-case scenario would be that we'd find the killer's DNA and run it through a state-wide database known as C.O.D.I.S., which holds the DNA of anyone ever incarcerated in a state prison. Even if the killer hadn't been in prison before, we could still use the DNA as a match when we found a suspect.

The worst-case situation would be that no DNA would be found, but I wasn't ready to entertain that scenario.

"What was she doing here?" I asked Coop, who was standing nearby.

"According to the kids who found her, they were all here together," he answered.

"How is that possible unless they're responsible?" I asked. "And why didn't you tell me this in the first place?"

"Hey, take it easy," Coop said soothingly. "You'll have to talk to them. Allegedly, they dared the girl to walk back here by herself, and she took the bait." He walked over and stood next to me, looking down at the body. "When she didn't come back, they walked down here to find her, and voila! They claim that no cars passed them on the way in, and there weren't any down here when they found her. They're all pretty torn up. I don't get the feeling that they're lying."

"That's a little strange, though, Coop, don't you think? Is anybody out talking to the nearest residents and farmers?"

"The uniforms are on it."

"Had I known this earlier, I would've blocked off the road from the asphalt on down," I murmured, irritated. "We may have been able to get tire tracks. Now that every cop car in the county is parked down here, it's pretty pointless."

"Don't look at me," Coop said defensively. "Naomi and I got here right before you did."

I was interrupted by the arrival of the Richland County Coroner and his assistant, J. P. Sanders, who, regardless of the circumstances, would have every officer at a crime scene laughing hysterically within minutes. In his late fifties, with gray hair and Coke-bottle glasses, J.P. has an unusual talent for lightening the most intense situation. To his credit, however, he will maintain the utmost professionalism when in the presence of family members.

He has never disrespected the dead; he merely tries to make it easier for us to cope.

J.P. is also the person you'd most want to consult with at a homicide scene. He could look at any evidence and tell you just about everything you'd want to know. Even though the county coroner is an elected position, everyone for the last thirty years has kept J.P. as the assistant—a smart move, since he knew more than all of them combined.

"J.P., long time no see," welcomed Coop. "How's business?"

"Dead."

I smiled as I watched J.P. eye Bob, who was fairly new to the crime lab and had yet to experience a crime scene with J.P. He was fresh, juicy bait. Coop winked at me. We all waited to see what J.P. would do next. He carried his suitcase-sized bag and set it down next to the van.

He started fumbling around in it as if looking for the most important of all tools, and I couldn't stop from bursting out laughing as he pulled out a large-brimmed black witch's hat and put it on his head. The hat was so large it fell over his eyes.

"That's just wrong." Coop laughed, wiping tears from his eyes.

J.P. had more gadgets and one-liners than anyone I'd ever known. I didn't doubt for a minute that when he was called here, he'd known exactly where to find the witch's hat—probably in his bedroom closet. But he wasn't finished with us yet.

Bob's mouth had already dropped when J.P. produced the hat. Now, he was watching intently as J.P. leaned over the victim, still wearing the hat, scanning the body up and down before stopping near the legs.

"Well. I'll be damned. Did anyone photograph this?"

Bob, who prided himself on covering every aspect of a crime scene, darted over to J.P. and put his hands on his hips. "What? I photographed everything!"

"You didn't photograph this, kiddo. Haven't seen one in a while, but this victim has a cheek-for."

"What the hell is a cheek-for?" Bob took the bait hook, line and sinker.

J.P. stood and kissed Bob's right cheek, sending Bob into a tailspin. He violently wiped his hand across his face.

"What's wrong with you? Are you crazy!"

Our laughter prompted Bob to stop and realize the joke he'd just missed. When he caught on, he was quite embarrassed.

"Oh, I get it. Very funny."

"You're lucky he didn't do the butt-for joke, Bob," Naomi laughed.

Once everyone regained their composure, J.P. removed the hat, put the jokes aside, and got down to business. He wouldn't do much here; right now, he was just looking over the body before they bagged it and took it away for more extensive tests. I saw him scrunch up his face and rub his chin as he looked at the marks on the victim's chest.

"What is it, J.P.?" I asked, realizing that he'd seen something.

"These burns," he said, pointing to the marks. "I would bet my wife's fat fanny they came from a fireplace poker. The point is a dead giveaway, no pun intended."

"How would someone keep it hot if there wasn't a fire nearby?" Coop asked. "With a blowtorch?"

"We'll know more by the end of the week. CeeCee, can you forward all your paperwork to me when you're done?"

•   "Of course," I told him. "I'll work up the case as fast as I can. How's a two-day turnaround?"

There wasn't much more for me to do here; the next step was to read all the reports on the incident and get my input over to J.P. It was near daybreak, and I was sure the distraught teens were ready to go home. They'd been waiting at headquarters with their parents for almost two hours now, and their imaginations must have been working overtime.

Sighing, I pulled open my car door and climbed in. I felt tired and cranky; it had been another long night, and I didn't do well with interrupted sleep—an unavoidable aspect of this crazy job. Now I had to deal with an unhappy group of people who wanted nothing more than to go home and forget what had happened that night at Mary Jane's Grave.

But it was my job to find out.

CHAPTER TWO

On my way to the station, I took a chance that Michael hadn't gone back to bed, and I called him from my cell phone. He slept even less than I did, and sure enough, he picked up after the first ring.

"It's me," I announced, "and I need your help." I briefly described the crime scene, and he listened without comment. Then I asked, "Honey, I need you to tell me if an *M* written in blood means anything."

If anyone would know, Michael would. Not only was he a certified profiler in sex crimes, but I considered him the go-to guy for just about anything involving the criminal mind. Years ago, when I was getting to know him, I'd been dazzled by his insights into why people kill each other. I respect Michael more than anyone I've ever known, including my father. A remarkable feat.

"An *M* in blood? That definitely sounds ritualistic," he said, confirming my growing suspicions. "Let me see what I can find out. From what you're telling me, the killer is a highly organized and educated individual."

"Great," I said gloomily. "Just what I need."

Picking up on my sour mood, Michael suggested, "Why don't you bring the file home tonight. Maybe I can sneak in a quick profile for you."

"I was hoping you'd say that," I confessed gratefully. What a prince.

Then he added, "Of course, it'll cost you."

"I'll be naked by nine," I shot back, laughing.

"Done deal. See you later, Cee."

When I arrived back at the department, I explained to the waiting teens and their parents what lay ahead. First I would take each of them back to the interview room individually to take a statement. Then they could all go home.

In a situation like this, there's usually at least one parent who puts up a fuss. This time it was the overweight, dark-haired man in his late forties who had his arm around the girl I'd seen crying hysterically when I first arrived at the crime scene.

"Excuse me, Sergeant. I'm Edward Nedrow, Ashley's father." He nodded toward his daughter. "I don't mean any disrespect, but these kids are pretty shaken up. Can't we do this more effectively later?"

"Mr. Nedrow, I know it's been a tough night for them, and I'll have your daughter out of here as soon as I can, depending on her cooperation. But right now, they're the only witnesses to a violent murder and, as far as I'm concerned, are all possible suspects. Yes, they claim they didn't see the murder occur, but they're the only ones, by their own admission, who were present. There's no other evidence to prove they weren't involved. Now, they can voluntarily come back with me and tell me their version of events, or I can take them into custody, read them their Mirandas, and let you and your attorneys sort out the rest. All the while they'll be sitting in the juvenile detention center. Remember, sir, at the very least, they were trespassing on private property."

I hated being so shitty with the man. Honestly, if it were my daughter, I'd feel the same as he did. But I had to flip off my emotional connector switch and get my job done. And in the back of my mind, the sooner I hustled these kids out of here, the sooner I could go home and get some sleep myself.

Mr. Nedrow hung his head in defeat, not that I expected any less, and muttered a soft "okay." But my short speech had produced looks of horror on the faces of the teens, especially at the mention of the juvenile detention center. I hoped the threat of incarceration would get them past their fears of betraying one another and inspire them to open up.

Since Mr. Nedrow had so boldly spoken out, I decided to start with Ashley. She was terrified. Her hands were shaking, and droplets of sweat began to form on her forehead.

"Have a seat, Ashley," I told her gently as we entered the small interview room. I was putting on my good-cop demeanor to get her as comfortable as possible under the circumstances. I just couldn't imagine being that age and seeing your friend dead only a few moments after you'd seen her alive and happy.

In that small room, I could smell that Ashley had been drinking. At first she denied it. She was under the drinking age at seventeen and knew she was in trouble. But I remained silent, staring at her until she relented and told me the group had shared a case of beer. Then, the dam having burst, she put her head in her hands and confessed what had happened.

The victim, seventeen-year-old Kari Sutter, had moved to Ohio from Vermont six months before. She immediately took the local kids by storm. She was pretty and popular, and everyone wanted to impress her.

Ashley and her buddies began telling her about Mary Jane's Grave, and the more she heard about it, the more she begged to see it for herself. Finally, they agreed to take Kari out there for Halloween.

"Kari loved a good scare," Ashley recalled, twisting her tissue into a wet ball. "She and I were always first in line for the latest horror movie."

"Since tonight was a full moon, we thought it would be perfect for our visit to the grave."

Apparently, the kids stopped for drinks at one of the boys' homes (his parents were conveniently out). They all rode in one car to Tucker Road, stopping where the asphalt ended and the dirt road began.

"It was Nate O'Malley's idea to dare Kari to walk to the grave alone. He said if she walked to the grave, pissed on it, and took a piece of bark from the tree, he'd let her drive his car for a week."

Again, tears rolled down Ashley's cheeks, and I handed her another tissue. "Kari was really brave. She took the bet without even thinking twice. I offered to go with her, but Nate said if I did, the bet would be off. He did let her take a flashlight, though, so she could find the tree." She blew her nose into the tissue and took a few deep breaths.

"Ashley, I know this is difficult, but did you see any cars around there? Not just on Tucker Road, but anywhere in the area?"

"No! I don't even remember passing a car on the way down there after we left Mansfield!"

I waited until she composed herself. "Want some water?" I asked, hoping to keep her talking.

"Please," she said, and I went out to the hall and got her a bottle from the vending machine. When I came back, she was a bit calmer.

"I'm sorry, Sergeant. I'm jus—I've never seen a dead body before." I thought she was going to lose it again, but she didn't. "We watched Kari walk down the road. I remember the light from the flashlight getting smaller and smaller. When she finally turned into the cemetery, it disappeared completely. I expected to see it again in a couple of minutes, but I didn't. After a few minutes, when she didn't come back, we stopped laughing and started waiting. Nate kept saying she was hiding back there, trying to scare us, but after a while nobody was laughing anymore." She took another drink from her water bottle and whispered, "It was so quiet."

They waited, according to Ashley, for at least twenty minutes before driving Nate's car to the grave to pick up Kari. Nate pointed the car toward the entrance, which illuminated the entire cemetery. That was when they saw Kari propped up against the tree.

"At first, I thought I was hallucinating. We all did, because no one said anything. But then Nate started to laugh, saying, 'Okay, you've got us,' to her. He thought she was playing a trick. It was Nate who got out and walked over to the tree. When he turned around and I saw his face, I knew it was no joke."

Ashley began to tremble, and I took her hand to steady her. "I started screaming for him to get back into the car. I was afraid we'd be next. Brittany was screaming and Kyle had his hands over his face." She paused, reliving the entire ordeal. "Nate ran to the car. He kept looking over his shoulder as if someone was following him. He was shaking and trying to get the car turned around, but he was so upset he couldn't! Kyle yelled at him to switch places and he did, and Kyle peeled out of there. We pulled into the first driveway at the end of Tucker Road, almost to Pleasant Valley and had the people there call nine-one-one."

I let her story sink in for a few minutes. I knew without a doubt that she was telling the truth. "Ashley, when

Kari was back at the grave alone, did you hear her scream or make any noise at all?"

"Nothing! We heard nothing!"

I could only imagine how scared she was, especially at her age. If I'd been there, I'd have been scared, too. "Is there anything else you can remember?"

She shook her head.

"Okay, honey," I said. I gently touched her shoulder, then went back into the waiting area to get her father. Before he retrieved his daughter, I gave him the name and number of a local therapist, which she was unquestionably going to need. He could find an attorney for her on his own. I was going to have a tough time explaining to the prosecutor why the only persons present at a murder scene weren't immediately charged and booked. I'd try to put him off as long as possible until I had further information.

Kyle Latham and Brittany Moore, both sixteen years old, told me almost verbatim the same story. It was sixteen-year-old Nate whose story deviated, just slightly. It was when Nate was running back to the car after seeing the body. He told me something the others hadn't— the reason he kept looking over his shoulder.

"I couldn't believe it. She was really dead. I was so scared I started running back to the car. I could hear everyone in the car yelling, but then I heard . . ."

"You heard *what*, Nathan?"

"You're not gonna believe me. It's crazy!" His face was pale, but he was managing to keep it together.

"Try me," I told him firmly.

"When I was running back to the car, I swear I heard a baby crying behind me."

I just looked at him. He seemed to be telling the truth, but it was ridiculous. The only explanation I could come up with was that he'd heard the echoes of the others yelling in the car. Sometimes people mistake the location of sounds when they're in an intense situation. In fact, I've heard officers involved in shootings claim that when they fired their guns, they heard nothing at all.

When I was finished with Nate, I found Coop and Naomi in Coop's office and filled them in on my interviews.

"A *baby* crying? Are you shitting me?" Coop was never at a loss for comments.

"Nope. I'm chalking it up to adrenaline. If the dirt samples show that Nate wasn't the only one outside the car, I'm going to polygraph them all. Anybody know the last time we had a call down in that area?"

"There was that robbery about eight years ago," Coop offered.

"I forgot about that. I think I was still in uniform when that happened." I tried to remember. Sometimes I felt like a senior citizen on the cusp of the century mark, rather than a young woman in her midthirties.

Eight years earlier, a carload of twenty-somethings went down to Mary Jane's Grave. Unfortunately, they had passed two carloads of thugs that were leaving the spot, having finished two cases of beer out there. When they saw the newcomers, the bad guys turned around and blocked the car in at the grave. Then, grabbing their handy ski masks, they pulled open the victims' car doors, robbed them and pulverized the car with a baseball bat. We caught them, of course, but the case had been a high profile one in the rolling hills of southern Richland County. Had this happened in the city, it wouldn't have even made the front page.

Which brought me to my next thought. "Damn, the media's going to have a field day with this, it being Mary Jane's Grave *and* Halloween." I knew that media attention could be a disaster in any investigation. Information in the public record could open the door to false confessions by local quacks and add long hours interviewing the wrong people. I'd found that it didn't even pay to ask the media not to print unsubstantiated theories. Some journalists had ethics that mirrored those of the criminals themselves.

"Well," Coop added, "at least no one's been going up into that house."

"What house?" I hadn't remembered seeing one.

"There's an old abandoned house up on the hill right above the cemetery. It's all boarded up and falling apart. A couple of uniforms and I checked it out, but it didn't look like anyone had messed with it."

I knew a local children's camp, Hidden Hollow, sat on the highest ridge away from the cemetery. In fact, I'd gone there as a child, but right now I couldn't even visualize where the house was. I made a mental note to go back to the cemetery in daylight to take a closer look.

"So," Naomi asked, "now what?"

"We do what we always do," I answered. "We wait."

CHAPTER THREE

"Wait? For what?" Naomi asked, wondering what I had up my sleeve.

"Nothing out of the ordinary. I'm still trying to sort this one out. Meanwhile, we wait for lab reports, final and preliminary. We wait for officer reports and for someone to start talking or bragging. We also wait for any anonymous tips. You know this, Naomi. We're in a holding zone right now."

"I guess you're right," she sighed. "Has someone run record checks on those teens?"

"Of course," I said, mildly annoyed. "I had Jerry run them."

Coop, sensing my mood, started talking about his own high school experiences at Mary Jane's Grave. They sounded the same as the rest of ours, mildly scary but ultimately uneventful. It was when he spoke of another incident that he got my undivided attention.

"I remember about fifteen years ago that a carload of kids from Madison High School got killed after leaving there."

"I don't remember that," I said, perking up.

"It was a highway patrol case, all over the news. Weren't you here in town?"

"Just get to the point and tell me what happened," I snapped.

"Grrrr!" he said with a grin. "I guess someone needs her beauty sleep. Well, supposedly four teenage boys were down at the grave drinking, smokin' dope, you know, what we all used to do. Anyway, according to the only survivor, they all pissed on the grave. On their way back, they hadn't gone a mile when they wrapped their car around a telephone pole. The kid who survived claimed that an old woman in white was standing in the middle of the road and the driver swerved to miss her. He claimed he was the only one who hadn't pissed on the grave."

"You said that was a highway patrol case?"

"Yup."

"Well, stories like that have been all over the Internet for years, Coop."

"Not fifteen years ago, they weren't."

I thought about it for a minute and realized he was right. I loved Coop to death, but hated it when he got one over on me.

I decided to look at the file, even though I couldn't imagine that the highway patrol kept fatal crash cases that far back, given how many there were each year. If all else failed, I could always get the name of the survivor from Coop and go talk to him myself.

After I finished my paperwork, which included the interviews, I saw it was getting late. However, I still had time to take care of something I'd been meaning to do for a long time. For some reason, I felt like doing it today.

Michael had been pressuring me to set a date for our wedding. I thought I would surprise him by getting the marriage license and bringing it home. I only had half an hour or so, since the courthouse closed at five.

I was whistling when I walked up the steps to the

courthouse, thinking how good my life was and how happy I was. But these thoughts quickly faded when I told the clerk my name and Social Security number to obtain the license. She looked confused when she pulled my information up on the computer screen.

"Ms. Gallagher," she said, looking at me with an odd expression on her face, "our computer is showing you're still married to one Eric Schroeder."

"That can't be," I protested. "We've been divorced for six months." My heart pounded in my chest as I struggled to breathe.

She gave me another look before walking away. I saw her go into an office and speak to a woman seated behind a desk, probably a supervisor. Good, I thought. Let's get this straightened out. Dumb civil servants, couldn't they keep track of recent records?

The woman behind the desk turned to her computer and typed something in, then spoke to the clerk, who finally came back out to talk to me. By this time, I had chewed my fingernails to the quick and almost lit a cigarette right then and there, wondering what the hell was going on.

"Ms. Gallagher, our records show where the request for the final hearing was entered, but no final divorce decree was ever filed. Did you attend a final hearing?"

"Of course I did!" I cried, my voice rising an octave. "I heard the judge say 'divorce granted' loud and clear." I was now on the verge of panic.

"Ms. Gallagher, that very well may be, but apparently someone dropped the ball. The final divorce decree was never filed with the courts. That was your attorney's responsibility. Therefore, you are still legally married and can't apply for a marriage license."

I was numb, sick and confused, my stomach now in knots, my happiness a distant memory.

"How could this happen?" I shouted. People stopped their chatter and looked at me, but I couldn't have cared less.

"Ms. Gallagher, I assure you that my supervisor checked to make sure it wasn't our mistake. I suggest you contact your attorney and inform him what happened. He should take it from there."

I didn't even answer. Instead I walked away, dazed. How on earth could I explain this to Michael, let alone tell Eric we were still married? I prayed it was all a mistake and tried to tell myself this wasn't really happening. Too bad Eric hadn't stepped up to the plate and married Jordan yet. We could have resolved this much sooner.

Michael and I had been through more rough patches than any two people deserved in a lifetime. It just wasn't fair!

On my way home I called Bill Warren, my attorney. His secretary began to tell me he was in a meeting, but I cut her off and demanded that she put him on the phone, or else. She could tell by my voice I wasn't in the mood for games, and a minute later Bill was on the phone.

"Hey, Cee," he began, but I had no time for idle chitchat. "What the hell happened, Bill? I thought you filed my divorce papers! But I just came from the court-house, and they never received them!"

He was quiet a minute and then assured me he would find out what happened and call me back, swearing up and down that he'd filed the final decree.

I dragged myself home, dreading what would come next. I found Michael in his study researching information on my bloody *M*. Thankfully, we had the house to ourselves since Selina and Isabelle were with Eric and Jordan for one more day.

Michael looked at my pale face as I stood in the door-way and immediately knew there was trouble.

"Cee, what's the matter?" he asked, alarmed.

I walked over and sat down next to him. I knew no other way to tell him other than to just blurt it out. I inhaled deeply, and said, "Apparently, Eric and I are still legally married."

He was so stunned he couldn't even speak. "Devastated" didn't even begin to describe the look on his face. You'd have thought I just told him I had a fatal illness. I did my best to comfort him, taking his hand and caressing his face, but all the while my heart was breaking for both of us.

I explained to him what had occurred at the courthouse, and after that, it didn't take long for his anger to rise.

"Damn! This will take another sixty to ninety days, CeeCee! Jesus Christ, why do I have the feeling that son-of-a-bitch Eric had something to do with this?" He began pacing across the room.

Michael rarely swore, but when he did I usually remained silent and just let him vent. Frankly, I didn't believe Eric had anything to do with this, but I didn't say so right then. Eric and Michael had a volatile past and usually blamed each other for their personal disasters when possible. It was the only juvenile aspect of Michael's personality, so I had learned to live with it.

"Please, sit down," I finally said, patting the space beside me. "Bill promised me he'd find out what happened. Chances are, some dipshit clerk put the paperwork on her desk and forgot to file it. If that's the case, he'll refile the final paperwork and it'll be done. Let's not make too much out of it, okay? You could at least be happy that I went to get our license today." I flashed a brilliant smile at him, hoping that would do the trick.

It did, and I knew the tantrum was over. I couldn't blame him. I probably felt even worse. We decided to go out and grab a light dinner before turning in early. I was exhausted, and with the impending press release in the paper tomorrow, I expected another busy day. However, there was nothing that could have prepared me for what I was about to learn.

CHAPTER FOUR

As I predicted, the local newspaper's front page headlined the murder. And to add a bit of flair to the story, the paper ran a section of excerpts from people who claimed to have had some pretty unusual experiences while they were at the grave.

I read through them and laughed. So many of these "oddities" had rational explanations, such as the sudden loss of cell-phone service while in the area. Hey, I haven't been able to get cell-phone service in the southern part of this county for five years. That's because there's no nearby cell tower.

As I was reading the reports, I realized that the reporter who'd written the story had attributed the excerpts he was quoting to a website. For example, a girl named Tracy wrote that three years ago she and two friends had been down at the grave and stabbed the tree with a knife. She claimed it began bleeding real blood. Evidently, this was not to be confused with the dark sap from the pine tree.

I saw nothing else in the article that grabbed my attention except the last account. Someone named Brian had claimed that when he and some friends were there four years before, they heard a baby crying. I found it interesting that this report matched the story that Nathan O'Malley had told us.

I picked up the phone and called the reporter, Max Cline. The two of us went way back, and I knew he'd give me the information I needed. He answered on the first ring.

"Cline here."

"Max, it's CeeCee Gallagher."

"CeeCee! Hey, glad you called! You got something for me on this murder?"

"Not yet. I actually need something from you. I was just reading your article in the paper on the murder and one of those excerpts jumped out at me—the one from Brian. I want to look at his whole story, Max. Can you tell me where the website is?"

"It's not a website, CeeCee. It came from a chat room."

"How'd you get it?" I prodded.

"Interestingly enough, one of the girls who works here took part in a chat room discussion on Mary Jane's Grave. The website was called Grave Addiction I think, and it was up maybe three years ago. She likes that spooky stuff, so she printed out the chat room transcript that day and hung on to it."

"So only the people who'd logged on to the chat room that day would've heard these stories?"

"I guess, unless the other people saved it, too. But I'd say it's unlikely. Why? It sounds like you're onto something. Give me a hint. I need it for a story I'm writing."

"Not yet, Max, but you'll be the first to know when the time comes."

It was highly doubtful that Nathan O'Malley had logged into the chat room three or four years ago. At the time, he would have been only twelve or thirteen years old. But as far as I was concerned, it still didn't matter.

Stories like that, once heard, are passed around for years. I was sure Nathan had heard the crying-baby story from somebody, but why he felt the need to throw it in after the murder I had yet to figure out. I would definitely have to talk to those kids again.

I spent the next hour on the phone with the highway patrol trying to find out if they still had the fatal accident report Coop had told me about. The guys assured me that if they found it, they'd fax it to me at once.

I knew it would still be some time for the preliminary lab results to come in, so I thought I'd go see the accident survivor in person. Coop had given me his name and I was getting antsy, sitting around feeling useless.

Now thirty-one years old, Gary Fenner was a sales manager at a local car dealership. I didn't call ahead for fear he'd hang up on me. After all, it was probably one of the worst experiences of his life and one he likely wouldn't want to talk about.

It didn't take me long to track him down to the new car lot. According to the salesman who greeted me at the front door, Gary was showing a young couple a sleek new SUV. He pointed to a tall, gangly, borderline homely guy whose nose took up most of his face. I walked over to him and pretended to look at a red Honda Accord. I always did like red cars, even though statistically they cry out, "Give me a ticket!"

"Good afternoon, ma'am. Anything special you're looking for?"

"Are you Gary Fenner?" I asked, even though I figured it had to be him.

"Yes, ma'am. Are you here on a referral?"

"Actually, no. I'm Sergeant Gallagher with the Richland Metro Police Department." I handed him my card. "I need to ask you a few questions. Is there somewhere we can talk?"

. He paled, his friendly smile replaced by apprehension. "Can you tell me what this is about, Sergeant? I'm working." He looked around nervously.

I explained what I wanted to talk about and watched his face go two shades lighter. I felt bad about making him talk about his past experience. It had to be hard for him. But it had to be done.

"I read about the murder today. I don't know how I can help you." He looked somber. "I don't know how my accident could be of any help to you at all."

My instincts told me he had more information than he was willing to share—information that could be helpful.

"Why don't you let me worry about that, Gary," I said soothingly. "Look, I just want to hear your recollection of events from that night."

He looked around again, as if searching for a way out. He didn't appear to be the type to take off running, but it was clear that the thought had crossed his mind. He began scratching the red hives that had appeared all over his neck. This guy was a walking ball of nerves. I did my best to try to calm him down.

"Gary, really, there's no reason for you to be nervous—you're not in trouble. I'm getting strange stories from these kids about the night of the murder and I just want to see if there's any basis in fact." I lowered my voice to what I hoped was an intimate tone. "I was told you had somewhat of a strange experience there, and I need you to tell me about it. Then I promise I'll get out of your way, okay?"

He sighed, then suggested we go inside to the employee break room. "I'm due for a break anyway," he said, "but I need to tell my boss I might need a longer one."

He ushered me into a small room that contained a coffeepot, about a dozen chairs, and some pastries.

Forcing myself to ignore the Danish, I gratefully reached for a cup of coffee while Gary went off in search of his boss. He was gone only for a few minutes before he returned and shut the door. I took out my tape recorder and explained that I'd be taping our conversation for his own protection. He slowly nodded.

"Gary, I want you to tell me everything you remember about the night of your accident. I know it was a long time ago, but anything you recall will be helpful."

He sighed. "You know, I've tried everything known to man to forget that night, Sergeant. I never thought I'd have to relive it. Even though it was a long time ago, I remember everything." He started playing with a pen that he pulled from his shirt pocket.

Gary began his story. He'd been a teenager at the time, and that previous July he and a few of his friends had gotten beer from their parents' refrigerators and gone drinking on Trease Road, a stone's throw from Mary Jane's Grave. Trease Road was a dirt road with little to no traffic on it, a prime drinking spot for local teens. I remember visiting it a couple of times myself in high school. The kids were going to a party later on, but it was his friend Jesse Walters who suggested they go down to the grave.

"Everyone was all for it, except me. I was always chicken when it came to stuff like that. The place gave me the creeps, even in daylight."

But Gary finally relented, giving in to his friends' taunts. After standing at the site for only ten minutes, Jesse suggested they all urinate on the grave.

"He said, 'Did ya hear that if you piss on her grave, you're cursed for life?' We were all laughing, still drinking, and Jesse walked right over and pissed on it. Cameron and Stevie did, too."

"But you didn't?" I asked. "Why not?"

"It wasn't about the curse and all that horseshit. It was just that I'd been raised to respect the dead, and I didn't feel right about pissing on anyone's grave."

Gary grabbed a coffee, threw in five packets of sugar and took a sip. He continued, explaining how the four of them had stayed a little longer, drinking and telling ghost stories. It was when they got into Jesse's car to leave that he got spooked.

"On my way to the car, I passed through an area that was freezing cold—I mean, I could even see my breath, and it was summer! No one else said anything, so I kept my mouth shut. I didn't want to sound like an ass." He started to rub his temples with both hands. "I remember Stevie asking if any of us smelled something burning. None of us did, and at first I thought he was just trying to scare me, but when I saw the look on his face I knew he wasn't joking. Right then, I just wanted to get the hell out of there."

Gary suddenly excused himself and dashed to the restroom just outside the door. I had a feeling he was going to lose his coffee. So far, nothing he'd told me was outrageous or unexplainable. Everyone's perceptions of sight, smell and sound can vary greatly, and being teenagers, one person's imagination could scare the hell out of the rest of them.

It was a good fifteen minutes before Gary came back into the room. I was beginning to think he'd finally decided to take off, his nerves getting the better of him. I reminded him where he'd left off, and he began to talk about the car.

"Anyway, like I said, I just wanted to leave. I felt better when we were finally in the car. Then Jesse turned the key in the ignition and the damn thing wouldn't start. The battery was dead. That's when I got scared. I kept telling Jesse to let me out—I was in the backseat—so I could walk out of there, but he was swearing at his car. It was brand-new. All of a sudden, the car just blared on. Jesse hadn't even turned the key again."

"If you were in the backseat, how could you see that Jesse didn't turn the key in the ignition?" I asked.

"He said he didn't, that's all. Stevie was in front and said Jesse didn't, too."

"Then what?"

"We left. Jesse drove like a bat out of hell down the road. When we finally came to the stop sign, they were all laughing like crazy. That's when I decided they were all pulling my chain." He paused.

"Go on."

"We had just made the turn when Jesse floored it. He got up to about eighty when I looked up at the dash to see how fast he was going. That's when I saw the woman." He stopped, and I saw he was beginning to sweat.

"Tell me about the woman, Gary."

"She was just standing in the middle of the road, wearing a long white nightgown. She was holding something wrapped in a blanket, and she was smiling." He bit his lip, the image clearly as vivid as the night he'd seen it. "She had really long red hair, and she was pretty but . . ."

"But what?"

"She was pretty but scary. I don't know how else to explain it, but once I saw her I yelled to Jesse, 'Look out!' That's when he jerked the wheel to miss her. That's the very last thing I remember until I woke up in the hospital and found out that everyone in the car but me was dead."

I waited a few moments, absorbing everything Gary had told me. Unfortunately, no woman had been found at the scene, and no other witnesses were alive to confirm his story.

"Gary, do you remember how much you drank that night? Were you drunk?"

"I know what I saw, Sergeant," he said firmly, looking offended.

"I'm not insinuating that you don't, Gary. I just want to know how much you'd been drinking or if you'd taken any drugs."

"I had, maybe, five or six beers, and yeah, I was buzzing. But I didn't do any drugs that night. Never have, never will."

I had asked Gary this question for several reasons. Alcohol consumption, drugs, and lack of sleep are just a few things that can cause hallucinations. I remember several years ago when I was working night-shift road patrol. I was so tired I thought I saw birds flying at my windshield and people ducking behind bushes. This was right before I fell asleep at the wheel and almost hit a telephone pole.

A sudden flash of light from an oncoming car could've caused Gary to think he was seeing a woman in white. At least that's what I tried to tell myself, since his story was so illogical. He was scared after being at the grave. Mix the fear with alcohol and I was surprised he didn't see the woman fly right at their car on a broomstick.

"Gary, I'm almost done. How many people have you told this to?"

"My parents and the state trooper who took my statement," he said matter-of-factly, but I knew he was lying.

Obviously, he had told more people than that. Coop told me about it, saying he'd heard it from his little brother. After Gary claimed he had told me everything, I got up to leave. "Thanks for your help," I told him briskly, ready to move on to other possibilities. "You can get back to your job. Looks like some folks out there may be in the market for that red Honda I had my eye on."

Gary murmured something and raced out to the lot, ready to assume the role of Supersalesman once again.

As I drove back to the department, I thought about our conversation. Gary hadn't told me anything that couldn't be explained rationally, and now I was more convinced than ever that Kari Sutter's friends had been connected to her murder. I just didn't know how yet. But gunning my engine, I swore that I'd find out.

CHAPTER FIVE

When I walked into my office, Naomi was waiting for me.

"Take a deep breath, CeeCee. We've been totally bombarded with calls since this article came out this morning." She was holding the paper out to me. "Every quack in the entire county has been calling about *their* experiences at the grave, thinking it'll help the investigation."

"Fantastic," I muttered, throwing my bag on my desk and sitting down. Just as I had predicted—damn, I hated being right.

"We've had two psychics call and say that Mary Jane contacted them this morning and told them who the killer was."

"Great, that'll save us a lot of work. Did you keep their numbers?" I asked, only half kidding, picking up my phone to check my messages.

She stood there patiently while I listened to my messages. There were twenty-three of them. Twenty were from the people Naomi was talking about, and I started to delete them, then changed my mind. They might be entertaining sometime if I was bored.

The other three were important. One was from Michael, another from the crime lab letting me know the preliminary test results were back, and the third was from Kyle Latham. He said he wanted to talk to me again. There was something he hadn't told me the first time.

"Gotcha now, you little bastards," I muttered while saving Kyle's message.

"Come again?" Naomi asked, perplexed.

"Kyle Latham just left me a message. He wants to talk again and said he didn't tell me everything. I just know those kids had something to do with the murder, and I think Kyle's going to be the first to break."

"Let me know what you find out," she said. "I'm outta here."

My first call was to Michael, to tell him I anticipated being home late. We now had both the girls and Sean, so I told him to order a pizza; I'd grab something to eat on my own.

My next call was to the lab. I was anxious to hear the results. Bob, who was out at the murder scene, answered on the first ring.

"Bob, it's CeeCee. Lay it on me."

"Wait a sec. I need to grab the file," he said. I waited impatiently till he came back with the information. "Okay, here it is. The victim died from manual strangulation with burn marks over her upper torso. They appear to have been inflicted postmortem, most likely from a fireplace poker. None of the soil at the grave site matches any on the shoes of the teens at the scene, except for Nathan O'Malley, and there's no match for any dirt inside the car. We couldn't find any blood traces inside the car or on any of the kids' clothing, and there was no sexual assault. So far, the DNA swab of the victim's neck turned up nothing."

To say I was disappointed would be an understatement. "So, to sum it up, you're telling me we don't have shit," I bit out.

"Sí, senora."

I was deflated and majorly pissed off. These kids couldn't be so smart that they wouldn't leave any evidence. Either that, or Bob was an idiot and did a terrible job of processing the crime scene, which I knew wasn't true.

"You're telling me you don't think any of those kids got out of the car?"

"Nope, only the Irish kid. Keep in mind, CeeCee, these are just the prelims."

I sighed, knowing I'd just hit a brick wall. It would be a miracle if the final results differed from the preliminaries. Now it was a matter of waiting for a break, from Kyle Latham I hoped. I thanked Bob and hung up. Then I had another thought and called Michael back.

"Michael, I forgot to ask if you came up with anything profile-wise on a suspect. There was no evidence left at the scene."

"Honestly, Cee, I haven't had much time to work on it. I've come up with a little bit if that helps."

"Just tell me this," I urged. "Is it possible that the four teenagers are responsible?"

"I highly, *highly* doubt it," he said firmly. "This was organized, sophisticated and well planned. Even if those kids watched every crime show on television, they're not sophisticated enough to stage that kind of scene. They wouldn't know that by just putting bare hands around a neck, more DNA than needed can transfer in a split second."

"But you still can't rule them out, right?"

"No, but I'd be looking for other suspects."

I thought about this for a moment. If there was a way for these teens to commit this murder and get away with it, I was going to find out. I was putting a lot of hope into Kyle Latham.

"Cee, you still there?" Michael asked.

"I'm here. I'm just extremely frustrated. I need to get going, honey. Are the kids okay?"

"They're fine. Isabelle is driving Sean around the yard in her Barbie jeep, and Selina is on the trampoline. We're waiting for the pizza. Get back here as soon as you can, okay? Even police officers need to eat."

"I'm practically on my way. See you soon," I promised.

Next, I called Kyle Latham's house and got the answering machine. I waited half an hour before trying again. This time, Kyle answered. We agreed that I would come to his house to talk to him since coming to the station made him nervous. I could understand that, and there was nowhere I wouldn't meet this kid, my only hope for vital information.

When I arrived at Kyle's house, I found him—and his parents—waiting for me. The three were seated around their dining-room table, an unmistakable look of anxiety on their faces. I felt a surge of hope, knowing their nervousness meant they were ready to reveal something that Kyle hadn't yet told us.

Kyle's father directed me to another room, his home office, and told me I could talk to Kyle in there. Evidently, Kyle wanted to talk to me alone. As he walked in, his father gave him a piece of sound advice. "Tell her *exactly* what you told us, Kyle. Don't sugarcoat any of it!"

I was now dying to hear what Kyle was going to tell me, but he wasn't exactly dying to tell me. When he closed the door and sat down, he began rubbing his palms across his jeans. I looked closer at him than I had the night of the murder. He was nice looking, his baby face starting to thin out with his age, and he seemed quite thoughtful.

I had done a brief check into the kids and found that none had a criminal record or been involved in any trouble at school. In fact, his files had revealed that Kyle was a straight-A student and a star soccer player.

"Kyle, you wanted to tell me something, so I'm waiting to hear it," I said for openers, trying to suppress my impatience.

"You're gonna think I'm crazy," he protested, clearly stalling for time.

"Tell me anyway," I said. "I'm a good listener."

"I didn't tell you this before because it's nuts." He took a deep breath. "That night at the grave, I did see someone else."

"Who?" My heart quickened.

"I saw a woman."

"You saw a *woman* at the grave?" This was hardly what I'd expected him to say.

"Yeah. When Nate and I got out of the car to switch seats, I ran around the back of the car, and something caught my eye. I looked at it. There was a woman standing by the edge of the woods."

"Why didn't you say anything about this before? What did she look like?"

"I didn't say anything because, um, she was a little different looking."

"Kyle, get to your point already." I was close to losing my patience.

"She, um, she had a white dress on, and she looked like, um, a ghost." He looked at the floor as if in shame.

I couldn't believe it. The ghost lady again? Frankly, I'd had enough of the woman-in-the-white-dress theory. Kyle Latham had answers for me, and I wasn't going to listen to another supernatural close encounter. I slammed my notebook on the floor and stood.

"You mean to tell me *this* is why you wanted to talk? Bullshit, Kyle, and nice try! Trying to pawn off a murder on a ghost won't work. You kids were the only ones at the grave that night, and someone better start talking before I start issuing warrants."

Kyle's jaw dropped, and he looked at me with real surprise. I couldn't believe his arrogance! To think that he thought someone in law enforcement would believe such a story! I opened the door and called his father back to the office. He looked bewildered as he glanced from me to Kyle.

"Mr. Latham, did Kyle tell you what he was going to tell me?"

"Yes, ma'am, he did."

"Please tell me you don't believe that crap."

"Sergeant, if you don't mind my saying so, I know my son and if he said that's what he saw, then he saw it. Kyle is not a liar. It took quite a bit of courage for him to tell you this." He was clearly struggling to maintain his composure, his hand resting on Kyle's shoulder protectively.

"I'm sure it did. Now, let me explain something. Your son and his friends are the only ones at the scene of a murder. There is no evidence to indicate that anyone else was there, human or ghost. If Kyle is worried about the trouble he's in, it'll be far worse if he doesn't start talking. The first one to cooperate usually gets the lightest sentence. If there's the slightest chance these kids had nothing to do with it, I'll apologize to each and every one of them, but I don't think that's the case." I looked at Kyle. "You can help me by telling me the truth, Kyle."

But his father had had enough, too. Enough of me. "Sergeant, I think you'd better leave. If you want to talk to my son again, it'll be in the presence of an attorney."

"That'll be fine. Just let me know if you change your mind."

I was angry when I left Kyle's house. My hopes were not only dashed, they'd been stomped on. I had been sure that Kyle was the break I needed, not another haunted grave story.

But before I'd reached the end of Kyle's road, I turned my car around and headed back to his house. I knew I'd be unwelcome, so I prepared myself for a verbal confrontation as I knocked on the door. Mr. Latham answered.

I tried a smile. "Mr. Latham, I know you don't want me talking to Kyle again, but if you wouldn't mind asking him a question for me I'd appreciate it. It's about the woman he saw."

At first, I thought he was going to refuse, but his face relaxed and he called Kyle to the door. Kyle didn't look at all happy to see me again.

"Kyle, about the woman you saw, can you tell me what color hair she had and about how old she was?"

He looked at his father and waited for the approving nod. "She was old, very old. Her hair was white and her face was old, wrinkly and scary. Is that good enough?"

"Yes, it is. Thank you."

At least now I had something. I had a lie. Kyle's description of the woman didn't match Gary's. Unless ghosts aged, both Gary and Kyle had merely fleshed out a description around the woman in the white dress, adding their own finishing touches. Kyle's description was so cliché it was downright corny: old, wrinkly, with white hair. He'd just described every witch mask from here to China.

CHAPTER SIX

After I went back to my office and typed up my interview with Kyle, I saw that it was late, close to eleven. I assumed everyone was asleep when I got home because the house looked dark when I pulled into my driveway. Seeing the light on in the study proved me wrong. Michael was in there, working on his own case files.

"You're up late," I greeted him, affectionately planting a kiss on his cheek.

"I have a trial next week and I haven't done a thing to prepare for it. Did you eat?" He continued to inspect the file in front of him as he spoke.

"No."

"There's plenty of pizza left in the fridge, but prepare yourself—the kids picked off most of the pepperoni."

"Actually, Michael, I'm not hungry at all. Can we talk for a minute? I want to tell you what happened."

He put his file down and gave me his full attention. I curled up on our comfy sofa and told Michael about my interview with Kyle and the story Gary Fenner had told me, explaining how I felt both of their stories were ridiculous.

"Why would they make up stories about the woman, Michael? It has no bearing on anything that happened to either one of them—well, maybe Kyle. Between

Nathan's crying baby and Kyle's ghost woman, I think they're trying to steer us in the direction of the supernatural, and the only reason I can think they would do that is they were involved somehow."

"Did you ever think that maybe they're not lying?" Michael never ceased to surprise me, one of the reasons I was so attracted to him. I could see he was serious by the look in his hazel eyes.

"Michael, don't tell me you believe in this ghost nonsense," I scoffed. "C'mon, you're an FBI man!"

He laughed, exposing his perfect smile. "That's not what I'm saying, Cee. But don't discount these reports out of hand. Maybe Kyle did see a woman standing by the woods."

"Okay, then, who was she?"

"First, let's start with Gary and his story," Michael said in a professional tone.

"I'm all ears," I said, my curiosity getting the better of me.

"It's entirely possible that there was a woman in the road," Michael continued. "I know you said that the descriptions didn't match, but did you find out whether there were any domestic calls the night of the crash in that area? Maybe a woman grabbed her baby and ran out of her house," he theorized. "Maybe she was trying to flag down Gary's car for whatever reason. Look, all I'm saying is that these kids may actually have seen women at the scene."

I mulled over his words for a minute. "Why would a woman be at the grave, then?"

"How do you know she wasn't with your suspects, Cee? Maybe she was a lookout who got away before the cops arrived, and they're protecting her, concocting the ghost story. Did they check for prints where Kyle said he saw her?"

"I don't think so. Their car was parked by the entrance, and I don't think Bob scoured the entire woods for prints. Plus, Kyle said she was extremely old, with white hair. Doesn't sound much like a bad guy to me. Not to mention, they're going to a hell of an extreme 'protecting' a friend. I don't buy it."

"I can't explain it right now. I'm just saying maybe it's something you should look into." He paused briefly. "Cee, getting off the subject a minute, I wondered if you've talked to Eric or your attorney yet?" He raised an eyebrow and crossed his arms, knowing I hadn't. In a way, it seemed he intentionally wanted to see me squirm.

I flushed. In fact, I had completely forgotten. I'd been so consumed by this case, everything else had been put on hold. I didn't need to answer Michael's question; he saw my face.

"I'll take that as no." His voice was low and strong, and he looked annoyed, with a touch of smugness. The man knew me very well.

I looked at him with pleading eyes. "Michael, I'm sorry! I promise I'll take care of it first thing tomorrow. I've been caught up in this case and I didn't—"

Michael put his hand up and interrupted me. "It's okay, Cee. When you get to it, you get to it. I know you have a job to do, but I'd like to see you follow through on your commitments. You'd expect the same of me, wouldn't you?"

I went over and laid my head against his chest and held him tightly. I knew I'd hurt his feelings by not making our life a priority, and I vowed to take care of the matter tomorrow.

After Michael and I had gone to bed, I couldn't sleep. What he had said earlier about the women kept going through my head. Since patience was not part of my vocabulary, I couldn't wait until morning to find out, so I got out of bed, slowly, so as not to wake Michael.

After throwing on a pair of jeans, a sweatshirt, and an old pair of sneakers, I grabbed a heavy-duty flashlight out of the garage and headed down to Tucker Road. I had already checked in the back of my SUV to confirm that my camera and tape recorder were in there. Figuring I'd be back within two hours if I floored it, I hopped in, popped in a tape, and took off. Michael would never even know I'd gone.

CHAPTER SEVEN

When I turned onto Tucker Road and saw how dark it was, I thought I should've waited until morning. I felt my old fears rise to the surface but fought them back. *I'm a cop, for Christ's sake!*

Gathering my courage, I headed toward the cemetery after getting on my police radio to tell the dispatchers where I was. It wasn't that I was worried about ghosts or dead witches, but if I ran into a group of drunks partying at the grave, I might need some help. There was supposed to be an officer parked at the grave to prevent curious locals from visiting the site after the murder, but to my surprise, no one was there.

I parked near the gate and considered leaving my headlights on for more light, then decided against it. The last thing I needed was to get stuck down here with a dead battery. As I got out of my car I remembered to grab my mini tape recorder and my camera, which I hung around my neck.

As I started walking toward the woods, I had a sudden thought and turned back to the car to grab my gun. Better safe than sorry. Then I started back toward the area where Kyle said he had seen the woman.

I pointed my flashlight toward the tree where Kari was found and scanned the cemetery. It was just as eerie as always. The broken tombstones were far apart from one another, all surrounding the large pine tree with a cross burned into the front of it. As I got closer to the edge of the woods, I pointed the flashlight down to look for any imprints, shoe or otherwise, in the ground.

At the exact area Kyle had been talking about, I actually got down on my knees and scoured the ground, inch by inch. I found a slight impression in the dirt, about a foot from a large maple tree at the edge of the woods. I couldn't tell if it was from a shoe or a hoof print, so I grabbed my camera and began to photograph it. I heard a noise behind me. Gun in hand, I whirled around, shining my flashlight over the cemetery.

Remembering my tape recorder, I quickly hit the record button, holding the recorder in the same hand as my flashlight. At first, I thought the noise sounded like a grunt, and knowing the woods can produce unusual sounds, I tried to brush it off.

A few years earlier, I'd been in a patch of woods at night searching for a rape suspect who'd escaped from a uniformed officer. I had been standing still when I heard a low grunt or growl, with heavy breathing behind me. Convinced I would turn around and face none other than Bigfoot himself, I was startled to see a large buck with a pretty impressive rack on his head. In retrospect, I guess I was lucky I hadn't been gouged to death.

I felt a chill go up my spine, and I shivered. It was brisk, but not as cold as it had been the night of the murder. I stood for a few more minutes and listened, but heard nothing. The sound was enough to make me call it a night and I quickly headed back to my car. Although it was probably a coyote or deer, I really wasn't in the mood to investigate.

The imprint I found could have been anything, and I decided to look at the area more closely in the daylight.

When I pulled out onto Pleasant Valley Road, a long, winding road that made its way through the foothills, I saw headlights coming from my right. They were far away enough that I had plenty of time to pull out onto the road, but in a few seconds the car was so close behind me I couldn't see its headlights anymore. It had to have been doing seventy-five, at the very least. The car stayed on my tail for another half mile before backing off.

I was annoyed, and had I been able to see the license plate, I would've called it in; the driver was probably drunk.

It was only when I was almost back inside the city limits and had made four turns that I realized the car was following me. I started zigzagging down side streets and called for assistance on the radio. Then I turned right on a dead-end street and threw my car into park. I jumped out with my gun and badge, ready to confront the driver.

He must've anticipated my move because he kept going straight by and I could only catch the back end of the vehicle, which looked like a dark compact car. It was only a few minutes before the uniformed officers arrived. Eric was the first one, and my father, the nightshift lieutenant, followed.

"CeeCee, what's going on?" Eric asked, a frown of annoyance on his face. I was suddenly aware of how drawn he looked.

I explained what had happened, and he radioed for the other patrol cars to check the area. I also reassured them that I was fine.

"I'll go look around for the car, CeeCee," my dad offered. "Call me tomorrow, and get yourself to bed. We've both been worried about you."

I didn't have a chance to protest because I heard my

cell phone ringing. I knew it was Michael, but just as I took the call Eric came up to ask if I wanted him to drive me home.

Michael must have heard him. "CeeCee! Where are you? Was that Eric?" he said, his voice rising.

"Michael, I'm okay. I'll call you back."

I knew Michael would be furious, especially since I hadn't explained what had happened. All he knew was I wasn't home at three o'clock in the morning and that when he called me, I was with Eric.

The officers checking the area couldn't find anything, so I asked Eric to write a report on the incident and forward it to me in the morning.

But before I got in my car I remembered something. I saw Eric standing with a group of other officers and realized this wouldn't be a good time.

"Eric, when you get a chance, I need to talk to you about something as soon as possible, if you can. It's personal."

"It's not the girls, is it?" He looked concerned again.

"No, no, of course not. It's us."

He looked taken aback. "Us? Well, why don't you meet me at the Corner Grill tomorrow night at six? I gotta go in early and I can grab something to eat while we talk. Jordan will already be at work."

"That'll be fine. I'll see you then," I said, disliking this whole business.

I already anticipated a confrontation with Michael when I got home, so it was no surprise to see him sitting on the couch in our living room, waiting.

"I can't wait to hear what you've been up to in the middle of the night," he said stiffly.

"Good, because I can't wait to tell you," I said with a grin, hoping to warm him up.

I sat down next to him and told him about my eventful

night. By the time I got to the end of it, his face had softened considerably.

"You know, the only thing I don't like about this whole business is the possibility that someone followed you tonight. God only knows how many enemies you make on some of your cases, which is why it wasn't very smart to go down there alone."

I nodded, knowing he was right.

"Just promise me that next time you'll let me know if you're leaving, okay?" he said quietly.

I squeezed his hand. "Okay."

When we finally went back to bed I was still fairly wired. By the time I had to get up for work, I had slept less than an hour. It was going to be another long, long day.

CHAPTER EIGHT

In my office, Naomi and Coop expressed their own concerns about what had occurred earlier. Coop wrote down the description of the car and said he was going to drive around the campgrounds near Tucker Road to look for it. I knew Coop was working on two other homicide cases, so I tried to tell him it wasn't necessary, but stubborn as always, he didn't listen.

I spent much of the day catching up on paperwork and listening to ridiculous phone messages from people desperate to leave their Mary Jane stories on my voice mail. When I was almost done for the day, I called Bob over at the lab.

"It's CeeCee, just checking in," I said wearily. "Anything more turn up?"

"Not yet, but we still don't have everything back," he reported. "Hey, I forgot to tell you this yesterday. For laughs, we took a sample of the burn mark from the tree. You know how some people claim it's spray paint or a carving, etcetera? Turns out it really *is* burned wood, and according to the lab, it's pretty old, too."

"I'm glad you had a few laughs, Bob, but that doesn't solve my case. Let me know when you hear something, okay?"

The "burn mark" Bob was referring to, according to

the legend, was the spot where the witch, Mary Jane, had reportedly been burned as she hung from the tree. I know of several instances where vandals have tried to set the tree on fire, so I dismissed his update on this historic evidence as just that.

Exhausted, I smacked the phone down and started gathering my briefcase, purse and files together. I'm not usually a nap-taker, but I suddenly found myself entertaining visions of a cozy snuggle under the covers when I got home. My visions didn't last too long, because Eric called to remind me of our meeting. I told him I'd be there in fifteen minutes and hung up, wondering if this was really a good idea.

When I walked into the diner and saw Eric sitting in the booth, I knew I was in trouble. I felt an involuntary tug at my heart and couldn't push away my feelings of regret. We'd been so happy once; invincible, we'd thought. And then it had all gotten screwed up.

I pushed these thoughts aside. Eric had also broken my heart, and now Michael had come into my life to heal it. "Settle down, girl," I told myself. "He's history, remember?"

As Eric stood and kissed my cheek, I turned away quickly and sat opposite him.

"CeeCee, you look great as always," he said with a grin.

Smooth talker, I thought, moving my purse around and not meeting his eyes directly. We exchanged pleasantries for a while, talking about his new son and our girls. I could tell Eric was getting more and more curious as to why I'd asked to speak with him, so I finally got to it.

"Eric, the reason I need to talk to you is that yesterday I went to the county courthouse. Well, lo and behold, I was informed that you and I are still legally married. For some unknown reason, the final paperwork was never filed."

His eyes opened wide, and he looked as stunned as Michael had. Now, for once in his life, Eric was actually at a loss for words. Then, to my amazement, he broke into a big smile. Maybe Michael was right, I thought. Maybe Eric did have something to do with it. If that were the case, I'd probably beat him right there with the ketchup bottle.

"What's so funny?" I asked, my eyes narrowing.

"Nothing. I thought you had bad news. This isn't bad news." He reached across the table and grabbed my hand. "Still being married to you is *not* a bad thing. In fact, this is the best news I've had in a long time."

Stunned, I pulled my hand away as Eric leaned back in the booth, playing with the paper that had earlier wrapped his drinking straw.

He sighed deeply. "CeeCee, every day, and I mean every single day, I think about us and what we used to have." He looked out the window. "I messed up—I know that. You did, too, but not like I did. I realize that, CeeCee. God knows if I could take it all back, I would."

I felt another tug at my heart, but this time it was out of guilt. I certainly wouldn't want Michael having a conversation like this with his ex-wife.

"But you can't take it back, Eric, and neither can I. What's done is done, and we have separate lives now—lives that involve other people."

"No, I guess we can't forget that Mr. FBI is in the picture, can we?" he shot back.

"I'm also talking about your new son, Eric, a child you had with another woman while you were still married to me!" I was getting upset. This was not what I'd anticipated. Maybe I'd been fooling myself, but I'd thought Eric would say, "Okay, take care of it and let me know when it's all done."

"You're right," he said quietly. "Things have changed

in our lives. But you can't look me in the eye and tell me you don't still think about us, or don't have feelings for me anymore."

Damn him! He'd hit a nerve, and I know it showed on my face. It wasn't that he spoke the truth; it's just that I was at a loss for words as this conversation took a direction I hadn't anticipated.

"That's what I thought," he said, looking pleased. "Look, Cee, why don't we sit on this for a while? Just think about it, okay? I know I have a new life and a new son, and I love him very much. But my relationship with Jordan has changed. It's just not the same as it was at the beginning. And it can't touch what you and I had. I'm pretty sure she senses that. She certainly wouldn't be surprised." He sighed, deep in thought. "This could all just be my ego talking, but maybe there was a reason for this delay." I had to admit, I'd already had that thought. "There's no hurry, right?"

I hadn't told Eric yet that I was planning on marrying Michael, but I'd assumed he knew we would eventually. Now I had to make things crystal clear.

"Actually, Eric, there *is* a hurry." I looked at him, fighting back feelings of nostalgia. "I'm marrying Michael as soon as this mess is cleared up. And yes, I'm in love with him. My feelings for you don't matter because they're buried beneath so much anger I don't think I'll ever be able to work through it all."

I felt tears well up in my eyes. "I made mistakes with you, I admit it. I kissed Michael while we were married, and I had feelings for him. But I told you the truth. But you—you looked me right in the eye and lied to me!" I was sobbing now. "For over six fucking months you were sleeping with Jordan, and the whole time, you lied to me! I think about all those nights that you came home, acting like everything was normal, and it makes me sick to my stomach. It's over, Eric!" I put my face in my hands and sobbed.

I didn't need or want this scene with Eric today. I was exhausted, with little sleep and awash with feelings I'd been suppressing for years. Dimly aware, I felt him sit down next to me and put his arm around my shoulders. With a big gulp, I pushed Eric away so I could slide out of the booth and stand up.

"My attorney will be calling for you to sign the new papers. It shouldn't take too long, Eric, and now I need to go."

"What if I refuse?" he asked, looking both defiant and broken.

"Please, Eric. That would benefit no one. The girls are settled with the way things are, and you need to stop being selfish for once and think about Brandon and Jordan."

He bowed his head as I turned around and left, and I admit it, I cried all the way home. Dredging up the heartache from our treacherous past had taken me by surprise, and now it felt as if it would never end—and it had to. Things change, and so do people. My life was with Michael now.

He was home when I arrived, riffling through a filing cabinet in his office.

"Hi, honey. Where are the girls and Sean?" I asked, looking around.

"They're next door visiting the neighbors' new puppy." He shut the cabinet drawer and looked at me, quickly taking in my red, swollen eyes. "What's wrong, Cee? Where'd you go?"

"I told you, I had to meet Eric for dinner to talk about the divorce papers."

Michael's face turned five different shades of red in a matter of seconds. Although he did his best to keep his cool, I saw a brief moment of adolescent jealousy under his stoic exterior. His color quickly returned to normal, and he made his best effort to show concern.

"No, you forgot to tell me about the dinner." He paused, letting his words sink in. "But I can clearly see it didn't go well. You okay, Cee?"

I thought back. Maybe I hadn't told Michael about dinner, although I thought I had. My insides lurched, knotting up.

"I'm sorry, Michael. I thought I told you. I didn't think the divorce was something I should discuss with Eric over the phone, so I met him at the Corner Grill because he was going in to work early. I didn't even eat! It didn't go well and I left."

"Why didn't it go well, and why were you crying?" His eyes stayed locked on mine, trying to read me.

I proceeded to tell him exactly what had happened, and I even told him how Eric had threatened to refuse to sign the papers.

Michael crossed his arms and leaned back against the cabinet, a wry smile on his face. "Well, isn't that something! I'd expect nothing less from Eric. Do you really think he wants you back?"

"Actually, Michael, it doesn't really matter," I said quietly. "I told him I was marrying you because I love you, and that's the only thing that matters. He just caught me off guard, that's all."

I went over to him and took both of his hands in mine. "Michael, this *will* end—and soon. These last two years have been so up and down it's got to level out somewhere. I'm going to be your wife, and nothing is going to stop that from happening. I love *you*."

I took his face in my hands and kissed him deeply.

"I love you, too, Cee," he whispered. "I just want you to be sure."

"Oh, there's no doubt in my mind," I said softly. I was even about to suggest we sneak upstairs when I heard the kids come in the back door.

"CeeCee!" cried Sean, running to me and giving me a tight hug and a kiss. A miniature version of Michael, he would no doubt break many hearts when he grew up.

Michael changed gears like the pro he was and told the kids to get cleaned up for dinner. I was so exhausted that, by the time dinner was over, I'd dragged myself onto the couch and put my head on Michael's shoulder to watch a movie with him and the kids. I was asleep within fifteen minutes.

CHAPTER NINE

I woke up in bed the next morning and realized at once that Michael had apparently carried me there from the living room couch. He was gone when I awoke, and I stretched luxuriously, feeling alert and refreshed. I took the rare opportunity to make animal-shaped pancakes for the kids before putting Isabelle and Selina on the bus. Since Sean had arrived a day early for his visit, our neighbor, a stay-at-home mom named Maggie, agreed to watch him.

I went to work earlier than usual and began combing every inch of the Kari Sutter murder case file. I could see that Bob was getting annoyed by my constant phone calls to the lab bugging them for the final test results. By afternoon, he had taken the phone off the hook.

I managed to sneak in a call to my attorney to get moving on the divorce paperwork as soon as possible. We had learned the original paperwork had somehow gotten lost by a temporary clerk. Worried about losing her job, she had kept quiet and never disclosed the error.

The errant clerk, whom I would gladly have strangled, had thankfully been terminated due to other errors on her part. As a result, there was technically no one we could hold accountable at this point.

To take my mind off my personal problems, I sat down cross-legged on my office floor to look at the photographs I had taken by the edge of the woods, along with the photographs from the crime scene.

Coop walked in, clearly feeling chatty. "And a good day to you, babe. Want to hear about how I keep busy?"

Resenting his easy familiarity, I shot back, "Forget the babe bit. What's up?"

He flushed briefly, then decided to ignore my rebuke. "I drove all over the county yesterday and didn't see anything that resembled your description of that car," he announced, sitting down in my one shabby chair. "I also listened to some of the messages the local kooks left on your phone."

I looked at him curiously. "I thought you had those two drug murders to work."

"Not much to work. We know who did it, and the warrants have been issued. I'm sure Detroit or Chicago PD will find them by the end of the month. The other detectives are working on the Harker Street shootings so I'm all yours, babe." He smiled.

I looked back at the photographs and began to check out the names on the tombstones. Coop had grabbed the case file off my desk and was flipping through it, but my attention stayed on the tombstones. Then I saw something I hadn't seen before. I turned to Coop, who had put the file down and was stretching out his legs.

"From the way it looks, we're at a dead end. Doesn't look like we have any more leads right now," he said with a yawn, clearly bored and looking for more excitement.

I held up one of the photographs. "Think again, Coop. I've got a lead right here. We're going to look into the history of Mary Jane's Grave."

"You've gotta be kidding me," Coop protested. "How

is looking into the history a lead? Hasn't every historian in the county researched Mary Jane's Grave?"

"Not like we're going to do it." I handed him the photograph. "Look at the new tombstone that the county put up. It lists the names of everyone buried in the cemetery."

"So?"

"They're all related, Coop." I needed him to understand where I was going with this. "It's mainly the Secrist and Berry families, and Mary Jane Hendrickson's name is second to last. I know that Mary Jane's real grave was the last one in the cemetery, but for some reason the county listed Ann Maria Baughman last."

"What does any of that have to do with the murder?" He still didn't get it. I groaned inwardly; patience was never my strong suit.

"Look, Coop," I said, "this recent murder was a very personal one. It required a lot of forethought. All I'm saying is we should be able to rule everything out, and we can't do that without a thorough investigation. I'm wondering how the Mary Jane legend got started in the first place."

"Don't know," Coop answered. "I know it was before my parents' time—they went to see the grave when they were teenagers."

"Mine did, too." I paused. "I heard she was actually an herbalist, and that was where the story came from. People back in the eighteen hundreds mistook herbalism for witchcraft."

"What the hell *is* an herbalist? I mean, I've heard the term and all, so I know it has to do with herbs . . ."

"Yes, that's exactly what it means, Coop." I snorted. "It's a person who uses plants, herbs and other home-grown stuff to treat ailments."

"Like that euthanasia stuff you take when you have a cold?"

I laughed hard enough to bring tears to my eyes. "It's echinacea, dummy, and yes." Actually, it felt like a relief to laugh—at least Coop was good for something.

I wiped my eyes. "Say, for example, you lived back in 1898 and got a sunburn. If you went to an herbalist, she'd give you part of an aloe plant to rub on the burn. Even today we use the plant's sap to heal burns. It's certainly not witchcraft."

"I think you're wasting your time," Coop said wearily, "but, hey, you're the ace. Just tell me what you want me to do."

"Nothing right now," I said, looking down at my watch. "I'm going to run over to the library to see what I can find out. Keep after the lab about those test results and call me if anything comes up."

Coop could be right, I thought. Maybe the history of the grave had nothing to do with the murder. But right now it was all I could come up with, and it felt better than twiddling my thumbs.

When I arrived at the library, I asked the librarian to find me everything she had on Mary Jane Hendrickson. She gave me an odd look and led me to the media resource room.

"Everybody comes here around the same time every year to read about her, and I'll tell you what I tell all of them. You'll be surprised at how unexciting she really was."

I sat down at the large wooden table in the center of the tiny room. Edna, the librarian, was a big woman with short, dark hair and glasses, and her bulk made it hard for her to maneuver between the table and the shelves.

However, she managed to grab album after album of news stories and threw them on the table. Each one produced a loud *whack!* as it landed in front of me.

"Everything you need should be in those," she said finally, dusting herself off. She pointed at the albums. "If there's something you can't find, it might be on microfiche. Let me know so I can get it for you." She eyed me over the rims of her glasses. "Is there anything else I can help you with?"

"No, thank you very much." I smiled as she shuffled off to her post at the front desk.

Suddenly, she turned back around and peered at me more closely. "Say, aren't you that policewoman I read about in the papers and saw on TV?"

"Yes, I probably am." I waited.

"Hmm, I thought so." She raised her eyebrows and walked out the door.

I shrugged and proceeded to attack the files. I ended up spending hours sorting through the news articles. The librarian was right about one thing—Mary Jane Hendrickson certainly seemed to have lived a boring life. Actually, there wasn't much written about her personal life, but there were stacks of articles about her legend. It was when I was reading her obituary that something caught my attention.

Mary Jane Hendrickson had been born in 1825 and died in 1898. The obituary said she had left behind a sixteen-year-old daughter, Madeline. I'm not much of a mathematician, but I could clearly add and subtract.

According to the dates, Mary Jane would have been fifty-seven years old when she gave birth to her daughter. I don't know of any fifty-seven-year-old woman outside the *Guinness Book of World Records* who'd had a baby at that age now, let alone in the 1800s. There had been no mention of Madeline being adopted, but I'm sure that possibility existed. For some reason, though, I had my doubts that she was the product of an adoption.

I checked again. No, it wasn't a misprint. Mary Jane had died at age seventy-three. I set the obituary aside, deduced that Mary Jane was Superwoman and continued my research.

I noticed it was dark outside, and I groaned when I looked at my watch. I had been there more than three hours. Michael probably wasn't home yet, either. I knew he was out meeting with federal prosecutors in Cleveland to prepare for their upcoming trial.

The kids were with our babysitter, so I called home to do a quick check on everybody. Selina said that Michael had called about forty-five minutes earlier and was on his way home. I told her I'd be there in about an hour.

Once I had gotten through all the articles, I looked at my handwritten notes. Mary Jane Hendrickson had lived on the property where Mt. Olive Cemetery now stood. She had married Joseph Hendrickson, but he died of smallpox in 1897. For the most part, Mary Jane had cleaned houses for a living, mainly for her sister and brother-in-law, Sophia and Samuel Secrist. I remembered seeing their names on the tombstone.

Several articles confirmed that Mary Jane had also been an herbalist. After Mary Jane's death, Madeline went to live with her aunt Sophia and had died in 1948 at age seventy-six.

Madeline's obituary read that she was preceded in death by her father, mother and infant brother. I couldn't find anything on the brother. That was the only time I ever saw him mentioned.

Madeline also had a daughter, Maryanne, who'd been born in 1899. I lost track from there. There was no mention of a husband of Madeline; her obituary said "Hendrickson" only.

Who was Maryanne's father? I made a note to go to the county health department the next day to get the whole family's birth and death certificates. And I was curious to learn more about this new character, the mysterious baby Maryanne.

Chapter Ten

I had gone long past the hour that I'd promised to be home, and I couldn't wait to get there. I needed to be with Michael and the kids. Unfortunately, they'd had a long day and, according to Michael, were pooped. He'd put them all to bed shortly before I came home, and then we'd talked for almost half an hour before climbing the stairs to bed.

As I passed Sean's room, I was surprised to find him awake and sitting up in bed in the dark.

I walked into his room and sat down beside him on the bed. "Sean? What's wrong, buddy?"

At first, he just looked at me with his huge green eyes—his father's. I noticed that his chubby little cheeks were puffing in and out, and I realized he was about to start crying.

"Honey, what is it?" I patted his leg reassuringly. "CeeCee's here. Tell me what's going on."

And then he did, and what he told me sent shock waves rippling throughout every part of my body. He said he wanted to ask me a question since he'd arrived here, but he'd been too scared.

Apparently, before Michael had picked him up to bring him here, Sean's mother had told him that she and his daddy were getting back together. She knew that Michael would be moving back in soon and that Sean wouldn't be coming here anymore.

As his tears began to fall, Sean moved into my arms, the saddest little guy I'd ever seen. My heart broke as I listened helplessly to his sobs.

"I won't ever see Selina or Isabelle or you again, will I?" he asked me, wiping his eyes.

I pulled Sean closer, and then I felt another presence behind me. Michael was standing in the doorway, and he looked as shocked as I felt.

"Sean, what exactly did Mommy tell you the other day?" he asked, sitting down on the other side of the bed.

I wasn't only confused and shaken—I was fuming. Maybe Michael had had enough of my conflicting feelings about Eric and had begun seeing Vanessa, his ex-wife, behind my back. This can't be happening, I thought. I refuse to go through all this again!

Sean rubbed his eyes. "Mommy said that you're leaving CeeCee because you don't love her anymore, and that you still love Mommy, and that we're gonna be a family again." He sniffed and grabbed my hand. "But, Daddy, I don't want to leave CeeCee!"

I stood, trying to sort out my feelings. There have been very few people in my life whom I've allowed myself to trust, and Michael was one of them. It had taken me a long time to begin to heal after Eric's betrayal.

I had to admit that I was probably jumping to conclusions, but the thought of reliving another four-way relationship nightmare hammered my sense of logic. I felt a lump in my throat begin to swell, and the tears reached the corners of my eyes. Michael saw my distress, but he stayed focused on Sean.

"Sean, remember when we talked earlier about Mommy? Honey, I think this has something to do with that. Mommy and I are not getting back together, and I am not leaving CeeCee, okay? Mommy might want that, but I don't."

Still unsure where Sean's announcement had come from, I gave him a kiss good night and walked toward our bedroom, dazed. Michael was behind me a few seconds later and closed the door behind us. I turned to face him, my chest heaving, and I felt short of breath. I struggled to keep my voice down.

"What the *fuck*, Michael?" I was trembling. "How can you accuse me of wanting to go back to Eric when you and your ex are in discussion about getting back together?" Despite my good intentions, I heard my voice rise.

"Please calm down and lower your voice," he said, a frown beginning to appear on his usually calm face. He went to the bed and sat down, then fixed a steely gaze on me,

"Sean told me about this when I picked him up the other day, but I didn't give it much thought. I figured his mother was just fantasizing again."

"Told you what?" I crossed my arms in front of me and tried to calm down.

"He said his mom has been crying a lot. I know she hasn't dated anyone seriously since our divorce, but I figured she just wasn't ready." He ran his fingers through his hair, and when he looked up, his face was drawn. Despite myself, I began to feel sorry for him.

"When I took Sean home the last weekend we had him, Vanessa acted odd. She was all dressed up as if she was going out, but she clearly wasn't because she invited me to stay for dinner." He paused. "Which of course, you know I didn't." He went on, "Before I left, she asked me if I regretted getting the divorce."

"What did you say?"

"I told her I felt bad that Sean had to grow up without both parents in the same house, but she looked so fragile, I didn't want to hurt her by going any further. She must've taken my answer and created a whole scenario—a faulty one—around it."

"I'd say your answer left all kinds of room for interpretation," I pointed out flatly.

"Maybe you're right," he sighed. "I had told her a couple of weeks ago that you and I were planning to get married, and she got really upset. She said when she left me, she thought she was losing me to you and hoped I'd get you out of my system and run back to her. When I called her bluff and filed, she decided to go along with it. Obviously, when I said I regretted that Sean wouldn't grow up with both parents, she misinterpreted and thought I was implying that we might get back together for his sake."

I stood there staring at him, trying to decide whether he was telling me the truth. Actually, it was pretty clear that he was. But I was still pissed off.

"May I ask why you never told me any of this until now?"

"Honestly, CeeCee, I never gave it much thought! Why this is coming from Vanessa now, I don't understand. I mean, there was almost a year when I was on my own without you, and she never said a word."

"If she had said something last year, would you have gone back?" I was almost afraid to hear the answer.

"Come on! You know I wasn't in love with Vanessa for the last two years of my marriage, even before I even met you. The answer is no." He held his hand out to me. I hesitated, then took it and sat next to him.

"I trust you, Michael," I said softly. "You've never given me a reason not to. But when Sean told me what Vanessa had said, I got scared. The thought of going through the same garbage I did with Eric was too much. I'm sorry I blew up." Hugging him fiercely, I let all the bad feelings evaporate. He felt good, and I was safe in his arms once again.

Michael nuzzled my neck. "Boy, the Irish in you really comes flying out when you're pissed off, doesn't it?"

I giggled as he brought his lips to mine, and when his hand moved to my hip, I moved closer and touched him where I knew he loved to be touched. Our love-making was different this time, and something inside me welcomed him in a whole new way. Afterward, we fell asleep holding each other, knowing that we were home together—and each other's home.

CHAPTER ELEVEN

The next morning, I got the girls off to school before heading to work. Sean, who usually went to kindergarten in Cleveland, was staying with us for a few days while Vanessa went out of town. We'd hired a babysitter to watch him while the rest of us were out during the day.

I decided to call the county health department rather than drive over there because I knew what I needed from them would take some time. In addition to the birth and death certificates, I wanted them to give me a list of the oldest living people in the county, preferably those who remembered their own names.

I was pleasantly surprised when the fax came in less than twenty minutes later. Evidently, the health department folks kept a list pretty close at hand. The employee I had spoken to had written a brief note on the title sheet of the fax, explaining that the list helped the county know when residents hit their magical nintieth and hundreth birthdays. Having survived so long, these super-seniors were rewarded with a card. Personally, I'd rather get a nice check in the mail, but hey, at least it was something.

I immediately faxed the list to our Communications Center to check and update all the addresses. To my amazement, I was faxed the list back within forty-five minutes. This might turn out to be a good day after all.

Scanning the list, I highlighted the top five. The list showed which residents had been born in Richland County. I wanted to start with those who lived in the southern part of the county first, as older people tend to stay with familiar surroundings, and I was hoping to catch a break.

I crossed out three of the top five and found another two who lived south. I grabbed the list and headed out the door. The first three stops were useless; one person was in a nursing home, one had died five days ago and the other had Alzheimer's. It was at my fourth stop that I detected a shred of hope.

Eighty-seven-year-old Walter Morris lived just south of the town of Bellville, about two miles from Mary Jane's Grave. He lived in an old, battered farmhouse that sat a couple of hundred yards back from the road. A large red barn that appeared to have survived a century of storms stood directly behind the house. Surprisingly, the lawn was well manicured. Someone was obviously taking care of it.

An old Lincoln with a white hardtop sat in the driveway. I ran a check on the license plate and was somewhat surprised when the dispatcher told me the car was registered to good old Walter, who still had a valid driver's license. Eighty-seven and still driving—God, I found that scary. On the flip side, though, at least I knew he'd be coherent.

I knocked loudly on the front door several times before I heard signs of life from within the house. As I heard the slow shuffling of feet moving toward the door, I tried to peer through the front windows. It was pretty hard to see anything through the inch of dirt on them.

Finally, I heard the door rattle and a moment later it was opened by the oldest man I'd ever seen.

Walter Morris, I presumed. The man looked as if he were two-hundred years old. This isn't going to work, I thought. I'd be lucky if this guy could tell me his birth date. He might've been tall once, but I couldn't tell since he was bent in half over his walker. He was completely bald except for a light covering of gray fuzz. He reminded me of an ancient baby chick. He squinted at me over the frames of his two-inch-thick glasses.

"Walter Morris?" I asked the obvious question.

"Yes. And who are you?" His voice was surprisingly deep.

"I'm Sergeant Gallagher of the Richland Metropolitan Police Department, and I was wondering if I could talk to you for a few minutes." I held out my badge, which he peered at over his glasses.

"They lettin' you gals carry guns now?" he asked affectionately. When he smiled, he revealed a gleaming pair of white dentures.

"Yes, sir, for a while now," I joked back, and immediately found myself liking him.

"Well, I'll let you in since you're so pretty." He reached over to the door to push it open, but I grabbed it quickly to prevent him from falling over.

"Have a seat over there, young 'un." He pointed to a couch in the living room, but I kept standing close to him to make sure he'd make it into the room without any help.

"I know what you're thinking, but sit, young lady! I've been gittin' around on my own for twenty years now, and I don't need any help." He was still smiling, clearly proud of his dental work.

I sat and waited as he made his way over to an old lounge chair in front of a window. It took a few minutes for him to turn himself around, put the walker to the side and sit down.

"There now, I ain't the quickest draw in the West, but I'll get there eventually. Now what can I do for you?"

Despite his physical deterioration, his mind appeared quite sharp for his age. I got the impression that he didn't receive many visitors, since he seemed thrilled to have someone to talk to.

"Mr. Morris, I—"

"You can call me Walt. No need to be formal."

"Okay, Walt. How long have you lived here?"

"My whole life. I grew up in this here house," he said, a touch of nostalgia in his voice.

This was exactly what I'd hoped for. Maybe Walter Morris could answer my questions after all.

"Now, what's this all about?" he asked, his gaze turning sharp.

"Mr. Mor—Walt, I wanted to know if you remember any of the Hendricksons, some folks who once lived around here. This would have been close to sixty, seventy years ago, so I can understand if you don't."

Walter's shiny dentures disappeared as his mouth tightened when he'd heard the Hendricksons's name. I hoped I hadn't hit a nerve. By the look on his face, I knew he remembered his former neighbors very well.

"Listen, young lady, I know what you're getting at, but take some advice from an old fart like myself. Some things are best left alone."

"Walt, I was just asking if you knew them, that's all."

He leaned forward. "Again, I know what you're getting at. I know all about the witch crap. I know what happened a couple of days ago, too. I still read the papers. Far as I'm concerned, the place has been and always will be evil."

"Now, Walt, you don't believe in ghosts, do you?" I

prodded. I couldn't take my eyes off him as I waited for his answer.

"Wouldn't know. I only know what happened when I was a child and that was enough for me to believe in that place. I never went back again." He let out a loud, gassy burp. "Sorry 'bout that. These kids nowadays don't know what their messin' with. They think it's fun and all, but look what just happened."

"What do you think they're messing with, Walt? Please tell me whatever you can. A seventeen-year-old girl was brutally murdered, and the killer is still walking around. I was hoping you might be able to help me."

"That girl is dead because she disrespected sacred grounds."

I silently groaned. I wondered if Walter was one of those superstitious people who never walked under ladders or used the number thirteen.

"I ain't superstitious, if that's what you're thinking," he said, startling me a little. Was the man a mind reader, too?

"I wasn't implying that you were," I said defensively.

"You had that look on your face, like you think I'm some fruit loop or something. I'm fine and I know what I know, and that's it," he grunted.

"Okay, Walt. Can you just tell me what you know?" I leaned back against the couch, trying to curb my growing impatience.

"I'll tell you what I remember," he began reluctantly. "But I was just a boy, maybe nine or ten, so my dates are kind of fuzzy. Me and the nigger kid . . . Oh!" He looked surprised. "I forgot you don't call them that anymore. One day, me and the colored kid that lived down the road was out catching crawfish and frogs down at the river. He asked me if I heard about the witch, and I told him I didn't know what he was talking about. Well, he told me that a witch had been buried at the cemetery, and he dared me to walk back there with him."

I sat forward. "I'm assuming you went?"

"Yup. Worst mistake I ever made in my life. It was near dark when we made it down there. I knew I'd be gettin' the board on my bare ass when I got home, but I didn't care. I remember standing there and looking at that tree when I heard the crying. The colored kid, don't remember his name, maybe Eddie? Edgar? I saw him get a scared look on his face like I'd never seen before. I turned my head to see what he was looking at, and there was the woman. She was standing at the edge of the woods. I even remember what she said."

My heartbeat went into overdrive. "She *spoke* to you?"

"Sure did. She was quiet enough, but I heard it. She said, 'I forbid violence.'" He stared off into nowhere as if he were reliving it. "She was crying when she said it. Normally, I wouldn't have been so scared, but she just didn't look like she was real or alive. . . . Do you understand what I'm saying?"

"Not really." I wasn't too convinced, and I asked what he meant to avoid hearing another ghost story.

"I'm not gonna explain it to you, then," he growled, his eyebrows furrowed. "All I know is we ran home as fast as we could. I was so scared that I even told my folks. The kicker was that they weren't surprised. All they said was to never go back, and to tell no one who or what I saw there."

I wasn't following him. "What do you mean, 'who'? Did you know the woman?"

"Oh, I know who she was all right. I found out years later. Don't expect me to tell you, though," he grumbled. "I'm eighty-seven, and I'd like to make it to eighty-eight."

"Walt, no offense, but what does all this have to do

with the Hendricksons?" I was more lost than when I'd arrived.

"You're not listening. The Hendrickson house stood inside the cemetery—it was a small family plot back then. What they didn't know then, and this is mapped on county documents, is that the ground directly behind the cemetery was used by the Mohawk Indians as a burial ground."

I couldn't help snorting. "My goodness, that's quite a busy place. Not only was a witch buried there, but an Indian burial ground? I bet if we kept digging, we'd find the first aliens buried next to Jimmy Hoffa."

Walt wasn't amused. "This wasn't meant for your entertainment, missy. You asked and I'm telling you."

I put my hands up in apology. "I'm sorry, Walt. Please continue with your story."

"All I know is the original Hendrickson place burnt down, and Mary Jane's daughter, Madeline, lived with the Secrists until they died. She stayed on after they left her the house." He took a deep breath. "She was a strange woman, a recluse according to people around here. It wasn't until I was a teenager that I found out Madeline had a daughter, Maryanne, living there with her. No one knew anything about her, and there was no mention of a father. Maryanne died in the late 1980s, I believe. That house has been empty ever since. However, there was talk that Maryanne had had a child, but no one has ever seen him or her. I do know I saw the girl around the Second World War and she looked so pregnant I thought she was gonna bust."

I waited for more, but Walt stayed quiet, staring off into space. I hoped he wasn't on the verge of falling asleep in the chair. I wanted to keep him talking.

"Walt, is there more?" I asked quietly.

"Not that I'm able to say. I've told you all I'm allowed.

People have kept quiet for over a hundred years, and it was meant to stay that way."

I couldn't help it. I was getting frustrated. "Walt, for crying out loud, you said yourself you're not superstitious. Why can't you just tell me everything?"

"You still don't get it, do you?" He sighed deeply. "There's only one thing I can tell you. . . . If you want to find out everything, start with Ceely Rose."

I was now thoroughly baffled. "Ceely Rose, as in the Malabar Farm murderer Ceely Rose?"

"That'd be the one. That was one evil woman. She's the one responsible for this whole mess."

I was shaking my head. "Walt, please, I'm really confused."

He began standing up and reaching for his walker. "Sorry, young lady. I may have said too much already, but if you're as smart as you look, you'll figure it out on your own."

I looked at him, incredulous, as he made his way to the front door. I didn't want to leave yet. He had me so puzzled I almost wished I hadn't come. As he stood at the door, I finally got off the couch. When I went to walk out, Walt put his hand on my arm.

"Listen, young lady, I like you. You're good people—I can feel it in my bones. No matter what, just remember to be careful."

"Thank you, Walt, you take care of yourself, too," I said, disappointment obvious in my voice.

I sat in my car for a long time going over everything Walt had said. I had taped the entire conversation, but I didn't need to listen to it right now; everything was still fresh in my mind. I think what threw me off guard the most was the mention of Ceely Rose.

I didn't know much about her except the basics. She had lived with her family on Malabar Farm back in the

1800s. Malabar Farm was a large, rolling estate nestled within the foothills. Bought by author Louis Bromfield in the 1930s, Malabar Farm served as the wedding site for Lauren Bacall and Humphrey Bogart. Bromfield left the entire area to the State of Ohio upon his death. Now a state park, it sits less than a mile from Mary Jane's Grave.

The Ceely Rose ghost has also been a local favorite. However, her story was quite real. Ceely Rose, a physically unattractive woman, lived with her family and had no friends or acquaintances. She was befriended by a local boy who felt sorry for her, and she mistook his friendship for a marriage proposal.

Not wanting to hurt her feelings, the boy said he couldn't marry her because her parents didn't approve of him. Angry and distraught, Ceely took flypaper, soaked it in water to extract the arsenic, and poured it over her family's cottage cheese. They all died. The county sheriff cornered her and got her confession, and she lived out the rest of her life in a mental institution in Lima, Ohio, where she's also buried.

The story goes that Ceely's ghost haunts the farm. If you drive past the house where she and her family lived, you can allegedly see her in the upstairs window. I remember taking a field trip to the farm in the first grade and hearing the story. It became so popular that a play was written and shown at the farm every year. It was simply called *Ceely*.

The first year the play was put on, the actors and actresses began to claim unusual experiences in the barn where the play was held. People got depressed, seemingly out of the blue, and they found that certain places in the room were colder than others—and I mean *really* colder. Sometimes the actors would have to wear sweaters in one area and take them off when they moved off to another one. Ghost-hunters tend to report that extreme cold seems to indicate the presence of other-worldly visitors. I say it's all a crock, but regardless of my opinion, Malabar Farm is regarded as one of Ohio's most haunted places.

Trying to put Walter's information together with Mary Jane Hendrickson and then attach it to my murder was just too much for me right now. Maybe Walter Morris was nothing but a crazy old man who liked to tell ghost stories. It was the first time I'd heard of a connection between Ceely Rose and Mary Jane, but it was a possibility I just couldn't afford to ignore.

CHAPTER TWELVE

It was too late to go to the Health Department to get the birth and death certificates, so I started for home. I found myself rubbing my temple and clenching my jaw as I drove. I usually do one or the other—or both—when I'm into information overload. I had so much to analyze I was tempted to disregard all of it and just focus on our present-day murder. Exploring the past made my head spin, especially since there was an extremely high probability that it had nothing to do with the current murder.

I had a pounding headache by the time I got home and went straight for the medicine cabinet. I was struggling to open the aspirin bottle when Michael stood in the doorway of the bathroom.

"Bad day?" He grabbed the bottle from me and popped the lid off on the first try.

"Not bad, just jam-packed is all." I poured four pills into my hand, grabbed the cup off the sink and filled it with water.

He looked at the obvious overdose of medicine. "Those may help your headache, but they'll also do wonders for your stomach and liver."

I ignored him and took the pills anyway. He shook his head as I brushed past him and into our bedroom to change my clothes.

Michael headed back downstairs. "You want a glass of wine, Cee? I'm going back to the office."

What a sweetie, I thought gratefully. "That sounds wonderful. I'll be there in a minute." I was so glad to be home. After I put on some comfortable clothes, I checked each child's bedroom and found the kids in Sean's room playing video games. They all ran to hug and kiss me when they saw I was home.

"Selina, do you have homework?" I stroked her hair.

"I did it on the bus." She didn't look away from the screen, focusing on jerking her joystick violently back and forth.

I was too tired to look at her homework anyway, so I padded down to Michael's office. He handed me a glass of wine before sitting on the small sofa that ran along the farthest wall. I sat next to him and noticed that he had a file on his lap.

"You still preparing for that trial?" I asked, stifling a yawn.

"Not really, just a couple of things to go over. Tell me about your jam-packed day," he asked attentively, reaching up and tousling my hair.

I told him everything, and I even had him listen to the tape recording of my conversation with Walter Morris. After the tape was finished, Michael continued looking at the recorder. His casual manner had been replaced by tenseness—I could always see it in his eyes.

"Well, Michael, what do you think? Is he crazy?" I asked eagerly.

Despite himself, he began to chuckle. "I've got to tell you . . . I have absolutely no idea, Cee." He handed the recorder back to me. "I can't begin to make heads or tails of what he's saying, but honestly, he doesn't sound confused or deranged to me. By the way, the alien and Jimmy Hoffa comment was really pretty funny."

I had almost hoped Michael would declare Walter Morris a stone-cold mental case so I could put the entire matter out of my head. I lay back against the couch, let out a loud sigh, and accepted my defeat.

Michael was sympathetic. "Honey, don't throw in the towel just yet. Check into this Ceely Rose person and see what you can find out. Who is she, anyway?"

I briefly told Michael about the murders that Ceely Rose had committed, as well as the haunted farm.

"There sure are a lot of so-called haunted places in this area," he said. "Richland County must be quite an attractive retirement center for wandering ghosts."

I had to laugh, which felt damn good. Michael went on to tell me that, as far as the history of the grave went, I was on the right track by checking the birth and death certificates. Sure, I knew that I was an excellent investigator, and people like me leave no stones unturned. But as usual, Michael made me feel much better about what I was doing. As soon as the aspirin kicked in for my headache, I drank the last of my wine and was more than ready for bed.

Tomorrow promised to be another significant day— and I needed my rest.

CHAPTER THIRTEEN

First thing in the morning, I headed over to the Health Department, waiting impatiently for them to unlock the doors at 9 A.M. When I had spoken to the employee who faxed me the list of elderly people in the county, I had also told her I needed all of the birth and death certificates from the Hendrickson family.

The clerk had said she would try to have everything ready by this morning. When I gave my name at the front desk, I was promptly handed an envelope containing the birth and death certificates of Joseph, Mary Jane, Ezra, Madeline, and Maryanne Hendrickson. Ezra was apparently Mary Jane's infant son, who had died, but there was no death certificate for him.

Briefly glancing at them, I noticed that there was no birth certificate for a child of Maryanne Hendrickson, at least under that name. Yet Walter had claimed she'd had a child.

Back in my car, I flipped through the certificates before driving to the police department. I was stopped at a red light downtown when I suddenly had one of my staggering insights. I felt a surge of adrenaline as I sped into the nearest parking lot, cut the engine and grabbed the envelope. This was too important to wait until I got to my office.

I sorted through the certificates until I saw the one for Mary Jane Hendrickson. I looked at the date. Her birth certificate showed she had been born in 1855, not 1825 as her obituary had read. If the dates on the obituary were wrong, then Mary Jane Hendrickson would have only been forty-three years old when she died. This made more sense, as Madeline would have been born when Mary Jane was twenty-seven, not the superhuman age fifty-seven that I'd previously calculated.

Assuming the year in the obituary was not a misprint, why had Mary Jane been aged? Dying at forty-three wasn't all that unusual back then, unless it had been the circumstances of her death that someone had tried to cover up.

I hurried back to my office and spread all the certificates on my desk in chronological order, birth to death. As I examined them more closely, I noticed that many of the dates seemed inaccurate. I wrote them all down on my notepad and listed them in order:

(infant son) Ezra Hendrickson—Born Sept. 1897, no d.c.

(father) Joseph Hendrickson—Died Nov. 1897, no b.c.

(mother) Mary Jane Hendrickson—Died March 1898, born Aug. 1855

(daughter) Madeline Hendrickson—Born April 1882, died March 1953

(Madeline's daughter) Maryanne Hendrickson—Born Nov. 1898, died March 1985

Ezra had been born only two months before Joseph died and seven months before Mary Jane had died. I wondered if he hadn't died shortly after birth. Madeline and Maryanne both had their maiden names on their death certificates, with no sign of a husband anywhere.

Sixteen-year-old Madeline had given birth to her daughter the same year her mother had died. If I counted back, she would have conceived the same *month* her mother had died. And lastly, all three women had died in March. Coincidence? What was I missing here?

I sat back in my chair and stretched my arms. Walter had said that Maryanne Hendrickson was pregnant around World War II; that would've put her in her mid- to late forties. I remembered reading an article that said Mary Jane Hendrickson had relatives in Holmes County, two counties away. I spent the next hour calling all the surrounding counties and their surrounding counties, looking for any marriage certificates for Madeline and Maryanne Hendrickson. I knew it would take quite a bit of time, but I had plenty of that right now.

Next on my agenda was finding information on Ceely Rose. I scoured the Internet looking at newspaper archives and finally found a website devoted strictly to her. There wasn't much more on it than what I already knew. I had a few more websites to check when I glanced at the date of the Ceely Rose murders. I felt every nerve in my body jolt into life and I gasped, "Oh, my God!" to my empty office as I stared at Mary Jane Hendrickson's death certificate.

Mary Jane's date of death was listed as March 3, 1898. Ceely Rose had murdered her family on March 3, 1897, exactly one year earlier to the day. Still looking at the dates, I realized I had my hands over my mouth and was breathing fast. What all this meant, I had no idea, but I knew I was getting closer to what Walter had been trying to tell me. What I had a hard time believing, other than the dates themselves, was that no one else had ever put all this together.

"Hey, Cee, what's the matter? Are you sick?" I looked up to see Coop standing in my doorway, a faint look of alarm on his face. I still had my hands over my mouth and he probably thought I was going to throw up, so I lowered them and grabbed Mary Jane's death certificate.

"Coop, you have to look at this!" I handed him the paper and sat back, feeling pretty proud of myself. A modern-day Sherlock Holmes, I was.

I had forgotten that Coop didn't know anything about the Ceely Rose connection I'd gotten from Walter, so I quickly filled him in. Then I brought him up to speed on why I had given him the certificate. I reached over to my computer and turned the screen to face Coop, the website on Ceely Rose still displayed.

"Look at the date of the murders," I said. Coop's eyes narrowed as he read the fine print of the old article. When he finished, he looked at me as if I had lost my mind. Evidently, he didn't get it yet.

"For crying out loud, Coop," I snapped. "Look at the dates! Mary Jane Hendrickson died on the same day Ceely Rose killed her family, only it was a year later."

He sat down and peered more closely at the death certificate. I started rubbing my eyes in frustration, trying to suppress the urge to call him a moron. I really adored Coop and he was a fantastic detective, but sometimes he could be pretty dense.

"It is weird, I'll give you that," he admitted, handing the certificate back to me. "But I still don't see what it has to do with the Kari Sutter murder."

"Maybe nothing. *Most likely* nothing, but there's that slim chance that all of this will lead me somewhere." I slapped my stack of files, elated at my newfound discovery, and decided to go home for the day. It was the first time in a while I had gotten out of work at a normal hour.

I stopped at the grocery store on my way home and grabbed some things for dinner. I rarely cooked. In fact,

I downright hated to cook. Luckily, I had found two men who liked cooking more than I did, so Michael, like Eric before him, usually made dinner.

My discovery made me so high, I decided to cook dinner. Sean was going home the next day, which made all of us sad, and I didn't have to work, so tonight would be special.

Michael started laughing as soon he walked into the kitchen after getting home from work. I was elbow deep in tomato sauce, splatters of it on my face, while I made lasagna. Since I didn't cook very much, I hadn't exactly mastered the art of doing it neatly.

"You're supposed to *make* the dinner, hon, not *wear* it," he mused. "You're cooking? Congratulations on solving your case."

"Very funny." I glared, wiping at my face. "I did make a discovery, though. I'll tell you about it later."

Michael couldn't help coming to my assistance. He rolled up his sleeves and essentially took over. I slipped away to let him roll out the rest of the meal. I set the table instead and a lovely job it was, too, if I say so myself.

Since it was a rare occasion for us all to sit down and eat together, the kids had a good time, laughing and telling stories. They were thrilled when Michael took us out afterward for ice cream. We had to carry the children upstairs to bed after they'd fallen asleep during the second video we had rented.

I was finally able to tell Michael about my small but interesting breakthrough. He was dumbfounded. "You're sure it was the same date?"

As I had with Coop, I didn't know whether to laugh or slap him at moments like this. Why neither of them thought I could read was a question I couldn't answer. Nevertheless, I kept my mouth shut and handed Michael my handwritten birth and death timeline, along with the certificates and the website page on Ceely Rose. He looked over each one carefully.

"I'd say, without a doubt, you're onto something," he murmured, still looking at the pages, hesitating at Mary Jane's birth certificate. "This gives old Walter's story a little more credibility." He put the pages down. "I'm trying to figure out why they changed the age of death. Her obituary reads that she died of cancer and dropsy at age seventy-three."

"Affirmative," I cracked.

He stared straight ahead, and I knew his wheels were in motion. Michael was thinking, and he was thinking hard.

"Find out how obituaries were obtained back then," he finally said. "See if people just filled out forms, wrote letters or what. There should be a local historian who could tell you that. You easily obtained the obituary, so it shouldn't be too hard to find the rest. It looks to me like the newspapers back then didn't verify much, so you need to find out who wrote her obituary and lied about her age. And good luck, because without that information, you're nowhere."

CHAPTER FOURTEEN

I lay awake in bed for a long time thinking about what Michael had said and what I had learned that day. I even got up a few times to check my notes for things I wasn't sure of. Eventually, I fell asleep and when I woke up I was surprised to see that it was almost noon. Michael, the sweetie, had let me sleep in.

After getting dressed and cleaned up, I spent the rest of the afternoon playing outdoors with the kids. It was a warm fall day, and the girls had gone into the backyard to jump on the trampoline. I was throwing a baseball back and forth with Sean while we waited for Vanessa to pick him up.

Normally, I don't have any contact with Michael's ex. In fact, we've never even been face-to-face with each other. However, after the incident with Sean the other night and knowing her not-so-hidden agenda, I decided not to hide, as usual, but to stand in my own front yard and let the chips fall where they may.

Michael had just gone inside to answer the phone when Vanessa pulled into the driveway. She must have been waiting for this moment to confront me because when she got out of the car, she opened her mouth and the verbal abuse streamed out.

"Well, well, well," she began. "How nice to finally see

you, CeeCee. I see you've got yourself set up nicely here with my husband and son." She leaned back against her car, her arms crossed in front of her. Talk about body language. "Then again, I would expect nothing less from a home-wrecking whore."

Unfortunately for her, that was a bad move. I used every bit of self-control to keep from lighting into her. My eyes instantly went to Sean, whose face held a look of horror. His chin was quivering as he tried to hold back his tears.

"Sean, honey, why don't you run out back and say bye to the girls, okay?" I sent a big, comforting smile his way, and it seemed to soothe him a little. He looked back at me and then at his mother, and then he sprinted toward the front door.

I knew he was heading for Michael, which was exactly what I wanted. Vanessa maintained her position by the car, her dark eyes fastened coldly on mine. I stared right back. She was just a few years older than I was and a little taller, her light brown hair pulled back into a ponytail. Before today, I had only seen her from a distance through her window; now, this close to her, I saw that she was quite attractive.

I wasn't about to let her comment go unanswered. "Vanessa," I said, trying to keep my voice calm, "if you don't like me, fine. I really don't care, but I would appreciate you not creating a scene in front of the children. As you can see, you really upset Sean."

For a split second, I thought she was going to walk over and slap me. "Don't you dare act condescending to me!" She stood straight and took a step toward me, hands on her hips. "I knew two years ago you were fucking my husband, and if you think that was fun to live with, you're sadly mistaken."

Her raised voice had attracted the attention of some

of my neighbors, and several heads were beginning to turn our way. That seemed to inspire her to raise her voice even more. "You have taken my entire family away from me, and you have the audacity to stand here and lecture me? I don't know how you can look at yourself in the mirror every day, you slut!"

"Vanessa! That's enough!" I heard Michael's angry voice behind me. Finally! I thought, relieved.

I was so angry I was shaking, and I could feel my blood boil. I have never been one to solve a problem by fighting, but for one moment, I wanted to walk over and smash her face in.

Let Michael handle it, I told myself. She's his problem, not mine. I turned around and went inside before I lost control. When I got inside, I stood by the open front window and watched as Michael berated his ex-wife.

"What the hell is wrong with you? You can't talk to her like that, and in front of Sean? You're out of your mind!" He was talking in hushed, angry tones, trying to keep his voice down.

"What do you expect?" she cried, clutching the car door for support. "This was the first time I've ever really been face-to-face with her. I mean she used to be a *model*, for Christ's sake!"

Michael stared at her, unable to believe his ears.

She continued, "Please, Michael, can't we try to work this out? I mean, think about Sean. Don't you think he deserves another try for us?"

She had sunk to a new low with that one. Using Sean to try to get Michael back was hitting below the belt. I was still shaking and getting crazy angry, a feeling I'm not used to. It felt as if I might break down, myself.

Even though I trusted him, I had to admit I was worried that when Vanessa brought up Sean Michael would fall right into her lap. Sean was, after all, the son he adored.

I watched as Michael put his hands behind his head and took a deep breath. "I don't understand any of this, Vanessa. Why now? Why would you get Sean's hopes up and tell him we're getting back together when you know damn well we're not!"

She grabbed the bottom of his shirt and tried to pull him to her, still crying. Michael resisted, and I felt so sickened I had to look away. When I looked again, she was wiping her face with a Kleenex she had gotten out of her purse.

"I never thought you'd actually want to marry her, Michael! I . . . I thought . . . I thought if I was patient, you'd get her out of your system and come back. That's why I didn't contest the divorce—I still thought you'd get over her! I still thought you loved me! I can't handle this, Michael. I can't! You can't marry her!"

For whatever reason, Michael walked over and put his hand on her shoulder and started talking softly to her, softly enough that I couldn't hear. That was it. Feeling the lump in my throat rise, with hot tears running down my face, I watched them doing their Dance of Love Denied, all the while covering my mouth with both hands so they couldn't hear me.

After a few minutes, I saw Michael turn and walk toward the house. I ran over to the couch and jumped on it, pulling my knees to my chest. I didn't want him to think I had been listening to the entire conversation.

When he walked in and saw me all scrunched up on the couch and saw how hard I'd been crying, he knelt in front of me, taking both my hands in his.

"CeeCee, honey, I am so sorry about this," he whispered, his face strained. "We're going to talk about this, believe me, but right now I really need to get her out of here. I don't want her driving Sean in the condition she's in."

My heart sank as I understood what he was saying, and I felt the tears returning.

"I know this is very difficult for you, but I'm going to have to drive Vanessa and Sean home."

I felt as if I'd been socked in the stomach. I was so stunned I didn't think I could breathe. "How are you going to get back here?" My voice sounded weak and tremulous. Take control of yourself, girl. He'll think you're as bad as she is, I scolded myself.

"There's a rental car place right down the road. I'll just drive to it and she can drive the rest of the way. It's only about half a mile."

Michael kissed my hands. "Please, believe me that all I'm doing right now is looking out for Sean. I don't think I could sit here for the next hour knowing she was driving him the way she is right now."

"Don't let her take him at all, for Christ's sake!" My voice was quivering. "If she's not stable enough to drive, she sure as hell isn't stable enough to care for Sean!"

Michael sighed, his eyes still locked on mine. "Look, Cee, you're right, I could do that, but tomorrow when she files a motion to find me in contempt of court for refusing to return him we'll be in a whole other mess." He paused for a moment, looking at the floor. "Please, I know this is difficult, but trust me, I know how vindictive she can be. If I drive her home, I can calm her down—it's easier this way. Once she's calmed down, I know Sean will be okay."

I couldn't respond; my throat was tight and my voice had taken a vacation. I wouldn't have known what to say anyway. I just couldn't believe that the day had turned out like this. I'm sure Vanessa was thrilled. Michael knew it was useless to try to talk to me right now, so he squeezed my hands and stood up.

"It'll only take me a couple of hours, and we'll talk

when I get back." He paused to see if there would be a response from me. Getting none, he continued, "All right, I'm going to grab Sean so we can leave."

He looked down at me for a minute or so, his face thoroughly pained, before walking out of the room.

After he left, instead of sitting on the couch and crying, I called our next-door neighbor, a teenage girl we used sometimes for babysitting. I asked her if she could come over and sit with the girls for a couple of hours. I had to get out of the house, and I didn't want the girls to see me so upset.

I yelled out the window to Selina and Isabelle that I had to leave for a few hours and that Laura would be watching them. They were still on the trampoline, jumping away, oblivious to the fireworks that had just gone off in the front yard. When I pulled out of the driveway, I had a vision in my head of Michael and Vanessa in the car. She had almost an hour to try to talk him into going back to her.

I tried to tell myself that I wasn't giving Michael enough credit, but it wasn't working. The fear in my heart was just as strong as ever.

To calm myself down, I drove to the Clearfork Reservoir, one of my favorite places to go and think. It was a medium-sized lake in the southern part of the county with pull-off areas and jogging trails all around it. Last year, a child's body had been found along one of the trails, a victim of our notorious child killer. I wanted to avoid that scene, so I drove to the north side of the lake. I didn't need any more depressing thoughts than I already had.

It was near dusk, but I didn't care. I pulled into one of the desolate parking areas that had an entrance to the jogging trail and picnic tables down by the water. If I'd thought about it, I would've grabbed a bottle of anything that contained alcohol to comfort me while I was there. It was a good thing I hadn't or I wouldn't have been able to drive myself home.

I found a picnic table on a small drop-off about six feet above the water and sat down to watch the sunset. I set my cell phone next to me. The only reason I had brought it was in case Laura needed to call me. Other than that, I didn't plan on answering it.

I hadn't realized how scary it was for me to think about losing Michael. All this time I had taken him for granted, always assuming he'd be there no matter what. And even as I sat on the picnic table for almost two hours, there was a small part of me that wasn't really worried. But I wondered if I should be. Sometimes I failed to see Michael as a human being, someone with feelings like everyone else. I always thought he would just love me forever and wasn't capable of having feelings for anyone other than me. Vanessa's intrusion into my perfect little life had made me second-guess my earlier feelings of security. Had I been kidding myself about Michael?

If the lights hadn't come on automatically in the parking area, I probably would've sat there even longer. But a noise got my attention; the distinct sound of a stick breaking. It was loud, too loud to be a deer or forest animal, I thought. The noise came from the woods to my left. There was an unlit jogging trail running through the middle of the woods. I sat on the picnic table a few minutes longer, straining my ears, but all was silent. Finally I decided to leave.

I had almost reached my car when I heard the noise again. This time I turned and, following the sound, headed right for the trail. Lakes and public parks were a haven for local perverts, and I assumed there was one watching me from the trail. I had my gun, so I wasn't too worried. I'd been in scarier situations than this.

I walked directly onto the trail, following it back about thirty feet or so and found nothing. Maybe I was wrong. Maybe it was a deer, I told myself, not that I could see a whole lot. Stupidly, I had forgotten to bring my flashlight.

Suddenly, I heard a light splash of water. I walked to the edge of the drop-off and looked down. That's when I felt the hands on my back, shoving me over the edge. It was only about a five- or six-foot drop, so I wasn't hurt, but the water was about four feet deep, enough to completely saturate me. When I stood up in the water, I heard sticks breaking and leaves crunching beneath the running feet of whoever had just pushed me into the chilly lake.

I climbed back up to the edge and sat down for a few minutes, shivering and listening. Whoever it was had gone. Obviously I had been pushed into the water so the person could get away without me seeing them. But I wondered whether it had been a pervert who didn't want to get caught, or if it had something to do with the Kari Sutter murder. Past experience has taught me that murderers have an overwhelming desire to fuck with the investigating officer.

I didn't think I'd been followed here, and I hadn't seen any cars behind me, but then again, I hadn't been looking for any.

I was a woman, and I was alone. I cautiously made my way back to my car, feeling a bit edgy. Finally, soaking wet, shaken and pissed off that I hadn't seen my attacker, I pulled out of the parking area and floored it, eager to get home.

As I drove, I tried to remember whether I had passed any cars pulled off to the side of the road when I first got to the park, but I couldn't recall any. I found myself looking in my rearview mirror often, just in case some-one was following me.

I couldn't believe how late it was when I pulled into my driveway. I knew Michael was back when I saw a small, dark rental car parked in front of the house. He was waiting for me when I walked in.

"Where have you been?" he demanded. "I really wish you'd answer your cell—" A look of surprise crossed his face when he saw that I was wet from head to toe. "CeeCee, what the hell? Why are you all wet?"

"Let me get some dry clothes on and I'll tell you." I waved him off, frozen inside and out.

After I changed, Michael sat down in the living room and waited for me to tell him what had happened. When I did, he became extremely concerned. "I'm go-ing to assume that, once again, you've pissed off some-one in this murder case. Did you call the police?"

"Don't *assume* anything, Michael. I have no idea who it was, as I said. It could've been—and probably was—just a local troublemaker."

Even though I didn't believe my own words, I said them anyway, just so Michael wouldn't worry.

"By the time the cops could've gotten there, the guy was long gone. As far as I'm concerned, there's not much to worry about. Except, of course, what happened today with Vanessa," I said, shifting to the topic that really con-cerned me.

Michael nodded, took a deep breath and leaned back against the couch. He was clearly tired. I didn't know if this was the best time to discuss it, but I couldn't wait any longer to hear what he had to say.

"How come you were at the lake anyway?" he asked. Was he deliberately refusing to change the subject?

"I needed to go somewhere and think. I was a little

upset earlier, to put it mildly, and I didn't want the kids to see me like that." My voice cracked a bit.

"I know you were upset, and I'm sorry. I just wanted to get Vanessa out of here with as little drama as possible." He leaned forward and put his hand on my back.

"Well, you were too late. She'd already won an Oscar for best dramatic performance by a wronged wife."

"CeeCee, I know what you're thinking. I love you. I don't know what's going on with her or why." He paused. "There's something I have to tell you, but I don't want you to flip out about it."

The familiar thud in my chest started again. I didn't think I could take any more surprises today and found myself holding my breath.

"While we were in the car together, she kept trying to get me to reconsider, and I continued to say no. Then she got pretty nasty."

"Nastier than calling me a 'home-wrecking whore'?" I asked, still smarting from her accusation.

"Definitely. When I dropped her off, she said if I didn't give it another try she was going to try to revoke my visitation with Sean, permanently, because of you." He breathed deeply and avoided looking at me. "She said you and your job put him in harm's way and that you're reckless. The press you've received from past cases will back up her claim. Obviously, since you and I have worked half of those cases together, she's yanking at whatever straw she can out of desperation. She never even mentioned my job—just yours. If I stay with you, I can't see Sean." He said this quietly, anticipating the explosion that was sure to follow.

However, it wasn't an explosion that followed but a steady stream of tears. I wasn't surprised in the least, and I think deep down I knew something like this was coming. I did my best to keep myself together.

"She can't just decide that you're not going to see Sean because she doesn't like the way your relationship turned out. There isn't a judge in the world who will listen to that crap," I declared, wiping away my tears.

"I explained that to her." He nodded, looking at me, his eyes sad yet resolute. "But she was pretty insistent. All I'm telling you is to prepare yourself because I have a feeling things are going to get ugly."

"What exactly did she say on the ride up?"

"She said when she left, she did it to get my attention. She thought I would come running home, away from you, but I didn't. She never thought I would file for divorce, because she thought I would back out. She's always hoped I would come back. When I told her you and I were getting married, she broke down completely." He sighed. "Like I said earlier, she's never told me any of this before."

"If she had, would it have made a difference?" Whatever his reply, I knew it would be honest. I braced myself.

"No, it wouldn't. I told her our marriage was over long before you came into the picture, but she didn't want to hear it. When we got to the rental place I said good-bye and left her and Sean.

"Cee, don't worry. I think she's just blowing smoke right now. She'll calm down eventually. She knows Sean likes coming here, and as much as you'll probably hate to hear this, there's a part of me that wants to believe she truly has Sean's best interest at heart."

"So how did you leave it with her?" He reached for me, but I pulled away and looked at him.

"She *demanded* that I get back with her, and I *demanded* that she get some counseling."

"This is really upsetting, Michael. I was worried that you were going to go back with her," I confessed, still shaken by the whole experience.

He looked shocked. "CeeCee, that's crazy! You know better than that!"

I nodded. There have been very few times in our relationship where Michael has seen my vulnerability. I don't know what he thought about it, and I've never asked him. I stood up from the couch and walked over to the front window and looked out, Michael came up behind me, put his hands on my waist, then turned me around to face him.

"Cee, you never have to worry—I love *you*," he whispered. He began kissing me. We made love right there on the living room floor, and I prayed the girls wouldn't wake up. I could only imagine their horror if they did, but miraculously, we were left alone. Afterward, we went to our bedroom and held each other as we fell asleep.

Unfortunately, my sleep was short-lived. Three hours later, Naomi called to tell me that another young woman had just been attacked at Mary Jane's Grave.

Chapter Fifteen

"You said attacked, not murdered, right?" I asked sleepily, noticing on my clock that it was a little past two in the morning.

"Right, she's still alive," Naomi replied. "She's at the emergency room right now and the crime lab is on their way to the grave. I'll meet you at the hospital in half an hour. The vic's name is Danielle Horton."

Although this was mostly bad news, it was also good. Thank goodness she was still alive and might be able to identify her attacker. If there was a link, we might even be able to solve the Kari Sutter murder case.

Now wide-awake, I quickly dressed and headed for the hospital. To tell the truth, I welcomed thinking about something besides Vanessa and Michael, who was still sound asleep and hadn't even awakened when the phone rang. This was a pretty strong signal that the previous day's events had exhausted him as well as me. I was still wounded, though. I wondered if he felt the same way after wrangling with his ex-wife.

The Mansfield MedCentral Hospital emergency room was always a nightmare. I can't remember a time when every room wasn't full, with cops everywhere and hysterical relatives and crying kids keeping the chaos level high. I usually said that I'd prefer two simultaneous root canals over being here in the emergency room, but to-night was different.

I looked up at the large message board that took up half the wall just inside the emergency personnel entrance. The board held the last names of patients in the ER and told what room they were in. I saw the last name Horton in room eighteen. Her name was written in green, which meant she was in fairly good condition. I was relieved to see that. Like the colors of a traffic light, names in green were stable, yellows were fair, and reds meant they were in serious to grave condition.

Her green status gave me hope that Danielle might actually be able to give me a statement about what happened to her.

After making my way through parked gurneys, wheel-chairs, hospital and police personnel, I finally found room eighteen. Two uniformed officers stood in front of it, and one of them, Charlie Fulton, a tall, dark-haired, burly man with a mustache, waved me over.

"Hey, CeeCee, she's in here."

"Whatcha got for me, Charlie?" I poked my head in the room, but the curtain was closed, hiding the victim.

"Group of kids down at the grave were drinking and raising hell. They're out in the waiting area with their families. So this here gal"—he pointed inside the room—"decides to go off by herself down a trail, and her friends can't find her for a while. One of 'em ends up finding her about a hundred feet behind the graveyard in the woods. She's out cold and has a head injury and burns. According to Captain Cooper, the first vic had burns, too."

"Yeah, she did. Think this victim can identify her attacker?" I asked hopefully.

"I don't know. She was still out when they brought her in, but I think she's waking up. Captain Cooper just got here, too."

Charlie stopped and looked at the other uniformed officer, a rookie named Bill Meadow. The two grinned at each other.

"Is there something else, Charlie?" I raised an eyebrow at him.

"I figure I better tell you this ahead of time. Those other kids are saying they heard noises and shit. You know, the spooks were talking at the grave." He smirked, clearly not buying it.

"Woooo," Bill moaned in his best ghostly voice.

"Lovely," I said, shaking my head. Men could be such babies. I walked into the room, pushed aside the curtain and found Naomi with Danielle's parents, hovering near her bed. Strain was etched on their faces as they looked up at me.

"Sergeant Gallagher," Naomi said, walking over to me, "these are Frank and Berniece Horton, Danielle's parents. She's starting to come around a little."

I looked at the bed and saw a dark-haired, heavyset girl with a bad complexion. She was experimenting with opening and closing her eyes, trying to absorb the strange new reality of being hospitalized. I empathized with her. I couldn't count the amount of times I had awakened in a hospital and didn't know where I was. It could be a frightening experience, especially for a kid.

Danielle's parents were seated just to her right and looked terrified. Her mother—who looked like a grown-up version of her daughter, but even chubbier—was chewing her nails, her eyes red from crying. Frank, her father, sat stiffly with one thin arm around his wife and peered at Danielle anxiously through his thick glasses.

"How old is your daughter?" I whispered to Berniece.

"Nineteen." Her eyes moistened, and she wiped at them.

I gave Naomi a serious look as I raised my eyebrows. She nodded, knowing what it meant.

"Mr. and Mrs. Horton," she began, acting on my silent request, "I know this will be difficult, but if we could all step outside for a bit so that Sergeant Gallagher can talk to Danielle, it would extremely helpful." She opened the curtain. "You may not know this, but in most cases crime victims lose their memory of recent events as soon as they regain consciousness. Whatever Sergeant Gallagher can learn from Danielle right now will help us catch who did this."

The Hortons looked at each other, with Berniece giving her husband a pleading glance. I could see that she didn't want to leave her daughter. But Frank nodded and patted her back. They slowly stood, and Frank waited while Berniece kissed her daughter's forehead.

"Mo-Mom?" Danielle's voice was low and scratchy. "Don't leave!"

"We'll only be outside the room, baby. This lady wants to talk to you." Danielle's eyes, now wide open, darted in my direction. "And you need to try to remember everything. We'll come right back in when she's finished."

I waited until everyone left before closing the curtain again. Then I poured Danielle a Dixie cup of water and pulled the chair Berniece had been sitting on closer to her bed. After I propped Danielle's head up on her pillows, she gratefully took the water and began sipping it. I sat down and got ready for my interrogation, knowing I had to go gently here.

Speaking slowly and quietly, I said, "Danielle, I'm Sergeant Gallagher with Richland Metro PD. I'm a detective, and I'm here to ask you a few questions about what happened tonight." She handed me the cup, which I took and set on the table. "And honey, take all the time you need." I threw in the "honey" to show her I was on her side.

She nodded. "Where should I start? Are my friends okay?"

"Start at the beginning when you all got together tonight. And, yes, they're all fine. They're waiting to see you when we're done here."

Danielle reached up and touched the large piece of gauze that covered her head wound. Then she brought her hand across her chest, where more gauze covered the burns. I desperately wanted to peek under the gauze and see what the burns looked like, but I knew now was not the time. Her face crumpled, and Danielle started to cry, tears pouring down her face.

I handed her a tissue and waited. I noticed that Danielle's hands were still filthy, her fingernails packed with dirt beneath them. The emergency room staff merely tends to patients' wounds and won't clean them up unless they're admitted later, especially a crime victim. They've had their asses chewed one time too many from us cops about washing away evidence. Her nails looked as if she had been digging into the ground with her bare hands.

Danielle took a deep breath, wiped her eyes and in a choked voice, began her story. "Well, a bunch of us got together earlier tonight to go on the haunted reformatory tour."

She was referring to the old Ohio State Reformatory in Mansfield. It's on the national registry and is, like many other places in Richland County, supposedly haunted. Numerous television shows and movies, including *The Shawshank Redemption*, had been filmed there, and every year around Halloween the prison puts on a "haunted" tour.

"When we got there, it was like a two- to three-hour

wait, so Jeff Mason said we should go to Mary Jane's Grave instead."

"Did everyone else agree to it?" I asked.

"Pretty much. I mean, some of us were scared because it's so far down in the hills. But we went anyway because getting scared was the point." She paused and listened to the announcement that came across the intercom.

"Code blue, room thirty-one! Neurology, code blue!"

Someone's number had just come up. I didn't pay much attention, but Danielle did. "Oh, my God! Is someone dying?" Her eyes opened wider.

I nodded. "You'll probably hear that a couple more times while you're here, Danielle. Try not to let it upset you." I tried to get her back on track. "So you guys went to the grave, right?"

She looked back at the intercom before continuing. "Yeah, we got down there late, like one in the morning or so. We grabbed some more beer from Jeff's parents' house first. Am I gonna get into trouble for drinking? I'm not twenty-one yet."

"Well, I don't know about your parents," I told her, "but the more you cooperate with us, the better things will go for you."

She sighed. "I don't want to go to jail. And my parents will probably kick me out of the house. It's not the first time they've caught me drinking."

"Don't worry about that right now, Danielle. Tell me what happened when you guys got to the cemetery." Jeez, didn't she realize she'd almost been murdered? Instead, she was more worried about getting in trouble from her parents and spending time in jail—which wasn't going to happen.

"We were having fun. We were jumping out of the bushes and scaring each other. Then somehow I wound up on a trail near the edge of the woods. It was really dark, and I didn't have a flashlight. The others had some, but I didn't see their lights, so I thought they were hiding and trying to scare me."

She swallowed and reached for the cup of water again. I handed it to her and watched as she drained it dry.

"While I was on the trail, I heard someone whisper my name. I thought it was the others, so I teased them by going farther down the trail." Her voice began to shake. "I didn't hear anything anymore, so I turned to go back. Th-that's when I heard it." She closed her eyes.

"What did you hear, Danielle?"

"You'll think I'm crazy, but I heard a loud woman's scream. It scared the crap out of me. Then the scream turned into a baby crying, and the air around me got so cold I didn't think I could move." She opened her eyes and looked at me. "That's when they started throwing things at me: rocks and sticks. I felt one of the rocks hit me hard in the back of the head, and I blacked out. That was the last thing I remember until I woke up here."

"Danielle, you said 'they' started throwing things at you. Who are 'they'?"

She started to sob. "I don't know! I couldn't see! You don't think my friends would do this, do you, to make fun of me? These are the first friends I've ever really had."

"No, honey, I don't think your friends did this. They all came here on their own to see if you're okay. They wouldn't have done that if they'd done this to you." I spoke softly, not knowing whether it was the truth but wanting to keep her mood positive. "Danielle, do you mind if I lift one of your bandages so I can look at the burns on your chest? I promise I'll be careful."

She nodded as she wiped a tissue at her eyes. As I lifted the bandage closest to her left shoulder, I prayed that Naomi had brought her camera since I had forgotten mine. Standing and looking at the same burn marks that had been on Kari Sutter, I seriously wondered why Danielle had not been killed. Kari Sutter had been alone for more than twenty minutes, but according to Danielle, her friends had been with her. Maybe that's why she'd been spared.

"And these burns?" I nodded at the bandages.

"They were there when I woke up." She sniffed. "Those hurt the worst of anything!"

I asked Danielle a few more questions, but they proved fruitless. Clearly, she hadn't seen who attacked her, and now she needed her rest—and her parents.

After I filled in Naomi on my interview with Danielle, I suggested that I take the other teenagers who'd been with her back to the department for interviews. My main question was whether they'd had any contact with the teens who'd been present at the Kari Sutter murder. Were they friends? I knew there had been nothing in the news about the strange sounds at the grave, and the others had been too far away to see the exact shape of the burns. These were loose ends that I needed to tie together.

"I told their parents to take them home, CeeCee. I've got all their information—names, addresses and such—so you can get hold of them later today. Why don't you go home and get a few hours of sleep? When you come back in, the crime lab might have something for us."

"Sounds good to me, except that I need you to take photographs of the burn marks on her chest. They match the burns on Kari Sutter. They're the exact triangular shape and length. And while you're in there, ask her if she or any of her friends knew any of the kids from the Kari Sutter murder."

"I'm on it. Now get out of here and hit the sack. You look like you need it—badly," Naomi ordered.

Although I hate anyone telling me what to do, I couldn't deny I was fading fast, so I headed back home to my nice warm bed and, I hoped, a few more hours' sleep.

CHAPTER SIXTEEN

I didn't think I'd be able to go back to sleep when I got home, so I was surprised when I felt Michael shake me, trying to wake me up. To my amazement, I'd slept in and my angel had already gotten the girls off to school and was ready to leave for work. As I sat up in bed, he handed me a cup of coffee. "How's the latest victim?" he asked.

"The good news is, she's alive," I mumbled, still trying to get focused. "And she's got the same wounds as the other one."

"Do you think it could be a hoax?" he asked, always the cynical FBI man.

"No, the burn marks on Kari Sutter's body were never released. No one would've known except the killer. This was the real deal."

With a final swipe at his hair, Michael started for the door. I jumped up and gave him a hug, and after he left, I took my time getting ready for work, still trying to clear the cobwebs. As I was walking out the door, the phone rang. It was Vanessa.

"Is Michael there?" she asked tersely.

"No, Vanessa, he's not. You'll have to try him at work," I said stiffly. I was about to hang up the phone when I realized she was still talking.

"CeeCee? Are you still there?"

"Yup," I replied. Did she want to apologize?

"Oh, I was just wondering. I don't suppose my husband told you what happened when he dropped me off, did he? He told me it's been a long time since he's gotten a blow job like that." She actually giggled, the bitch.

"As usual, Vanessa, your trailer-trash upbringing is showing. As for the blow job, I made up for it this morning," I purred calmly. Then I slammed down the phone.

Honestly, I didn't know how much more of this I could take. The woman had no shame at all, spiraling down to the crudest level of human interaction. I wondered where she'd learned her social skills—maybe at a women's detention center?

I thought about calling Michael but decided against it. I'd tell him later if I felt like it. I knew she was lying, but I was beginning to wonder how long she'd be able to keep this up. The phone began to ring as I walked out the door for the second time, and I knew it was her, probably furious with my parting shot. I didn't answer it because I knew it would upset her even more not to have the last word.

I wasn't in my car for five minutes when my cell phone rang. It was Michael. "CeeCee, Vanessa just called me—" he said in rather clipped tones.

"Oh, I'm sure she did," I interrupted.

"She said you called her and told her she was white trash and taunted her with our sex life. She was crying."

"What?" I had to laugh, her claim was so ridiculous. "This woman is seriously ill!" I practically screeched. Then I told him what had really happened, and he was quiet.

When he didn't speak for a minute or so, I began to get angry. If Michael dared question whether I was telling the truth, I was going to go off the deep end.

But he didn't. Instead, he sighed into the phone. "All right, I'll take care of it. I'm sorry she upset you. You know how unstable she is. Just let me know if she calls back."

Oh, I'll let you know, all right. Because if this keeps up, I'm gonna get a restraining order against this nutcase, Michael's feelings be damned.

I could only put up with so much of this behavior. Yes, I understood that she was frustrated, and for that reason I'd been trying to tolerate her. But she'd have to grow up and accept the changes in her life—or else.

I put the Vanessa situation out of my mind as soon as I got to work. God knows, I had more pressing things to take care of. First on my agenda was to schedule interviews with the other teenagers who had been with Danielle at the grave. There were six altogether, and I figured it would take up most of my day, if not all of it.

I called and scheduled appointments with each of them, and while waiting for them to arrive I went online to search through the websites on Ceely Rose. All of them gave the same facts I already knew—except one. While most of them claimed that Ceely had murdered her entire family, one site stated that an older brother, Randall, had survived the murders. Fortunately for him, he had been out of town when the murders occurred.

Hmmm, I thought. Very interesting. Then I began a search through local archives for Randall Rose. I immediately came upon his obituary, not the original, but a statement of facts about his death. There wasn't much to it. He had apparently fallen off the roof of a barn and broken his neck.

There was only one problem: the date he died was recorded as March 8, 1898. This was five days after Mary Jane Hendrickson had died and exactly one year and five days after his family was murdered by his only sister.

I didn't know what any of it meant, but I printed the page to add to the file. I wrote a note on the page to go look at Randall's grave at the Pleasant Valley Cemetery, directly between Mary Jane's Grave and Malabar Farm.

That was the most I could do right now because the secretary of Major Crimes had just informed me that the teens were here, two with their parents because they were under eighteen.

As I'd expected, the interviews took up most of the day. Everyone gave a similar account of Danielle's attack, and for the most part Danielle's description about when had they arrived at the grave was accurate.

Yes, they all admitted, they'd been drinking and scaring one another. However, the other teens, unlike Danielle, claimed that they'd stayed together and hadn't gotten separated. They claimed that they'd merely turned around, and suddenly Danielle was gone.

When I questioned them about the other teens at Kari Sutter's murder, they said they'd never heard of them.

The accounts that Charlie gave me were the most interesting. The whole group had told me that as soon as Danielle disappeared, their flashlights suddenly lost power. Three of the kids then went down the road to get help because they'd heard about the earlier murder and had started to worry about Danielle.

The other three stayed put, but as they walked around yelling for Danielle, they described more "strange things" that began to happen. First, a sudden steep drop in temperature got their attention big time. The teens claimed that it became so cold they were actually shivering—a tad unlikely for early fall.

Next, they reported that someone started pitching rocks and sticks at them from the woods and that they heard a baby crying noisily. And last, sitting beneath the pine tree that appeared to have blood running down it, they all saw a gray-haired old woman dressed in white.

That was the last straw. At that point, the terrified teens ran as far as they could from the mysterious woman perched under the tree, heading away from the gate and toward the back of the cemetery. And that was when Jeff Mason tripped over Danielle's body, lying on the ground. One look at her and everyone freaked out, because Danielle looked dead as a doornail.

If memory served me, Walter Morris had told me that Mary Jane Hendrickson's house stood at the back of the cemetery before it burned down.

Meanwhile, Danielle's friends had returned, reporting that help was on the way. Mysteriously, their flashlights were working again, and even more mysteriously, the old lady had disappeared. The temperature had begun rising back to normal and the kids could hear the approaching sounds of sirens.

The only thing I could figure out from all this was that Danielle had been left alive because the killer realized the other teens had gone for help. He or she only had time to put the burns on Danielle and drag her to the back of the cemetery. None of the kids had seen anyone else either before or after their arrival at the grave, other than the old woman by the tree.

After the last teen left, I sat at my desk staring at the door. It was now more than a coincidence that all the witnesses were claiming to hear and see the same things, but it couldn't be real, could it?

How could this stuff be? I thought. Maybe it was special effects or someone who really knew how to stage a prank. Either way, the supernatural trappings were meant to distract the witnesses, no doubt about it.

I looked at my watch and saw it was getting late, but it

was still light enough for me to run over to Pleasant Valley Cemetery and snap a few pictures of Randall Rose's grave. Before I left, I checked with the crime lab to see if they had come up with anything. According to Bob, the news was the same as for the Kari Sutter murder—nothing.

I called Michael to let him know what I was doing. It was near dusk when I arrived at the cemetery, so I grabbed my flashlight just in case. Unlike Mary Jane's Grave, Pleasant Valley Cemetery stood along the side of Pleasant Valley Road. Anyone driving by could read most of the headstones.

Walking through the tombstones and reading the names, I saw they were all members of the same families: the Moffets, Mengerts and Tuckers. I also noted that these were also the names of roads that ran off of Pleasant Valley, telling me they were important, land-owning families back in the day.

The Rose family was buried in the back, and I noticed that there was no road named after the Roses. Oddly enough, they were joined in eternity by Randall, who was buried in the very last row beside one member of each of the other families. Four plots, their headstones about five feet apart, made up the last row of the cemetery. No one else.

After I took a few pictures of his grave, I turned to walk away. For some reason, though, I looked over at the grave next to Randall's, and the one next to that one, and so on, before I stepped back and looked at all four graves in front of me. Then, with a shudder, I read the names and dates out loud.

Randall F. Rose
Died, March 8, 1898

James L. Mengert
Died, March 13, 1898

Albert M. Tucker
Died, March 18, 1898

Gerald T. Moffet
Died, March 23, 1898

To my amazement, all the men, all in their early twenties, had died five days apart—within twenty days of Mary Jane Hendrickson's death. I whipped out my trusty camera and took enough pictures to fill an entire memory card.

For some reason, none of the men, including Randall, had been buried with the rest of their families. Instead, they'd been hidden in the back. Now I had to find out why.

CHAPTER SEVENTEEN

As I drove home, I still couldn't figure out how no one had made this discovery before. The notion that maybe someone had and then tried to hide it occurred to me, but I decided to put it aside for now and concentrate on getting home to my waiting family.

I was almost there when Michael called me. "Are you going to be home soon?" he asked, his voice tense.

I felt a chill run through me. "I'm almost there now. Why?"

"I'll tell you when you get here. I called Laurie to watch the girls for a while so we could talk."

My heart skipped a beat, then another one. "Sounds serious," I said, trying to sound calm.

"It is. I'll see you soon." And then he hung up.

By the time I pulled into the driveway, I was a nervous wreck. I was sure this had something to do with Vanessa and had to keep pushing away my alarm bells signaling that Michael might be going back to her.

When I walked into the living room and saw him sitting on the couch drinking whiskey, I became really concerned. This was a man who rarely drank hard liquor. I sat down next to him and put my hand on his.

"Michael, what happened?" I asked gently.

In reply, he handed me the papers he was holding,

and I felt my heart sink. I had only to read the line, *Vanessa A. Hagerman; Petitioner vs. M. Michael Hagerman; Respondent,* to know what this was—a motion filed by Vanessa to revoke his visitation rights with Sean.

"That vengeful bitch," I murmured, shaking my head in disbelief as I read the papers. According to the papers, the cause of the motion was, of course, me. Vanessa claimed that my past high-profile cases put me and my own children in danger, that I was reckless in doing so, and that I had no regard for my own children, let alone hers. She claimed that when Sean was here, he was at risk from the "criminal element" that I have, by being on the force, "chosen" to surround myself with.

Depositions were scheduled for two weeks from today. Still trying to appear calm, I handed Michael the papers.

"Her claims are ridiculous," I told him, biting out the words. "I'm a law enforcement officer, for Christ's sake. So are you! Of course we're around criminal elements. I can't believe a judge would sign this crap!"

I was beyond angry.

He nodded and handed me another piece of paper. "This was just dropped off a little while ago."

It was a subpoena for me to attend and give testimony at the deposition. I threw the subpoena down, stood up and headed for the phone. Michael was right behind me.

"CeeCee! What are you doing?"

"I'm calling Vanessa. I've had just about enough of her bullshit."

"You can't call Vanessa! She'll take that as a threat, and it'll get brought up in the testimony. Please, Cee," Michael pleaded.

I turned around and saw his face. The man was tortured, deep frown lines creasing his forehead. I could see that this was killing him, which in turn was killing me. I grabbed him and began to cry.

"So we can't see Sean until this is over?" I said through my tears.

He pulled away and looked at me. "No, there's no temporary order in that motion. I've already called my attorney and he said everything stays as is until the final hearing. Actually, he didn't think there was any reason to be concerned about this."

"How can he say that? It's your son!" I protested.

Michael led me back to the living room, where we both sat down again. I wiped the tears from my eyes and felt myself calming down somewhat. It was then that I had a thought—one that made me shudder—but I had to suggest it.

"Michael," I began quietly, "maybe if you moved out she'd drop all this. Just for a little while, until she calms down."

He looked horrified. "Forget it, CeeCee! I am *not* giving her what she wants—and I'm not letting her manipulate us. We'll let the court settle it."

"But custody cases can take months, Michael, even up to a year."

"I'm aware of that. Just don't bring that up again, okay? I'm not leaving you." To my relief, I saw that he meant what he said.

There was no point in arguing with him; he was as stubborn as I was. So we sat quietly for a while until an idea dawned on me. "She just threatened this yesterday, Michael. How'd she get the paperwork drawn up, filed, signed, and served in one day?"

"I noticed that the papers were filed with the court last week," Michael replied. "She's obviously planned this for some time. I guess yesterday was her last attempt before having me served."

The pain in his voice returned and I swore at Vanessa for hurting this man I loved so much. If Vanessa had been standing here, I would have wrung her neck with my bare hands. I've never had so much contempt for a person as I did for her right then.

I was so keyed up that I decided to join Michael with my own glass of whiskey.

"Michael?" I put my hand on his arm and looked at him intently. "Are you okay?"

"I'll be fine, honey, don't worry. I just hoped that she'd give this up, but apparently I was wrong." He sighed. "You know, I'm pretty tired and I think I'm going to go to bed. You coming?"

"Honey, I'm too wired. I'll be up in a bit," I said, giving him a kiss and watching him wearily climb the stairs.

I sat up for another hour after I put the girls to bed, trying to figure out a solution to this nightmare. I ended up feeling more frustrated than ever.

Since I wasn't able to fix my personal life, I found my thoughts drifting to my case. I realized I needed to find out how each of the four men whose graves I'd found had died. After that, I had to figure out how they were connected with everything. And only one person could tell me what I wanted to know—Walter Morris.

CHAPTER EIGHTEEN

I didn't sleep much that night, mainly because Michael didn't. He was restless and kept getting out of bed to walk around. I hated to see him like this, but there was nothing I could do. He was already dressed and ready for work when I got up, and he was unusually quiet and distant most of the morning until he left. My heart ached for him.

I decided to skip going to my office and drove to Walter Morris's house. Thoughts about Michael hovered around me during the entire drive until I pulled into Walter's driveway. I grabbed the photographs of the men's tombstones and arranged my notes before knocking on his door. After five minutes without an answer, I was getting ready to leave. Walter's car was there, but I assumed he was still in bed. It was early, but it wasn't that early.

As I turned to leave, I heard the familiar shuffling of feet coming from the other side of the door. Walter finally opened the door. By the look on his face, though, he didn't seem too happy to see me.

"Oh, it's you, young lady. Forget something last time, did ya?" He eyed me suspiciously.

"Actually no, Walt, I didn't. I happened to discover some other information that I'd like to talk to you about, if you're willing."

He stood there looking at me, and I suddenly knew that he wasn't going to let me back in.

"I told you all I can tell you, young lady. I'm sorry you wasted a trip back down here, but there's nothing else to say." He started to close the door.

I put my hand on it. "Walt, please. I have some pictures I want you to look at, and then I'll leave. You can look at them right here—I don't even have to come in," I said in my most enticing voice.

Walt reached up, took off his glasses, and began rubbing his eyes with one hand, the other holding on to the walker. "All right, young lady, let's see those pictures. I've never been one for rudeness, and I don't intend to start now."

I shuffled through my folders, quickly in case he changed his mind, and pulled out the digital photographs of Randall Rose's grave and the others, thrusting them forward. He reached out and grasped them in his gnarled fingers.

I didn't know how good his vision was, but he only looked at them for a few seconds before handing them back to me. A strange, defeated look was on his face. He let out a deep sigh.

"Can you tell me anything about those, Walt? I don't know if you're aware of this, but those men died right after Mary Jane Hendrickson did, including Ceely Rose's brother."

"Yep, it's a bit strange, isn't it, young lady?" he said cryptically.

"Yes, it is, and I think you know why," I said. I was getting a bit impatient with his game-playing.

"Maybe I do, but you'll have to figure it out on your own. You've come this far, right? Now you'll go the rest of the way." He paused. "You can't come back here anymore, Sergeant, it just won't do. No one is supposed to talk about this, ever."

"If no one was supposed to talk about it, how did the story get started in the first place?" I countered with a somewhat forced smile.

"Because someone *did* talk. Now be on your way, young lady."

Walter shut the door as I stood there flabbergasted once again. He dangled important information before me, and then shut the door in my face. It was infuriating.

When I got back to my office, I logged on to my computer to research the deaths of James Mengert, Albert Tucker, and Gerald Moffet. It took quite a while to find anything, but I got lucky with James Mengert, who drowned in a nearby pond. Then Albert Tucker apparently choked to death on a piece of food. I couldn't find any cause of death—odd or ordinary—on Gerald Moffet, but I'm sure it was along the same lines as the others. They had all died of "ordinary, everyday" accidents, but the timing was sure one hell of a coincidence.

Feeling stuck again, I pulled the file on the robbery that had taken place at the gravesite several years ago. I had only briefly skimmed through it earlier, but now I was paying closer attention to the interviews with the suspects. Several had casually commented on some unusual occurrences while they were robbing a carload of teenagers.

First, each of the suspects claimed that the car had "died." The lead suspect had said, "I don't know, it just died. It's never done that before." Second, one of the suspects said he thought the car had caught fire because he smelled something burning, but no one else did.

All of the suspects, prior to the robbery, were at the

grave and tried to cut the pine tree down with an ax; predictably, it wouldn't budge. After that, they tried to set the tree on fire, but instead, one of the suspects ignited his own arm. Clearly not one of the brightest in the group.

In one interview, the suspect had claimed, "I don't know what the deal was, but that tree didn't want to come down, so we gave up."

And last, not one of the suspects had a prior criminal record. They were former straight-A students and college graduates. All of them claimed they didn't know why they did it. "Something just came over us, I guess."

For these young men to put on ski masks, grab baseball bats and surround a carload of teenagers, then beat and rob them, was extremely unusual. All had been sentenced to at least ten years in prison.

I threw the case file aside and stretched. I knew I was missing something, and then suddenly it came to me. I grabbed the photographs from the Kari Sutter murder and began flipping through them, stopping at the large photograph of the bloody *M* painted on the tree. I set it aside and grabbed my timeline of the Hendrickson family. I hadn't paid much attention to it earlier, but taking another look at it, I realized that the first names of all the Hendrickson women started with M: Mary Jane, Madeline, and Maryanne.

Could it be a coincidence? I didn't think so, but I had to remind myself that anyone wanting to toss a clue to investigators could've written M for Mary Jane only, not knowing about the others. I noted this in my file as Coop came striding in.

"Anything yet?" he asked. My clenched jaw was my response. "Oops, I guess not," he noted, then pretended to back out of the room.

"So what are you up to?" I asked, closing the file.

"Getting ready to leave. Naomi has her monthly checkup this afternoon, so I'm taking off early."

Last year, during the Carl James Malone case, Naomi's skull had been severely fractured. Now she had to have monthly exams to ensure that her neurological system kept working properly.

"Everything okay with her? No problems?" I hadn't asked in a while and I felt bad.

"Nah." He waved off my question. "She's as good as gold. Sometimes she jokes around with me, though. The other day we were eating dinner and she looked right at me and said, 'What's my name?' I'm telling you, Cee, she scared the shit out of me."

I laughed loudly. We had all been tense when Naomi was in the hospital, but she had come through as good as new and with an even better sense of humor, apparently.

When Coop left, I tried the lab again. Bob told me if I called one more time he'd take the final results, when they came in, and stick them up his ass, and I'd have to climb in and grab them if I wanted them that badly.

Wearily, I shook my head as I hung up, then looked at my watch. I had an hour to kill, a rare phenomenon.

Grabbing my bag and keys, I decided to have a look at Malabar Farm. It would probably take me less than an hour, and then I'd sneak home early. It was Eric and Jordan's time to take the girls, so I had to get them packed and ready to be picked up.

On the way down to Malabar Farm, I realized I hadn't heard from Michael all day, which was unusual. I tried to call his cell phone, but he didn't answer. I hoped he wasn't trying to avoid me so he could give me more bad news in person at home. Actually, I didn't know how things could get much worse.

When I pulled into the long paved drive leading into

the farm property, I was again struck with how inviting and picturesque it was. Certainly, it wasn't your typical site for a ghost hunt. The Bromfield House, or "mansion," as it were, sat high up on a hill to my right. The Malabar Agricultural Library sat on my left, across from the Malabar Hostel, and the Ceely Rose House was ahead around a large curve. I parked in front of it and got out, my camera in hand, ready to shoot anything that looked interesting.

It was a simple two-story, white aluminum-sided house with dark green wooden shutters. I walked onto the front porch and tried to open the door, but it was locked. I took a couple of photographs and looked up at the window where, according to local legend, the ghost resides. Seeing nothing but the reflection of a large maple tree that stood beside it, I packed up my camera and headed home.

On my way, I tried to call Michael several times, but there was no answer. So I was somewhat surprised to see his car in the driveway when I got home.

"Hi, Michael. I'm back!" I called. I heard the shower running, so I quickly packed the girls' things and got them ready to go. Jordan would be there in fifteen minutes to pick them up.

Michael came outside just as Jordan was pulling in. He gave the girls a quick hug and a kiss on their cheeks before going back inside. He hadn't said a word to me, and I didn't much like the foreboding that was growing inside me. I kept it together while I helped Jordan put the suitcases in the car and said good-bye to the girls.

Then I marched right back into the house and found Michael in his office, looking out the window at Jordan's car as it drove down the street.

"Michael?" I said, but he didn't respond. "Michael, are you okay? Is this about last night?"

He shook his head and ran his fingers through his hair. "Sit down, Cee." His voice was quiet and held a note of sadness.

Apprehensive and on edge, I sat on the couch. "Oh God . . . What now, Michael?"

He sat next to me. "I had these served on me today." He reached over to the table beside the couch and grabbed a set of papers, handing them to me.

The papers were a temporary motion filed by Vanessa to revoke all Sean's visits, pending the outcome of the custody case. A judge had signed the papers, which now meant Michael couldn't see Sean until the matter was resolved, which could take months, if not a full year.

I'd been wrong thinking things couldn't get any worse. I felt the familiar lump in my throat rise and a jolt through my stomach. Next came the tears.

"Did you call your attorney?" I whispered.

He nodded and cleared his throat. "He's trying to get the hearing date pushed up so we can take care of this sooner." He bowed his head and spoke softly. "She won't even let me talk to him on the phone, Cee."

I felt so many simultaneous emotions I wanted to throw my head back and scream. I was sad, angry and devastated, but most of all, I was torn into little pieces by Michael's anguish. I pulled him into an embrace, and we just held each other for several minutes.

"Michael," I said, while stroking his hair, "I'm so sorry."

He squeezed me harder. "I don't know how I'm supposed to go for months without seeing him. I can't do it."

I wanted to tell Michael that this could easily be solved if we just bumped off Vanessa, but I didn't think he'd be amused—especially since I was only half kidding.

After barely eating dinner, Michael went to bed early, emotionally wiped out. I stayed up and finished an entire bottle of wine, which did nothing but add to my own emotional imbalance. Then I headed to bed.

The next morning when I woke up, I was astonished to see that Michael was gone. I'd thought I'd heard him earlier but was too sleepy to call out to him. He obviously hadn't fallen asleep and decided to head to work early.

Hungover and depressed, I was looking forward to working all day about as much as standing in front of an oncoming eighteen-wheeler. And then the day really turned to crap when the phone rang. Vanessa.

"Hi, CeeCee!" She sounded upbeat.

I began to shake. "You've got a lot of nerve calling here. As far as I'm concerned any communication will be done through the courts, and you are *not* welcome to call my home again!"

"Now, now. Let's be fair. You know how you can end this," she chastened me, the lilt still in her voice.

I imagined a number of ways I could eliminate Vanessa—permanently—from our otherwise happy lives, then decided to see where she was heading with this. "Really? How's that?" I was sarcastic.

"I'll tell you, but you need to listen carefully."

I should've hung up, but didn't. "I'm listening, Vanessa."

"First of all, he won't win. You both need to realize that up front. My brother knows the domestic relations judge well. They're tight. Shall I say more?" she goaded.

"How can you do this to your son?" I demanded.

"I'm not doing anything to my son because I know you're going to go along with me. He'll see his father."

I was confused. She had me so shaken that each of my two million nerves seemed to stand on end. I knew that to continue a conversation with her would likely be a game of Russian roulette so I bit back my reply and waited silently.

"I'm assuming you're there, CeeCee, so I'll finish. The only way Michael will see his son again is if you break it off with him, and I mean *entirely*. No relationship, no living together, and clearly no wedding." She snorted. "I know you won't tell him this, because if you do, I'll tie this up in court for years. Do you hear me? Years! If you really love Michael, you'll quit being so goddamn selfish and let him go. For his son."

She waited for a response, then, getting none, continued, "As soon as I get word that you two are kaput, I'll let Michael see Sean. And don't even think about trying to sneak around behind my back because I'll refile the motion. Again, you're going to do it in a way where he'll never know this conversation took place. I'm waiting for an answer."

She had me, and I could've died right there in my kitchen. I had to suppress the urge to threaten her life, but I had no other choice. She was probably recording the conversation in case I did, editing out the blackmailing part, of course.

Once again, I was being faced with giving up Michael, and this time, I didn't think I would be able to cope. It was me or his son. I thought back to Michael in his office and how devastated he was, and I knew I couldn't see him like that again. Sean was his whole world.

"If I do this," I said, trying to ignore the voice within that was yelling *Wimp! Tell her to go to hell!*, "you'll let Michael see Sean?"

"Yes, of course I will."

I paused. "Give me a few days, and it's done."

I slammed down the phone, and then I lost it. I cried so hard I thought I'd pass out. I was screaming and berating myself for putting off the wedding, because if I hadn't, we'd already be married and she'd have a tough time trying to coerce me into giving up the man I loved. I didn't think I'd be able to face Michael and tell him it was over, but I had to. Vanessa had left me no other choice.

It took me a long time to get myself together. Even then, I felt dazed as I drove to work. When Michael called just as I was pulling into the police department parking lot, I said, "I can't talk," and hung up. This was not like me at all, and he had to know something was wrong.

I wouldn't have believed it, but when I got to my office, Naomi was waiting for me. And yes, she had more news to ruin my day.

CHAPTER NINETEEN

"I hope you didn't have anything planned today, because guess what we get to do?" Her sarcastic tone told me something unpleasant was coming.

"Let's have it," I grumbled, throwing my bag and keys on my desk.

"The storage room is being sprayed. Sooo, we have to move all the boxes of old files over to this building. After that, we have to go through all of this year's boxes and pull the reports that haven't been scanned onto the computer yet and give them to records. I have a list." She flopped into a chair and sighed. "Needless to say, it's going to take us all day. Coop's gonna help."

I couldn't deal with this today. "Why do we have to do it? Thirty clerks in the records department have nothing to do all day."

"So said the sheriff, that's why. Some of those cases are confidential, and he wants us to do it. Not to mention, some were never closed out, so we have to see which ones need to be." She stood up to leave. "If you have something that needs to be done with any of your cases today, let me know and I'll assign one of the other detectives to do it. I'll meet you at the storeroom in a little while. If you want to go home and throw some jeans on, feel free."

I put my face in my hands and felt like crying again. I should've called in sick. I hadn't taken a sick day in more than ten years, and if ever I needed one, today was the day.

I took Naomi's advice and went home to change my clothes. I threw on an old pair of jeans and a sweatshirt with a T-shirt underneath, in case it was warm in the storeroom. I had been in the storeroom before, and it was filthy.

My head was cloudy all day. I felt like a robot: lifting boxes, sorting through files, checking off lists. Nothing seemed real. Every time I thought about going home and facing Michael, I got downright ill. Naomi and Coop noticed. Both asked me what was wrong several times throughout the day. I told them I had a headache and didn't feel well. I wasn't lying.

At the end of the day, we weren't finished with all the files yet. Naomi said we'd finish them tomorrow.

"I'll stay and finish them," I volunteered.

Naomi looked at me strangely. "That's okay, go home. You said you weren't feeling well, and quite frankly, you don't look so good. We'll have them finished by late morning."

"Really, it's not a problem." I didn't want to make too much of an issue of it. "The girls are with Eric, and Michael will be late . . . I've got things to do tomorrow with my case, and I'm feeling much better, so go. I'll take care of it." I produced a halfhearted smile.

Naomi kept looking at me, her eyes narrowing. "CeeCee, I don't mean to pry, but is everything okay at home?"

I rolled my eyes and kept my smile. "Yes, things are fine. Not to worry. Shoo!"

That was the downfall of being a cop; you had to

work with other cops and it was hard to get something past them.

I called Michael and prayed I would get his voice mail. I was in luck. I told him not to wait up for me. I would be very late. I tried my best to sound normal, but even hearing his voice on the message stirred my emotions. I couldn't face him until I thought of a reason to break it off. Otherwise he would know immediately something was wrong, and he'd start badgering me about it.

I took my time with the remaining files. I went so slow, it was after midnight when I finally crossed the last file number off the list. I was exhausted. Michael should be asleep by now, and as tired as I was, I would be asleep within minutes when I got home.

As I predicted, he was asleep. After I took a quick shower, I set my alarm two hours early so I could be gone by the time he woke up. I wasn't allowing myself much time for sleep, but I couldn't face him.

I felt just as dreary as the day before when Naomi called me on my way into the office. "You need to go down to the grave first thing. I'll meet you there." She sounded out of breath.

"Why?"

"It's nasty. Apparently, the township was mowing the cemetery this morning when they found a dead dog. Not a big deal, except this dog was completely skinned and supposedly has a bunch of ritualistic crap around it." I heard the *beep, beep, beep* as she opened her car door. "By the way, I can't believe you finished all that last night. Thanks."

"Naomi, why are we going down there? It's just a dog that was probably mutilated by some sicko fascinated with the murders. It's not a person."

"You're probably right, but we should at least look at it and snap a few pictures." Her car was now accelerating; she was on the move.

"All right, I'll see you in a few," I conceded, while I made a U-turn.

On my way down to the grave, my cell phone rang. I saw Michael's number, so I didn't answer it. After a few minutes, the ring from my voice mail went off. I listened to the message:

"Hey, baby, it's me. I'm getting ready to leave and was just wondering when you're going to be home tonight, since I haven't seen you in a couple of days. I really miss you, and I love you. Have a good day."

My chest went into a spasm, and for a moment I had my phone in my hand ready to call Vanessa and tell her to take her deal and stick it right up the farthest reaches of her ass.

But I remembered that Michael had once told me that her brother, a Cleveland Police officer, was married to a judge's daughter, a domestic relations judge. Her brother had probably told his father-in-law over dinner what a horrible person I was. No doubt the judge's mind was already made up before the hearings even began. Typical of our justice system. It was nothing but a farce. Phone calls were made, money was passed, judges and juries were prejudiced, all of it happened every day. I put my phone down and fought back the impending tears. Michael had sacrificed everything for me, and now it was my turn to make the mother of all sacrifices—our relationship and future marriage.

I parked next to Naomi's car in front of the gate to the cemetery. I saw her and several township employees standing around a white mass in front of the pine tree. I was only a few feet away when I could clearly see the burn marks on the dog's skinned body. Burn marks that matched Kari Sutter's and Danielle Horton's.

"You've got to be kidding me," I mumbled as I took in the entire scene.

The dog was lying in a red circle, presumably its own blood, with its own skin torn up in pieces next to the carcass, forming a crude *M*. Flies had already come and gone, so the maggots were feasting away. One of the township workers looked like he might vomit.

"I'll get the crime lab down here." Naomi sighed, as she turned and walked toward her car.

I got all of the township employees' names, looked at their shoes and asked where in the cemetery they had been. Then I sent them away and declared the area a crime scene—for the third time this month.

Waiting for the lab techs to arrive, I started walking the perimeter of the cemetery and came across something that hadn't been found in the earlier crime scenes: a footprint. It wasn't one of the employees' prints, and it was also very fresh.

"Naomi!" I called over my shoulder. "Bring me a flag, a ruler and a camera!"

Naomi fumbled around in her trunk, then brought the items over. I took the small bright orange flag from her and stuck it in the ground about an inch from the footprint. I laid the ruler directly next to it. Stepping back, Naomi and I looked down at the print, which was longer than the ruler.

"That is one helluva long shoe print," I pronounced.

Naomi nodded. "What is that? Size thirteen? Fourteen?"

"Definitely not a woman's print."

"When the lab gets here, we'll have them make a plaster cast of it. At least there's some treads in it. It's a start." She looked toward the gate, anticipating the arrival of the lab.

After I took a few photos of the shoe print, I continued to walk the perimeter of the cemetery but found nothing else. The crime lab technicians, once they arrived, complained about having to bag up the dog for an autopsy. Considering the mood I was in, I didn't want to hear it and I snapped at them, something I have never done before.

"Just bag the goddamn dog, and quit your fucking bitching!"

My dressing-down turned the heads of everyone around us. I never disrespected a member of my department as I had today. The township employees were down by the gate and heard every word. Naomi shot me a stern glance, walked over to the technicians and calmly told them to get the dog bagged up so we could all get out of here.

As I walked over to my car, I was treated to enraged stares by the technicians, some of whom I had known for years. It was all I could do not to burst into tears right there in the cemetery.

I tossed my camera into my car and was ready to drive away when Naomi came over to my window.

"CeeCee, shut the car off," she ordered.

I left it running. "I need to go, Naomi. I have things to do."

"Not until you tell me what the hell has been up your ass for the last couple of days." She was angry. "I've never heard you talk to any member of this department like that. You owe them an apology!"

I tried to stay calm, but my voice began to shake. "Naomi, please, I'll apologize later, and I don't want to talk about this right now. I have to go."

With Naomi still at my window, I pulled away. I wasn't

even to the end of the road before my dam broke. I turned onto a side road, put my car in park and sobbed.

When I felt able to drive again, I drove around for a while before going back to my office. I was somewhere near the county line when my attorney called.

"CeeCee, good news! Your papers are ready. All you and Eric have to do is come in and sign them. I'll file them tomorrow, and it'll be a done deal."

I had a thought. "Have you called Eric yet?"

"No."

I took a deep breath. "Do me a favor and don't call him right now, okay? Just hang on to the papers and don't file them."

I had found my reason to break up with Michael.

CHAPTER TWENTY

"CeeCee, I don't understand," my attorney said. "You said you couldn't get this done fast enough."

"I know. Trust me, it won't be much longer, but I just need a few more days. I can't explain it right now."

I rubbed my head after hanging up with my attorney. I anticipated today being one of the longest days of my life. I had been driving around for more than an hour and was sure Naomi was livid by now.

When I walked in my office, Naomi was there with Sheriff L. Richard Stephens, our head honcho.

Naomi couldn't talk about my whereabouts too much in front of the sheriff, so she just asked me casually, "CeeCee, where you been?" She looked concerned.

"I was looking for a witness," I lied, and then changed the subject. "Sheriff, how have you been? I haven't seen you in a while. "

"I've been busy campaigning. It seems my opponent has been hitting the northern part of the county hot and heavy."

I sat at my desk and genuinely smiled. "Sheriff, the only one around here who believes you have to worry about this election is you. It's in the bag."

He shook his head. "I don't know. I don't ever say that. In this type of thing, anything can happen. My luck, this guy will find a picture of me in a strip bar wearing a bra on my head from 1980."

I laughed and so did Naomi. The sheriff took a seat in front of my desk and flipped briefly through the Kari Sutter file.

"Anything yet?" he asked.

"Nada."

He threw the file back on my desk. "You know, I remember that murder down there back in the eighties. I never thought something like that would happen again."

Naomi and I shot looks at each other.

"I never heard of another murder down there. Why didn't the papers flash back on it? When was it?" I asked, stunned.

The sheriff looked just as surprised. "You never knew that? I thought for sure you did." He looked at Naomi, who also shook her head. "I don't know why the papers didn't bring it up. Probably because no one was ever convicted. I think it was in . . . oh, let me think . . . I'm pretty sure it was springtime, 1986. "

"In spring of 1986 I was in the seventh grade, Sheriff," I said.

"Thank you for that bit of information, CeeCee," he quipped. "I don't think I could have possibly felt any older until you just told me that. I was a sergeant of road patrol then, for Christ's sake."

Naomi smiled and added, "You look wonderful for your age."

"All right, ladies, quit while you're ahead. Now, I'm trying to think who investigated that case. I remember the victim was a young girl, and her friends were the suspects. They were all rich kids and got acquitted." He looked down at the ground, thinking. "If memory serves, the girl's mother killed herself a few years later."

He had gotten my wheels spinning. "Sheriff, I need to see that case, the entire case."

"Whew, CeeCee, I don't know. You guys were in the storeroom files yesterday, right?"

Naomi and I nodded.

"I'd check there first. If it's not there, try the cold-case unit. They may have it since technically it was unsolved."

The cold-case unit investigated every homicide deemed unsolvable by major crimes. Cold cases took years to solve and lots of money. Nonetheless, the unit seemed to be on a roll lately. In the last six months they'd solved two murders from the late 1970s.

I already knew that trying to find a file from 1986 would be like trying to find a needle in a haystack. After the sheriff and Naomi left, my phone rang. It was Bob with my final test results from the Kari Sutter murder.

"I've decided not to make you get these out of my ass, CeeCee. You ready?" Bob asked.

"Ready with bells on. Go ahead. "

"Don't get your hopes up. It's pretty much the same as the prelims. The blood on the tree was the victim's, no other DNA. The cut on the wrist was with precision, probably a razor blade. No fibers, no sexual assault, and the material from the victim's hand was over one hundred years old."

I was thrown by the last result. "What did you say? What material?"

"The material in her hand," he said calmly.

I was getting irritated. "*What* material in her hand, Bob? You never said anything about finding material in her hand."

He was quiet, and when he finally spoke, it was weak. "I didn't?"

"No!"

"Oh, well, um, the victim's right hand, the one that

wasn't cut, had about a two-square-inch piece of material in it. I'm sorry—I thought I told you." He seemed nervous.

"You never told me," I growled. "You said it was over a hundred years old? What does it look like?"

"Um, right, it was very old." He coughed into the phone. "The material probably used to be white, but it was tinted yellow from age. It was a type of thick lace. "

"I'll be there in a minute."

Taking the elevator to the basement where the crime laboratory was, I couldn't help wondering what else Bob had forgotten to tell me. I'm sure he had heard from the other technicians about my mood at the cemetery this morning and most likely didn't want to deal with me. I was at a point where I couldn't have cared less.

Bob was waiting for me at the entrance to the lab, holding the material in a clear plastic bag, along with photographs of it, something he clearly anticipated me asking for. He apologized again for not telling me about it, and I in turn apologized for biting his head off. While I was on an apology streak, I poked my head into the lab and apologized to the technicians I had yelled at while at the cemetery, explaining I was having a bad day and that I didn't mean to take it out on them. They were quite forgiving, considering the circumstances.

I still hadn't heard anything about any marriage certificates for Madeline or Maryanne Hendrickson, so I spent the remainder of the day catching up on paperwork—typing interviews, making copies and so forth. I found myself continually looking at the clock, somehow hoping it would stop completely so I wouldn't have to go home. Michael had called twice, neither of which I answered.

CHAPTER TWENTY-ONE

An hour after I was supposed to leave, I called Eric to check on the girls and talk to them. After that, I drove around for two hours. I was trying to figure out how I was going to tell Michael. I decided since there was no easy way to do it, it was time to go home. My stomach was in knots.

I saw Michael looking out the window when I pulled into the driveway. I realized this would probably be the last time I would ever see him do that and suppressed the urge to cry again. I closed my eyes and put my head against the wheel. I didn't think I would be able to go through with this. I had to keep telling myself it was for Michael and Sean. I was doing the right thing.

I put on my best game face and walked toward the house. He opened the door before I had a chance to turn the knob.

"Honey, where have you been? I've been calling." He reached over to hug me, but I pulled away.

I walked to the kitchen table, set my bag and keys down, took off my jacket and hung it in the closet. Michael stood by the door, looking at me with apprehension.

"Did you have a bad day? We can talk about it," he offered tenderly.

My chest felt like it was going to explode, and I was trying hard to not let him see me trembling and breathing hard. I was on the verge of panic. Looking over at a picture of Sean on the wall, I closed my eyes and inhaled deeply.

"Michael, I do need to talk to you, but not about my day. Let's go sit in the living room," I said stiffly, without emotion.

His expression showed grave concern. I could see him trying to read my face for signs of what I wanted to discuss. Since Michael could usually read me like a book, I had to be very careful. He sat down, still looking directly at me.

I cleared my throat. "There's something I've wanted to talk to you about, and now seems as good a time as any, considering the mess with Vanessa."

I could see he was holding his breath.

I did my best to maintain eye contact with him. If I looked away, even for a slight second, he would know I was lying. I knew that what I was about to say would shatter his world, and it was killing me.

"Michael, this is very hard for me to tell you, but you need to know the truth." My heart was pounding so hard I was sure he could see it through my shirt. "Last night when I told you I was closing files out in the store room, I lied—I was really with Eric."

He looked devastated, but I had to keep talking or I wouldn't be able to finish.

"We were talking and we . . . we decided to put the divorce on hold and give our marriage another try."

Michael stood, and I saw his eyes begin to water. "Please tell me that again. I don't think I quite understood what you just said."

I looked at him. "What I'm trying to tell you, Michael, is that I still love Eric, and I can't marry you. It's not fair to you." I made a grave mistake and briefly looked away when I said I still loved Eric. I couldn't help it. Michael caught it immediately.

"You're lying." His eyes, still watering, were dead on mine.

"No, I'm not. Michael, don't try to look for reasons to make you believe this isn't happening, because it is." I felt the tears coming and I stood, turning my back to him until I could make them go away.

He turned me around. "I know what you're doing, and it's not going to work." He got right in my face. "You think that there's a chance I'm going back to Vanessa, and you're playing it safe by getting back with Eric, right? Well, it's not going to happen!"

I backed away from him, feeling the bile rise in my throat. I honestly thought I was going to be sick. "What are you going to do to stop it, Michael? Huh? Nothing! That's what! You think I want to deal with your psychotic ex-wife for the rest of my life?" I laughed. "Hardly. No-body, including you, is worth that grief!" I was getting hateful, but he'd never believe me if I didn't.

He stood staring at me, looking as if someone had just run him over with a truck, tears now streaming down his cheeks.

"Please, Cee. This isn't you. Something's going on . . . Please, talk to me," he begged, and took a few steps towards me.

I backed away. "Michael," I lowered my voice. "The only thing going on is that I'm still in love with my husband, the father of my children. Maybe this will help you believe what I'm telling you: Eric and I slept together last night. That's why I was late. I really didn't want to have to tell you that." I paused to let the words sink in. "It's over, Michael. I'm sorry." I held my head up defiantly and placed my engagement ring on the table in front of me.

Something changed in Michael's face. It went from pure devastation to sheer hatefulness. I have never been hit by a man I was in a relationship with, but I genuinely thought tonight might be the first time. Not that I wouldn't be completely shocked if Michael laid a hand on me. He was too good for that.

The tears were gone from his eyes, but he continued to look at me with utter contempt. Remaining silent, he turned to leave the room, then turned back and faced me again.

His voice was low and scratchy. "You are the worst mistake I have ever made in my life. I gave you everything, and you have just shit all over me. I will always regret the day I met you, CeeCee." He was breathing heavy. "So help me God, I never, and I mean never, want to see your face again. I hope you're happy. I'll be gone within the hour."

His words hit me like daggers before he left the room, sending shock waves rippling through my body. The emotions I had been holding in were violently fighting their way to the surface like a raging volcano. I grabbed my car keys and ran out the door, shaking so uncontrollably I could hardly get my keys in the ignition. I knew I had to quickly find a place to park because I wouldn't be able to drive.

I was a block away when I pulled into the parking lot of a pair of tennis courts. I jumped out of my car and began running, to where I don't know, when my volcano finally erupted. I fell to my knees. I was sobbing, my chest was heaving, I was soaked with sweat, and I was screaming. Even when I found out Eric had been having an affair and we finally decided to divorce, I had never felt pain like this. It was excruciating physical pain.

I thought of Michael, the way he felt, the way he

smelled and how much I truly loved him, and my pain worsened. I honestly thought I was dying.

Dear God in heaven, please make this go away! my head screamed. It didn't go away. I continued to cry until I actually started vomiting. I remember once, during the Murder Mountain case, Eric said he was leaving me because I was going to West Virginia with Michael to find the killers. I was upset then, certainly, but nothing like this.

It was when I had a vision of my daughters that I began to calm down. They needed me, and they didn't need me a basket case. I had to pull it together, not for myself, but for them. I also knew that very soon Michael would be seeing Sean, and that's what was most important.

I was still on all fours in the gravel parking lot when I began taking long, deep breaths to try to calm down. I finally made my way back to my car, but I didn't think I was quite ready to drive yet. My eyes felt like they were the size of baseballs. My head, tingling and achy, felt like a hot-air balloon, and my stomach was still queasy. I also had a loud ringing in my ears that didn't seem to be going away.

It was forty-five minutes before I felt able to go home. When I drove down my street and saw my house, dark and uninhabited, I felt the earlier emotions begin to come back. Doing my best to fight them off, I pulled into the driveway and went into my empty house.

Michael had left a note for me on the kitchen table:

CeeCee,
I will make arrangements in the next couple of weeks to pick up the rest of my things. I would appreciate it if you were not here when I do. I would've liked to have seen Isabelle and Selina be-

fore I left, but now it doesn't seem possible. Please
tell them I will call soon. Not that you gave him
much thought, but Sean will be extremely upset by
this. I would prefer that you do not call him. I will
take care of it.
Michael

Oh, the irony. If he only knew how much thought I
had given Sean. I had given him more thought than my
own daughters. After reading Michael's note, I wondered how I would explain to them why Michael left.
They would both be very upset, Isabelle more so.

I went upstairs and saw that Michael had taken most
of his clothes from the closet and all his toiletries. I sat
on the closet floor, looking at the empty hangers and
began crying again. I ended falling asleep in my closet
and not waking up until an hour before I was supposed
to leave for work.

When I opened my eyes I was hit with everything
again, and realized I wouldn't make it through the day.
I left a message on Naomi's voice mail, telling her I
wouldn't be in because I wasn't feeling well. I knew
she'd be suspicious, but I didn't care. I crawled into bed
and slept on and off most of the day, with bouts of crying in between. It was not only crying and sadness I had
to deal with, it was also anger.

I had more violent thoughts of what I would like to do
to Vanessa Hagerman than I ever had about anyone in
my life. It would be downright scary if I were to see her
right now. I also went over and over ways to get myself
out of this, almost coming up with a realistic solution
but not one good enough. I thought if I filed a formal
complaint with the Cuyahoga County Bar Association
against the judge and Vanessa's attorney, that it would
do the trick. Then I realized that it would be her word

against mine. I should've been smarter and taped our conversation, just as I assumed she was doing with me. However, now that Michael had left, I would only look like a bitter ex-girlfriend. It was hopeless.

I called in sick the next two days. My answering machine was flooded with calls from Naomi and Coop. I think one of them even stopped by the house because I heard knocking, but I didn't answer the door. By the end of the second day, I was at least able to function, meaning I could get out of bed. I had convinced myself that there was nothing I could do, and that I needed to get on with my life. Still feeling like I had a cement block in my chest and a lump in my throat, I talked myself into going to work. On my way in, I stopped at my attorney's office and signed my divorce papers, telling him to call Eric to do the same. He said they would be filed by the end of the day. I wanted closure on everything.

Naomi and Coop, knowing I hadn't called in sick that day, were waiting in my office. They jumped all over me the minute I walked in, wanting to know if I was okay, what was wrong, why didn't I answer the phone or the door, telling me how worried they were, and that they almost had someone break in to check on me. It was what Naomi said last that got an emotional reaction from me.

"When I called Michael, all he would tell me was you weren't feeling yourself."

I was stunned. "You called Michael?"

Coop and Naomi exchanged confused glances. I realized I was giving myself away, and I needed to fix it quickly. I wasn't ready to tell everyone yet what had happened. I needed some time.

"It's just that . . . you really shouldn't bother him, Naomi. I just had the flu, that's all. I was asleep most of the time and didn't hear the door or phone."

"Okay." Naomi looked at me peculiarly. "If you want to

take it easy today, I can get some other detectives to help you."

"Don't be ridiculous. I have a lot of catching up to do, and I'm more than capable." I sat down at my desk and started grabbing files and throwing papers.

I wasn't paying attention when Coop left my office and shut the door. Only when Naomi took a file out of my hand and laid it on my desk did I notice. She pulled a chair over to me and sat down.

"CeeCee, I know you're telling me you had the flu, but in all honesty, I don't believe you." She looked at me solemnly. "I've never seen you like this before. I hope you know you can talk to me."

I tried to smile. "Really, Naomi, you're making too much of this, I'm . . ."

I lost it. I suppose I was trying too hard to put on a show and my emotions got the best of me. I became hysterical there in my office, putting my face in my hands and sobbing. No one has ever seen me do that before.

Naomi was speechless. Only briefly. "CeeCee! Oh my God! What happened?" She grabbed the box of tissues off my desk and began handing me one after another.

For reasons unknown, I confessed everything to Naomi. Truthfully, it felt good to talk to someone about it. She was even more shocked.

"I can't believe you, of all people, would let someone bully and blackmail you like that! CeeCee, you have to tell Michael!"

I looked up from under my tissue. "No! Naomi, I just told you, there's no other way." I inhaled in short, hic-cupping breaths. "You have to promise me right now that you will not say a word to anyone, especially Michael."

It took her a few minutes, and I honestly thought she was going to refuse and tell Michael everything.

Nevertheless, she finally relented, nodding her head, tears in her own eyes.

"CeeCee, I can't imagine dealing with this." Her voice was quiet, soft. "After all you two have been through . . . this isn't fair. How are you going to handle this?"

"I don't know," I sniffled.

Naomi sat with me for half an hour while I cried, finished and attempted to pull myself together. She kept shaking her head, completely flabbergasted at the situation. I knew how she felt.

I was so tired of being an emotional train wreck, I was desperate for a distraction. I found it when I looked down on my desk and saw my notes from the sheriff's story on the 1986 murder at Mary Jane's Grave. Naomi saw me looking at them.

"You find something?"

"No, I just decided I'm going to spend the day looking for this murder file." I held up the notes.

She stood up to leave. "If you need to talk, call me. Will you be okay?"

I sighed and gave a halfhearted smile. "For now."

CHAPTER TWENTY-TWO

As I promised, I spent the entire day searching for the old murder case. It was a wonderful way to get my mind off my disastrous personal life. And as I predicted, it was like trying to find a needle in a haystack. I started with the boxes we had transferred from the storeroom. Trying to find the ones marked 1986 was a feat in itself.

I didn't have a report number to go by, so I had to flip through each file, skimming for the location. Since the department averaged about 150,000 calls per year, this would take me weeks. However, since the sheriff told me he remembered the murder occurred in spring, it narrowed my search considerably. I sectioned the boxes off, between March and April of 1986 but had no luck. I made another attempt at February and May but still came up with nothing. It was my call to the cold-case unit that struck gold. I silently scolded myself for not checking with them first.

When I called them, a detective with more than thirty years on the department, Greg Tolander, knew exactly what I was talking about.

"Hell yeah, we got that case, CeeCee. I'm actually surprised you hadn't called earlier since there was another murder down there. I figured you'd want to see this one."

"I didn't even know about it until a couple days ago. You do have everything? Photos, statements and all?"

"Yup."

"Anywhere near solving it?"

"We already solved it. It was those kids, no doubt about it. But since they were all acquitted, we have to hang on to it. All it does is take up space."

"I'll be over shortly to get it."

I felt a tad euphoric over the revelation of the file's whereabouts. Not ecstatic by any means—the dark cloud of the Michael situation was still hovering—but it was a welcome feeling nonetheless.

I decided to take the file back to my office. It was the end of the day, and I could've gone home, but all I'd do there is sit and stare at walls.

As I got to my desk, my attorney called and said, "Congratulations, you're officially divorced!" I couldn't say I felt like celebrating.

I grabbed a cup of strong coffee before I settled in to review the case file. Reading the file, I felt a sense of gloom come over me, and it didn't have anything to do with Michael. The case itself was depressing.

The victim, sixteen-year-old Melissa Drake, was a somewhat backward girl with very few friends. According to the statements, a popular boy at school who had just broken up with his girlfriend befriended Melissa. The boy, Derek Solis, took a genuine interest in Melissa, and she was thrilled. Along with having a new boyfriend, Melissa was sought out by a new group of friends, popular girls, including Derek's ex-girlfriend, Meghan Dearth. It was all a ruse.

Living by the old adage, keep your friends close and your enemies closer, Meghan Dearth set forth an intricate plot to kill Melissa Drake. And it appeared she succeeded. For months they took Melissa with them wherever they went: to the mall, to the movies, out to eat and to the best parties in school. Melissa was in seventh heaven, having never known a social life before.

Her heaven turned to hell in March of that year when Meghan and the others—Nicole Harstein, Alexis Kemper, Sydney Whitlow, Dillon Anderson, and Daniel Griffin—decided to show her Mary Jane's Grave. The children of local attorneys, doctors and judges, they took Melissa there and dared her to kiss the pine tree.

She had just bent over when the first strike came, and then the next and so on. They had beaten Melissa Drake to death with rocks. Meghan Dearth had felt humiliated to have been dumped for a backward, plain and unsociable girl like Melissa Drake, so she got her revenge. Furthermore, she got away with it.

No one talked. The parents provided their alibis and even testified to the fact. According to them, the teens were all at home. Only once did Nicole Harstein tell one of the investigators what really happened. Even so, when the case went to trial, she retracted it all and claimed the detective coerced her. There was so little physical evidence, each of them was found not guilty. According to the detective who interviewed Nicole Harstein, Daniel Griffin did the actual killing. The rest of them handed him the rocks.

I put down the statements and looked at the photographs of the crime scene and body; it was brutal. Melissa's head had been caved in on both sides. I hoped that she blacked out with the first blow. I shivered, thinking back to when Naomi's head had been crushed with a rock.

When I finished viewing the photographs, I looked at the background of all the suspects. They were all clean, straight-A students except one, Daniel Griffin. He was a twenty-two-year-old high school dropout with an extensive criminal record. One of his prior charges was a felony conviction of cruelty to animals. He had taped a bottle rocket to the side of a kitten with duct tape and lit it. He served only three months in the county jail for it. There was another conviction of cruelty to animals, but the file didn't give the circumstances.

My question was why were these other kids hanging around with him, and how did they know him in the first place? He was clearly the odd man out. At the time of the murder, he was living at the YMCA. The parents of the others covered for Daniel as well, knowing if they didn't and he took the fall, he would talk.

According to Nicole, Meghan kept urging Daniel on and screaming, "Kill the bitch! Do it!" She also claimed that Meghan was giving Daniel sexual favors in return for his part in the murder. Nicole said that she and Meghan were out driving around one night and found Daniel walking down the street in a rough part of town. Allegedly Meghan said, "He looks perfect for the job. Pull over!"

Nicole denied knowing what Meghan was talking about, but she pulled the car over anyway. It seemed as if all the girls were terrified of Meghan. I couldn't imagine why. Nicole said that Meghan got out and stood outside the car whispering to Daniel for almost fifteen minutes. When he got into the backseat with Meghan, Meghan ordered Nicole to start driving while she gave Daniel a blow job. Meghan's father was a municipal court judge who retired about five years ago. I'm sure he was quite proud of his daughter's actions. Knowing cops as I do, I guarantee the detectives told the judge everything. I never liked girls like Meghan Dearth, and I could never understand how other girls followed them.

All the girls were seventeen years old, and all were

tried as juveniles, another indication of their parents' standing in the community. Anybody else would have been bound over as an adult in a heartbeat. When I looked at their pictures, I thought back to the time of the murder. I was just turning thirteen, and I don't ever remember hearing about this. My father was still a patrolman back then. I'd have thought he would've mentioned it. He always came home and told me about cases like that.

I put the photographs down, and wrote a list of things I needed to do. I was very interested in finding out the circumstances behind Daniel Griffin's other conviction. It was in Richland County in 1984, and luckily I had a report number. I also wanted to track down all of these kids. They didn't talk then, but maybe they would now. Years of guilt may have taken its toll on some of them—except Meghan Dearth. People like her don't ever change. But even if they confessed the whole crime now, they could never be tried for it by reason of the double-jeopardy law.

Melissa Drake had been murdered in March, the same month all the Hendrickson women died. I highlighted the date of the murder and threw the file aside, stretching my arms and back. Only now did I realize how late it was. Since I had nothing to go home to, I wanted to stay and finish looking through the file. I only had a little more to go.

The last section of the file was the follow-up after the murders, including the suicide report of Melissa's mother that had been taken a year later. Someone had made a copy and put it in her daughter's murder file. It saved me from having to look for it. Melissa's twin brother, Nicholas, and their father, Martin, survived Melissa and her mother. After Lucinda Drake's suicide, Martin and Nicholas moved out of state to parts unknown. I couldn't blame them. I don't know that I would've stayed around here either.

I closed the file and sighed. It was heartbreaking. It made me appreciate that my problems didn't amount to shit, considering what other people have gone through.

I took my notebook and tried to sum up what I had so far, which was essentially nothing. I had a century-old legend and two murders twenty years apart. Throw in another attack and a skinned dog, and I almost laughed at myself. None of them had anything to do with the others. I knew that, so why was I hell-bent on solving all of them? Because it gave me something to do, and I always held out hope.

Looking at my watch again, I recognized that I would only get a few hours of sleep tonight before coming back in to work. I had already accepted that sleep would be minimal for the next year or more, until I got over Michael.

After gathering my things, I walked out to the parking lot. I was somewhat surprised to see Eric and Jordan standing by his cruiser, kissing each other good-bye. Since she was still in uniform, I assumed that she worked overtime for half of the night shift with Eric. We exchanged uncomfortable pleasantries for a few minutes, and I asked about the girls. They were with a babysitter until Jordan got home and were doing fine. I gave a slight wave before heading to my car, which was parked in the back of the parking lot.

Eric and Jordan had left by the time I opened my car door, and as I had that night at the lake, I had the peculiar feeling I was being watched. I scanned the parking lot and didn't see anything out of the ordinary. There were always cars there twenty-four hours a day. If someone was watching me, I probably wouldn't know it anyway.

Once inside my car, I turned on my dome light so I could see while I put my bag and purse on the passenger seat. Unexpectedly, I was hit with another emotional attack. I began sobbing, put my face in my hands and lay my head on the steering wheel. I wished I could keep this from happening, but I figured it was something like the flu. My emotions came in waves as they saw fit, and there was nothing I could do about it.

I don't know if it was seeing Eric and Jordan happy or the prospect of going home to an empty house that triggered my breakdown. It was probably both. Nevertheless, it took me only a few minutes to settle down, unlike the hours it took before. I was making progress.

When I got home, I was moderately amazed all it required was an entire bottle of wine and two hours to fall asleep. Three hours later, I was ready to head back to work.

Chapter Twenty-three

The entire next week wasn't much better. With the girls back, I told them that Michael was out of town for work. I needed to get myself mentally stronger so I could be there for them when I gave them the bad news. Two days after finding the Melissa Drake murder file, I was served with a notice that stated my appearance at the depositions was no longer needed; they were canceled. I guess Vanessa kept her word. I couldn't help wondering if they were back together. That thought alone sent me into emotional chaos.

Needless to say, having the girls around was rather therapeutic since I couldn't fall onto the floor in a poignant mess when they were there. I learned to control my feelings a little better, like the old days. Michael had yet to call and make arrangements to pick up the rest of his things. I began to wonder if he ever would. I knew he despised every part of me and probably didn't want to come back here. That hurt.

Naomi and Coop treated me like a fragile china doll. They were constantly asking me if I was okay and stopping by my house. I assumed they thought if they didn't check on me every five minutes, they'd find me hanging in my garage. I told them they were being ridiculous, but they knew how Michael and I felt about each other, and they knew what we had been through.

It was near the second week after Michael left that Danielle Horton called me. She wanted to come in and talk. She said she remembered some other things about the night she was attacked. I didn't get too excited because I anticipated more ghost stories. I was partially right.

When Danielle came to see me, she looked much better than she had the night in the hospital. Her head was almost healed, as well as the burns. She said the doctors told her the burns would definitely leave scars, but they weren't painful anymore. When she began to tell me what she remembered, she appeared very uncomfortable, wringing her hands and playing with her hair.

"I don't know if this means anything, Sergeant, but I was taking a shower last night and I totally remembered that when I was on the trail, I saw someone standing in the woods." She blew out a highly audible sigh of relief that she was able to tell me.

"Are you sure it wasn't one of your friends?" I asked.

One chubby hand went directly to stroke her hair. "No, I mean, I'm positive it wasn't, because this guy, or person, was soooo tall. I mean, like, huge. None of my friends come close to that."

She was onto something, I'd give her that. She most likely was describing the person whose footprint that I had in a plaster cast locked away in evidence.

"Danielle, do you remember anything else about him? Did you see his face, clothing, anything?"

She shook her head. "It was dark. I just saw, like, the outline of him. Ya know what I mean?"

I had a thought. "If I drove you down there could you

show me exactly where you saw him standing?" Maybe I could get another print and match it.

She shook her head aggressively. "I can't go back there, Sergeant. I'm sorry! I haven't told you the rest of it yet!"

"I'm listening."

"You're gonna think I'm crazy, but"—if I heard someone say that one more time, I believe I might be the one ending up in a straitjacket—"after I blacked out I remember waking up for a few seconds, and I was actually standing on my feet." She drew in a deep breath. "I was disoriented, ya know, confused, and I heard something behind me. Oh my gosh, I can't believe I'm telling you this, but when I turned around . . ." She began to cry. "There was a lady behind me!"

She cried for a little while until I prodded her to continue. I put my pen down, knowing I was about to hear about the woman in white again.

"Sh-she was standing less than two feet from me, and her eyes, her eyes were red!" She sniffled.

"Danielle, what do you mean they were red?" I tried not to sound disbelieving, even though I was.

"You know when you break blood vessels in your eyes? Kinda like that, except it was the entire eye, both eyes!" She put her hands up to her face for just a second. "The next thing I remember, she reached out and grabbed my neck, and her hand, her hand was all black and burned, and you could see the bone!"

"Then what?"

"That was the last thing I remember until I woke up in the hospital. I suppose I could've imagined it, right?"

"Most likely, Danielle. You were scared anyway, being at the grave. The mind does funny things to people, but you're sure about the man in the woods?"

She nodded.

"I'd really like you to go down there and show me," I said before she could protest. "Danielle, I'm a police officer. Nothing is going to happen to you there. And if it makes you feel any better, we can take more police officers with us. You want to find out who did this, don't you?"

She gave a slight nod.

I had three uniformed officers meet us at the grave. I would've had other detectives go, but I think seeing officers in uniform and their marked police cars was far more comforting.

It was evident that Danielle was edgy while at the cemetery. She kept looking back at the officers, making sure they were still there. She wasn't quite sure where the trail was but found it near the back, behind the large pine tree. I hadn't even known it was there. We had walked about twenty feet on the trail, into the thick overgrown woods, when Danielle pointed to her right.

"There, over there by that tree. That's where I think he was standing."

I tried to make my way over to the tree without getting pricked to death, but the woods were full of briars. I was a bloody mess by the time I walked the entire five feet. It was clear around the tree, but I saw nothing. It had rained considerably over the last few days, so any prints most likely got washed away. My legs and hands took a beating for nothing, but I remained hopeful regardless.

As we were leaving the cemetery, Danielle muttered something that made me slam on my brakes and look at her.

"What did you just say, Danielle?"

"I just said I'm gonna start spending my weekends at church instead of here, that's all. I was just kidding."

I had a brainstorm. All the attacks had happened on

weekend nights, and we were a week away from Halloween.

"Danielle, can you call your friends and have them come, with their parents if need be, to the police department?" I asked eagerly.

"I suppose." She looked suspicious. "Why?"

"I'll tell you shortly."

I had to hurry if I was going to organize my plan. It was late afternoon already. Once back in my office, I called Coop and Naomi. They sensed the anxiety in my voice and came into my office immediately.

"What's going on? Did you come up with a suspect or something?" Coop asked.

"Nope. We're going to bait him." I waited for their response.

They looked perplexed. Naomi spoke first. "Bait who?"

"The suspect, or suspects."

She looked irritated. "CeeCee, please tell me what you're talking about since you lost me the minute I came in here."

"Every attack and murder has happened on a weekend. Today is the Friday before Halloween." They weren't getting it yet. "I've called Danielle and her friends down here to help us bait this guy. We're going to station ourselves around the cemetery, incognito of course, while they drive in and pretend to party like they did before." I waited to see if they caught on. Coop did first.

"I get it. You're assuming the suspect will be there tonight watching for cars. So we can catch him if we send one in, right?"

"Exactly."

Naomi pondered this for a while, taking a seat in front of my desk. Ultimately, as captain she had to give the final approval.

"You realize the chances of this guy, or whoever, being there and us catching him are slim to none, right? I mean, anyone, I don't care how bright they are, would anticipate something like this, wouldn't ya say?"

I nodded. "It's at least worth a shot. We can have the road blocked off at Pleasant Valley and Hastings East Road to keep other cars from showing up down there. From what I understand, they're disregarding the gates that were put up from Kari's murder. They won't drive past a marked cruiser, though, so at least we can control this."

She stood up. "All right, I'll pull the other detectives together. Plan on meeting in the conference room in half an hour for a briefing, and bring the list of equipment you'll need."

I quickly drew a sketch of the cemetery and marked where I needed detectives placed. I made copies for everyone. Next, I had to confirm that Danielle and the others were willing to participate, a small tidbit I hadn't shared with Naomi. After serious coercion and promises that their children would go home in one piece, the parents and teens agreed.

The plan was that they would drive down to the cemetery close to midnight, park their car and get out with what appeared to be a case of beer. Of course, they would be drinking from empty beer cans. They would simply act like they were having a good time. Meanwhile, the other detectives and I would be situated throughout the woods with camcorders, night-vision goggles, advanced audio recording equipment and most importantly, our guns and handcuffs.

After the briefing, we were getting ready to leave when I had a moment in my office, simply standing and staring at the wall, thinking of Michael. Naomi came in and saw it.

"CeeCee? You okay?" she said quietly. "Have you heard from Michael?"

I broke out of my stare and sighed. "I'm functioning, barely, if that's what you mean, and no I haven't, nor do I expect to ever hear from him again."

She narrowed her eyes and looked like she was going to say something, but decided against it before turning around to leave. When she got to the door she stopped, but kept her back to me.

"You know, CeeCee, things have a funny way of working themselves out . . . trust me on that." Her voice was still quiet, barely above a whisper. "I'll meet you outside."

I knew she meant well, but this was one of those things that couldn't possibly work itself out. Michael and I were done, and I was slowly beginning to accept that, although I didn't feel that I would ever be completely over it. With my heart heavy, I grabbed my bag of equipment and went outside to meet the others.

CHAPTER TWENTY-FOUR

We were at the grave almost five hours before Danielle
and her friends were due to arrive. That gave us time to
set up and, with luck, maybe the suspect would show
up early to do the same. It took us two hours to get situated and put everyone in place, and another three
hours of sitting there in the dark woods, freezing. That
was three hours of me wondering what Michael was doing. My conclusion was always the same: he was with
Vanessa. Coop, who was next to me, noticed I was distracted.

"C'mon, CeeCee, you need to stay focused tonight,"
he whispered.

I nodded and tried to shake the visions out of my
head. It didn't work, but seeing the oncoming headlights of Danielle's car did. I sat straight up, anticipating
and ready for anything.

"Here we go," I whispered to Coop.

I radioed to the other detectives that the car had arrived, and to keep their eyes and ears open. Coop and I
were at the edge of the woods where the road ended.
Danielle pulled her car right up to the gate, so Coop
and I had to duck to avoid being spotlighted.

They all piled out of the car, whooping and hollering
and passing around beer, just as we had instructed

them to do. One of the first problems was that they started blasting the car stereo, some type of reggae-rap-dance mix. We wouldn't be able to hear anything. Coop didn't seem to mind, though. He did a slight, jerky movement that fairly resembled the dance of the Scarecrow in the *Wizard of Oz*. I couldn't help giggling.

"What the hell was *that?*" I whispered loudly.

"It's called crunking. You need to brush up on your moves, girlfriend," he whispered back.

"I know what crunking is, and that wasn't even close. That was more like the hillbilly crank," I chuckled.

"Very funny."

I tried to get serious again. "They need to turn that goddamn music down. I can't hear anything."

As if she heard me, Danielle slowly walked over to her car and turned the music off completely. She also turned her car off and grabbed three fully charged flashlights that we had provided and passed them out to her friends. They began walking toward the large pine tree that loomed over the rest of the cemetery. I was too far away to hear much of what they were saying.

They all stood around the tree in a circle, and began to act out a mock séance, something else we had planned. I was sure if anything were to happen tonight, it would happen in the next several minutes. The teens were holding hands and mumbling, with a few giggles in between, "Bloody Mary, Bloody Mary."

This went on for five minutes before they stopped, obviously under the impression that it wasn't working. They continued to hang out and pretend to drink beer and tell ghost stories. Naomi radioed it was time to call it quits since there was nothing to indicate the suspect was here. Coop let out a low whistle, a sign to Danielle that it was time to leave. As the teens were gathering the beer cans off the ground and heading to Danielle's car, something happened.

I wasn't in a position to see what she was looking at, but one of the girls with Danielle stopped walking and turned to look at the woods to her right. What followed was a scream that made my hair stand up on end. All the teens dropped their flashlights, leaving the cemetery in complete darkness, and started running in different directions. All of them were yelling and screaming.

Naomi was screaming too, on the radio, telling us to move in. I went to grab Coop, but he was gone. Over the sounds of the screams and yells I heard something I couldn't possibly believe. It began low and gradually got louder until it hurt my ears. It was a baby crying. I was spinning my flashlight around trying to see where it was coming from when I heard something behind me. I turned around to see what it was and my flashlight went dead.

In a flash, I saw a shadow move to my right. Hearing the leaves and sticks break, I knew it was a person, and not one from our party. Everyone else was in the cemetery trying to get the teens together and calmed down. As the sound moved away from me I gave chase.

The faster I ran, so did the person in front of me. He or she knew the woods, no doubt about it. He was zigzagging back and forth through the trees and briars. I tried to keep up, but since I couldn't see my own hand in front of my face, I had to rely on sound alone, and it wasn't working. Branches and briars scratched my face and arms, and when I finally felt a large briar bush catch me in the leg, I knew I couldn't go any farther without tearing a patch of skin off. I stopped, but I heard the running continue in front of me until it completely faded away.

"CeeCee!" I heard Coop yell from a distance.

"I'm over here!"

When Coop made his way to me, I grabbed his flashlight and looked at my leg, which was caught and bleeding.

"Ouch! Jesus! Your face is all scratched up. What the hell were you doing?" Coop asked as he began to delicately pull the briar branch from my leg.

"I was chasing our suspect, that's what!"

"You were?"

I told Coop about my relatively short foot pursuit and he was irritated at himself.

"Damn it, I knew I should've stayed back here with you! I'd have caught the fucker."

Coop and I walked back to the cemetery and to the commotion of all the teens. The girls were crying, and the boys looked rattled. Naomi was trying to figure out what exactly happened. The girl who I saw look behind her was the first to speak.

"When we were walking to the car, I heard something, and I turned around to look. At first I thought it was fog, and then the harder I looked at it, it looked like some old lady! It scared the shit out of me!" she cried.

"Did anyone else see it?" I asked.

They all shook their heads and started talking at once. When they heard their friend scream it scared them so they all started running. When they heard the baby crying they started running faster and tried to hide in their car. I asked Naomi if any of the cameras were pointed to the area where the girl claimed to have seen the woman. She shook her head.

"No, they were all on the cemetery and the edges around it. She's talking about behind the clearing. The other detectives didn't see anything either. We all heard the baby, though," she whispered.

"What *was* that? A recording, maybe?" Coop asked.

"Probably, although it was high-quality sound equipment, I'll give you that," I said. "I'll be anxious to listen to that again when we get back to the department. Coop, did you radio any marked cruisers to patrol where these woods end, in case the suspect comes out?"

He nodded. "They're thick woods. I've already called a K-9 officer down here to see if he can pick up a track where you said you first heard him."

We gathered the teens and took statements from them before driving each one home. By then I was tired. I decided viewing the video from tonight could wait until morning. After I got home, morning came quickly. I slept very little.

It was supposed to be my day off, but I had a lot to catch up on. Selina and Isabelle were going back to Eric and Jordan's for their week, so I decided to work for a little while after I dropped them off. I dreaded the thought of the girls being gone, because I would face the empty house again, and my emotions, for the next week.

Once in my office, I viewed the video several times. It was exactly as I remembered it. The sound of the baby crying was very clear and seemed to be coming from all around the cemetery, not just one particular area. The other detectives had already searched for hidden sound equipment or wires, but found none. After I was done with the video, I spent the rest of the afternoon catching up on paperwork and organizing the files.

On my way home, I had to fight the strong urge to call Michael. I was so tired of being tired and tired of being sad and tired of being depressed, I didn't think I could take one more day of it.

CHAPTER TWENTY-FIVE

I spent the next several days re-interviewing all the witnesses. I like to do that because even if they remember something after the first interview, chances are they won't call me and tell me about it. Unfortunately, this wasn't the case now. Everything they had told me was exactly as it had been before.

One afternoon I started looking into Maryanne Hendrickson. I knew she died quietly in 1985, but I had a lot of questions that needed to be answered. There was never a mention of occupations with either Maryanne or Madeline, and I wondered how they survived financially. I knew Mary Jane cleaned houses, but that certainly didn't leave anything for her survivors. Maryanne's body was discovered a week after her death only when the mailman noticed she hadn't been getting her mail and called the police to check on her.

Walt spoke of a child that Maryanne had. I still hadn't heard from any of the counties about birth or marriage certificates. At the present, there was no proof that Maryanne had a child, who would now be in his or her fifties or sixties. Coop had tracked down the letter giving notice of Mary Jane's death through the county historical society. The letter, written by Madeline, tells of her mother's passing, stating that cancer was common at her age, which she quoted as being seventy-three. Again, I didn't know how anyone could've missed this. It told me that Mary Jane was not a frequent visitor to town, nor did she have many friends. No one questioned it. Madeline went on to write that Mary Jane was now joined with her beloved infant son who, she claims, died at birth. There was no record of the baby's death anywhere. All of this continued to confuse me, especially when I remembered that Walt told me Ceely Rose was the key.

It was when I was scanning through the websites on Ceely Rose that I saw the notice for the play based on her life was being put on tonight. A great excuse to stay away from home. I called Coop and Naomi and in no uncertain terms I demanded they go with me to watch the play. They didn't argue. They thought it was great that I wasn't going to go home and sulk all night. We made arrangements to meet at Malabar Farm fifteen minutes before the play, since the play was being held in the barn there.

Coop and Naomi were already there when I arrived. I was surprised at the amount of people there. Nearly every seat was full. Earlier, when I had been looking at the websites on Ceely Rose, I had come across an old picture of her. She was quite hideous, to say the least. I relayed this to Coop and Naomi.

"Maybe she had some disfiguring disease that made her crazy," Naomi proposed.

"I don't think so. From what I could tell, the rest of her family weren't exactly supermodels either. Shhh, the show's getting ready to start," I whispered.

Surprisingly, I enjoyed the play. Coop and Naomi did, too. After it was over, I went to the stage to speak to the play's writer and producer. Everyone else had left. The writer, Matt Simon, was more than happy to talk to me. At first.

He told me that when he first started putting the play together there were unusual occurrences. The barn where they staged the play was built from pieces of the mill where Ceely's father had been the operator. He didn't give that too much thought until he had several incidents of the lights pulsing and turning on by themselves.

Three days before opening night, during their last rehearsal, the entire barn went black. No lights, no sounds, no nothing. Matt told me they tried everything, but nothing worked. Matt said he stood in the middle of the barn and said quietly, "Please, Ceely, we can't tell your story without your help." After that, he walked over to the switch, flipped it on and everything worked. He also talked about going to her grave at the Lima Mental Institution.

"It was weird. It was a very cloudy day. As soon as I walked over to her grave, there was just a slight bit of sunshine coming down on her tombstone, but nowhere else."

Matt believed the place Ceely haunted the most was the women's restroom in the little building next to the barn. He talked of people claiming there was an extreme sense of dread when they walked in. They'd also heard Ceely giggling and her footsteps walk around the barn a lot. Matt said they'd all figured out how to deal with her. They usually say, "Knock it off, Ceely," and she stops.

"Ceely has made us all believe that there are good ghosts out there, and that she's one of them. She only wants to play and get attention," he said cheerily.

"This is about a woman who brutally murdered her family, and you talk about her like she's a saint you're paying homage to. Play and get attention?" I tried not to sound too condescending. "No offense, Mr. Simon, but I just don't get it. Outside of all the ghost story nonsense, I find it very disconcerting that you and your staff are praising this woman."

His smile faded. "I'm sorry, Sergeant, but yours is only one opinion. We like Ceely. I'm sorry if you don't understand that."

"I *don't* understand it. When Charles Manson drops dead, I highly doubt a hundred years from now people will be putting on a play and saying Charlie's a good and playful ghost!" I couldn't hide the sarcasm in my voice.

He nodded. "Well, Sergeant, if that's all the questions you have, I really need to start putting everything away. Thank you for coming."

He walked away, leaving me standing there with Naomi. Coop was near the entrance to the barn, talking to one of the actresses. Naomi startled me a little by agreeing with me. I assumed she would chastise me later for being rude to Matt Simon.

"You know, CeeCee, I was thinking the same thing when he was talking. He was acting like she was this wrongfully convicted woman who was put to death and now they're all trying to make it right. I totally agree with you." She chuckled. "Instead of walking around this barn and the restroom, she ought to be burning in hell."

"Be careful, Naomi. She's listening, and you don't want to piss her off!" I snorted.

We caught up with Coop by our cars. He told us a few of the stories that the actress had told him.

"She's as nutty as the writer, but she said they used to take the audience on a wagon ride past the old Rose house before the play began. There was a new girl who'd started and on her first wagon ride, she came up to my girl and was like, 'That was a cool effect having someone in costume standing in the window at the Ceely

Rose house!' Of course my girl says there was never anyone in costume up there."

I remembered something. "There was never any mention of the surviving brother, Randall Rose, and I forgot to ask Matt Simon about it."

"I wouldn't bother," Naomi said. "I don't think he's very fond of you at the moment. He probably won't answer any more questions."

I nodded and said good-bye to both of them before sitting in my car for a while. Reflecting back on the play, I still couldn't find a connection between Mary Jane Hendrickson and Ceely Rose. I thought about going in and asking Matt Simon, but he wouldn't know. I knew more about both Mary Jane and Ceely than most people at that point.

I drove around a bit before going home. When I pulled away from the farm, I felt a deep sense of dread, and it wasn't from Ceely Rose. I was trying to find anything to keep from going home. I thought about going to a movie, but realized it was probably too late.

I thought about what I had said to Matt Simon, and I was right. Here, people were praising Ceely Rose, glorifying her crimes and keeping her name alive. On the other hand, there was this other woman, Mary Jane Hendrickson, who did nothing wrong. Now she'd been branded a witch and people were urinating on her so-called grave. If the stories were true and Mary Jane was haunting the cemetery, it was no wonder. I'd be pissed, too.

CHAPTER TWENTY-SIX

Ultimately, I decided to bite the bullet and start toward home. It was late enough that I was hoping I would be able to fall asleep soon. When I turned onto my street, I was deep in thought, which is why it was only when I got to my driveway that I felt my heart stop. Michael's car was there.

Initially, I didn't know what to do. My first thought was to back out and drive away, but I had to see him. I couldn't help it. I knew he was there getting the rest of his things, and I also knew I was the last person in the world he wanted to see, but even knowing I shouldn't, I pulled into the garage.

The familiar thud in my chest from my heart beating so fast was back, trailed by shortness of breath and shaking. Seeing him was the worst thing I could do right now. It would only send me back into the tailspin I'd been trying to get out of so desperately. It had been almost two weeks since he had left. Opening the door and walking into the kitchen, I subconsciously held my breath.

He was leaning back against the counter facing the door, waiting for me with his arms crossed. He looked as though he had lost some weight, and he had about three days' growth of beard on his face. He seemed as exhausted as I felt, but he still looked wonderful. Trying to keep from running over and taking him in my arms was a feat in itself. I crumbled inside at the sight of him, and it was too much to take. He was staring at me with an intense look on his face, but he said nothing. I realized, as hard as it was, I needed to keep up my charade for his sake. I could barely mouth the words this time. My voice came out in a squeak.

"Michael." I sounded hoarse. "You shouldn't be here. Eric will be here any—"

He put his hand up. "Stop, CeeCee."

I did stop. I was too tired to try to convince him anymore. I stood and looked at him. He uncrossed his arms and put them back on the counter, sighing deeply, while looking at the floor and then back at me. I stayed silent, because I knew any minute I would burst into tears. He spoke first, and it was so quiet I barely heard him.

"You know, I've never had anyone close to me die before." I became alarmed thinking something had happened to someone we knew, but he continued, "That said, I don't know any other way to explain how incredibly horrible these last two weeks have been for me." His voice was as scratchy and hoarse as mine was.

I felt the rush coming, and I tried to fend it off. That didn't stop my eyes from filling with tears, though. I continued to maintain my silence and let him talk.

"Never in my life have I felt pain like that. It physically hurt, and quite frankly, I didn't think I would get through it. I think about what I said to you the night I left, and it makes me sick . . . especially now that I know the truth."

"Michael, I don't know what you're talking about," I barely whispered.

"I know, CeeCee." He stood straight, his eyes piercing right through me. "I know about Vanessa."

I didn't answer. I could only stare back at him. If he was bluffing, I didn't want to give it away. There was no other way for him to find out unless Naomi called him. If she did, she would certainly hear about it from me. It didn't matter, though. At that moment, Michael started nervously pacing back and forth across the kitchen.

"When I left here, Cee, I didn't think I'd even be able to drive. You killed me. I was up the entire night wondering how this happened. I kept thinking this wasn't like you, when it dawned on me: I'd just answered my own question. It wasn't like you because it wasn't true. I figured that out on the first night." He stopped pacing and leaned back against the counter again. "The only problem was, I had to figure out why, and that would take some time."

I should've known better. Michael was an experienced, top-notch investigator. The fact that I thought he would just walk away from us with no questions asked made me feel quite idiotic.

He continued, "I had that trial, so I couldn't do anything for a few days, which made things worse. But when I drove down here three days later, my suspicions were confirmed a little more, although not completely yet. I was in the parking lot one night you worked late in your office. I saw you walk out while Eric was kissing Jordan. It didn't seem to me like you two were back together. I also saw you walk to your car and start crying. Of course, it was all I could do not to run over to you. It killed me to see you like that."

I knew someone had been watching me that night. It was Michael.

"If you knew then, Michael, why didn't you say something? Why wait almost another two weeks?" My eyes were flooded with tears.

"Because I needed to figure out why you did this in the first place." He took a deep breath. "Anyway, I thought there was a slight chance that you were telling me the truth, that Eric hadn't told Jordan yet and that you guys were just putting up a front. When I called and found out that your divorce had been finalized after I'd left, there was no more room for doubt. I knew it had something to do with this custody thing, but I couldn't quite figure out how. I called Naomi."

Now he knew the truth. I still didn't know what to say because it didn't solve anything as far as Sean was concerned.

"CeeCee, when she told me everything about what Vanessa had done, I was completely bowled over. My heart absolutely broke for you and what you've been through, and God forgive me, the words I said to you when I left." He wiped his watering eyes. "So, needless to say, I knew I had to take care of this before I talked to you, knowing how stubborn you are. To make a long story short, the custody case is over, CeeCee. Vanessa dropped the motion, and I guarantee she will never file one again."

My jaw dropped. It was over? How? I looked at him to make sure I had heard right. His nod told me that I had. All I knew was that I had Michael back. The trauma from the last two weeks caught up with me in an instant. I fell apart completely. I fell to my knees, put my face in my hands and sobbed uncontrollably. I realized now that Naomi had known all along when she'd told me that things have a way of working out.

Only when I felt Michael's arms embrace me did I truly comprehend that my nightmare was over. Feeling him hold me and touch me was all I could take. I grabbed him and held him for dear life, sobbing into his shoulder while we both sat on the kitchen floor. He held me just as tight, gently stroking my hair. We sat like that for what seemed like an hour before I began to relax. Sensing it, Michael took my face in his hands and pulled me close.

"Listen to me, CeeCee. Promise me you will *never* do something like this again, do you hear me?" His voice cracked. "We do things together, no matter what. If there's a problem, you come to me and we'll work it out. Promise me."

I could only nod. Being this close, I couldn't help pulling his face to mine and kissing him, something I thought would never happen again. It didn't stop there, for me or him. I was tearing at his shirt just as he was at mine and within seconds we were making love on the floor in a passionate frenzy. I almost felt like I was dreaming and had to keep telling myself this was real and he was home.

We moved our lovemaking from the kitchen to the bedroom, where it continued for most of the night and into the early morning hours. I didn't want to let him go, even when he got up to get a drink of water. I'm pretty confident he felt the same way, since he followed me downstairs when I remembered I hadn't locked the house.

At one point, lying in each other's arms, I asked him how he managed to get the custody case dropped.

"You really want to hear this right now? All right, but first tell me how your face got all scratched up. Was it from your stakeout at the grave the other night?"

I sat upright. "How'd you know about that?"

Even before I finished my question, I saw the small smile creep across his face and I knew. Naomi had been giving Michael a daily report of my schedule.

"Never mind." I lay back down. "Tell me about Vanessa."

"When Naomi told me what Vanessa had done . . . By

the way, don't get mad at Naomi. I didn't give her much choice but to tell me. At any rate, I was beyond furious, to say the least. I was up for forty-eight hours trying to figure out a way to get us out of this mess, and there was only one thing I could do. When I called her and told her I had moved out and you and I were done, she was ecstatic. She kept insisting that I come over for dinner and talk about her and me, so I agreed."

I sat up again. "What? Why?"

He laughed. "Relax and I'll tell you. I had it all figured out and hoped she would play into it, which of course she did. When I got there, I was thrilled to see Sean, of course, and he kept asking about you. She was pissed about that."

"I can only imagine." I smirked.

"After dinner, I played nice, very nice. I acted like I was interested in getting back with her and even went so far as to bad-mouth you." He saw me wince. "Don't worry, as much as I hated to do it, it was the only way she would believe I was being truthful. Plus, she was drinking. It was only a matter of time before she confessed everything. She was so goddamn smug and proud of herself I wanted to smash her right in the face, and I've never even thought about hitting a woman in my entire life. The upside to all of this was I had my tape recorder on and recorded the whole shebang."

"Did you sleep with her first?" I said weakly. I couldn't help asking.

"Of course not!" He looked shocked. "As soon as she told me, I made an excuse to leave. Needless to say, she came unglued. She had this unrealistic vision of us re-newing our wedding vows that night, I think. The next morning, first thing, I called my attorney and played the tape for him and told him what needed to be done. By the end of the day, he had been on the phone with Vanessa's attorney. After playing him the tape, he told him a complaint would be filed with the bar association to start with. Next, the FBI was going to open an investigation into the domestic relations judge for corruption, along with an ethics investigation into her brother by the Cleveland Police Department. It took less than an hour and several phone calls to Vanessa by her brother and her attorney for her to drop the complaint."

"That was when I got my notice that the depositions were canceled," I reflected. "I assumed you and Vanessa had gotten back together."

Now it was Michael who sat up. "God, CeeCee! I wish you would give me a little more credit. I still can't believe you would think, after everything we've been through, that I would walk away from us so easily. Yes, I was thrown when you told me you had slept with Eric, and I let my emotions cloud my judgment, but I knew something was wrong with the whole picture that night." He lay back down and sighed, caressing my face, which was nestled on his chest. "I'm just glad this nightmare is over."

"You and me both," I whispered.

I still felt traumatized, as if I had been in shock for several weeks and was just coming out of it. My mind and body were tired, and being here now with Michael didn't seem real.

I looked at the window and saw the sun coming up. I let out a low groan.

"I can't believe I have to start getting ready for work soon. I predict this is going to be a very long day."

"You don't have to work today," Michael said matter-of-factly.

I sat up, confused. "Of course I have to work today."

"No, you don't. You have the day off, courtesy of your captain." He was smiling. "I talked to her before you guys went to the play last night. She knew what was coming. She knows you have more important things to tend to today."

"Let me guess, the important thing being you!" I nudged him playfully.

"That's part of it." He reached over and grabbed his pants off the floor and took something out of a front pocket. I couldn't see what it was. "The other part is as soon as the courthouse opens, you and I are going to be there to get our marriage license." He took my hand and slipped my engagement ring back on my finger. "And then we're going to celebrate." His face turned serious. "I can't ever lose you again, Cee."

I felt the tears returning, except these were different tears; they were from unreserved happiness. Michael pulled my face to his, brushing his lips gently over the wetness on my cheeks. Soon after, we were making love again.

If not for the marriage license, we probably wouldn't have gotten out of bed all day, but we were both anxious. I took the last two weeks as a sign that anything is possible, no matter how secure one feels in their life.

As Michael promised, we were at the courthouse when it opened and had our marriage license in hand within fifteen minutes. Michael said he was taking me out to dinner that night to celebrate, but made the wonderful suggestion of going home and getting some sleep beforehand. We were both emotionally and physically exhausted.

We slept longer than anticipated, but neither of us complained. When we were getting ready to go out to dinner, I took a brief moment to call Naomi. I assumed she was dying to hear from me. She answered her phone immediately.

"Naomi, it's CeeCee."

"CeeCee! How are you?" She seemed nervous.

She wanted me to bring up the topic first, and I realized she thought I might be angry with her.

"I'm fine. Most importantly . . . thank you."

She gasped into the phone. "He's there! CeeCee, I'm sorry I told him, but it was just *so wrong!* I'm assuming everything's okay now?"

"It will be if you agree to be my maid of honor."

She let out a light whoop into the phone. "Oh my God! Of course! CeeCee, I'm so happy for you. Take this time and enjoy it, please. Don't worry about work. It's not going anywhere." I could hear Coop in the background wanting a play-by-play. "Listen, CeeCee, enjoy tonight. I want details later!"

I was lightly laughing to myself when I hung up. Never in a million years would I have ever thought that Naomi Kincaid-Cooper would be my maid of honor. Now I realized she was probably the best friend I've ever had.

Michael and I enjoyed our night together immensely. We ate, drank and even danced a little. I think both of us kept silently wondering if fate was going to try to screw with us again, both of us still recovering from the shock of it all. Nonetheless, we savored every moment.

That night, I slept soundly for the first time in weeks. My mind and body were screaming for more than two hours of rest. I actually slept eight full hours. I woke up feeling almost myself again. I was refreshed, content and ready to tackle my first day back to work since Michael had come back.

Everyone noticed the change in my demeanor and appearance. Naomi was, of course, the only one who commented on it when she saw me walking down the hall toward my office. She was standing outside the secretary's door.

"Well, this is certainly an improvement. You look better, and I'm guessing you feel better. Am I right or wrong?"

I smiled. "Definitely right. I feel better than I have in weeks—obviously."

"If you're not doing anything for lunch, get with me. You can give me the gritty details then!"

I agreed to meet her for lunch, if I could get caught up on some things. I started pulling sticky notes full of messages off my desk when my gaze caught my handwritten notes on the Melissa Drake murder. I had forgotten several things I had wanted to do, including finding out the circumstances of Daniel Griffin's first animal cruelty conviction. I figured now was as good a time as any to go downstairs and dig through the files. This time I had a report number, so it wouldn't take me as long.

I was whistling and singing most of the way to the storeroom, feeling like a teenager in the throes of her first crush. I was even more jubilant when the box I was looking for was right by the door. I flipped through the files, reading all the numbers, until I came across what I was looking for. Instead of taking the file back up to my office, I decided to look at it here. That way, if there was nothing of consequence in it, I wouldn't have to make a second trip down.

I opened the file and begin flipping through the pages, but didn't find what I was looking for. When I stood, still holding the file, a small brown envelope fell out of it onto the floor. Photographs. I set the file down and grabbed the envelope. When I pulled the first picture out, I felt my blood run cold.

It was a photograph of the animal victim of Daniel Griffin's crime: a dog that had been skinned alive.

CHAPTER TWENTY-SEVEN

The dog in the photograph eerily resembled the dog found at the cemetery, minus the burn marks and ritualism. Daniel Griffin had been twenty years old when he committed this crime. He had served nine months in the county jail before being released and put on probation for a year.

One would think since he had a prior conviction of the same, the judge would have come down a little harder on him. Then again, this is Richland County; clearly not much changes in twenty years. This is the only county in which a convicted child molester might not serve a day in prison and only get probation.

Feeling my pulse quicken, I grabbed the case file and photographs and almost jogged back upstairs to my office. There were a lot of things I needed to find out and confirm before I got too excited about Daniel Griffin. He would be in his midforties by now, if he was even still alive.

I called the Communications Center and gave them the names and Social Security numbers of all the suspects in the Melissa Drake murder. I asked them to locate a current address and phone number, if possible. It should have been easy if they were all still living in Ohio because the checks would be done through the bureau of motor vehicles. If any of them had recently moved out of state, the BMV would note that on their record and list the state where they'd obtained a new driver's license.

I was tapping my fingernails on my desk and chewing my bottom lip when my phone rang five minutes later. They had located only two of them.

"Damn!" I cursed into the phone.

"Sorry, Sergeant." The dispatcher was nervous. "If you want, we can try to do an NCIC search on the national database if that helps. It'll take some time and they'll have to have committed crimes to show up."

"It's not your fault. I wasn't yelling at you. Go ahead with the NCIC thing." I had a thought. "Also, check the last names locally. Maybe I can track down their parents or relatives if they're still around."

"Will do, Sergeant."

They had located Meghan Dearth and Nicole Harstein, two of the more important ones, but not Daniel Griffin. Meghan Dearth was in Cincinnati, and Nicole had just moved to Indianapolis from Dayton a month ago. I was actually closer to Indianapolis. I looked at my watch and figured I could be there, talk to Nicole for twenty minutes, and get back by the end of the day. It would take me three and a half hours to get there, three if I took a marked cruiser.

I had to talk to her in person since I already knew she would probably hang up on me if I called. Same with Meghan Dearth. I couldn't help finding some joy in meeting Meghan Dearth. Few times in my life I've had the opportunity to go up against someone like her. Each time I've walked away with the upper hand, leaving them to feel as small as an amoeba on a grain of sand. That was exactly what I intended to do with her, whether or not I got any answers. The sad and realistic fact was that she got away with murder, and I find that disgraceful to say the least.

I would go to Cincinnati tomorrow since it was a four-hour drive. It's one of my favorite cities, and I wondered if Michael would want to go with me. I thought after I was done talking to Meghan, we could go have dinner on one of the riverboats. I called him.

He couldn't go to Cincinnati and was less than thrilled that I was driving to Indianapolis, mainly because I would be late getting home. *I already miss you like crazy,* was his reasoning. I assured him it would still be daylight when I got home. Then I hung up.

I informed Naomi what I was doing and canceled our lunch date before gathering my things and heading out. Once on the interstate, I called a friend at Indianapolis PD, Detective Ron Armbruster. Ron and I had taken several training seminars together and kept in touch every couple of months or so. He was thrilled that I was coming and agreed to meet me at a restaurant on the west side. He was going to drive by Nicole's house first, to make sure she was home. If not, he would try to track her down before I arrived.

I had forgotten how much I loathed the drive to Indianapolis. Once you get to Dayton, the ride is fine, but the stretch of Interstate 70 from Dayton to Indianapolis is awful. It's nothing but flat cornfields the entire way. I was hoping I wouldn't get stuck in traffic in Columbus and counted myself fortunate when I didn't. I actually arrived at the restaurant twenty minutes early. Ron was already waiting for me.

"CeeCee Gallagher, how the hell are ya? Oh, forgot, it's *Sergeant* Gallagher now. Whoo, whoo, whoo!" Ron gave me a tight squeeze.

In his late forties, Ron was overweight with thinning brown hair, a large bulbous nose and rosy cheeks. He always reminded me of one of the Campbell's Soup kids. Ron was one of the nicest people I've ever met.

We went inside to grab a quick lunch and get a game plan together. Plus, it gave us time to catch up. Ron had driven past Nicole's house and saw a brand-new Lexus, registered to her, in the driveway.

"She lives in a hoity-toity gated community, definitely high up on the food chain. Chances are she doesn't even work. I'm sure her hubby is quite the sugar daddy. Oh, her married name is Judson."

I nodded. "I know, it showed on her driver's license. By the way, what a sexist thing to say about having a sugar daddy," I kidded. "She could be a doctor or something."

He rolled his eyes. "I doubt it."

"Pig."

We finished our lunch and joked with each other some more before going to Nicole's house. I left my car at the restaurant and rode with Ron, since he knew where he was going.

When we pulled through the gates, I was in awe. My house was fairly large by normal standards, but these homes were utterly gargantuan. I'd estimate that the lowest priced home was at least five million dollars.

Ron made his way to a cul-de-sac at the end of the first road, turned into the driveway of one of the colossal homes and parked behind a black Lexus SUV that stood just outside the garage.

"Good Lord!" I looked up at the home. "What do these people do for a living?"

"Who the fuck knows. All I know is I'm in the wrong job. I estimate this house is twelve thousand square feet, minimum, and it's one of the smaller ones."

"And to think, I thought I was the shit, living in a six thousand-square-foot house," I remarked.

"Your house is six thousand square feet? Jesus Christ! You guys on the take up there in Mansfield or what?"

I giggled as I got out of the car. Ron was still shaking his head and mumbling, "six thousand square feet," as I rang the doorbell. After several minutes, we still hadn't gotten an answer. Ron walked up and pounded so hard on the door I thought he'd break it.

"Probably need a goddamn PA system to hear the fucking front door in this house!" he griped.

It was another couple of minutes before an intercom, which was situated by the doorbell, came to life.

"Hello?" A woman's voice came through the speaker, almost in a whisper.

"Oh this is fuckin' beautiful. Goddamn rich people!" Ron muttered.

I turned around and socked his arm before putting my finger up to my lips to shush him.

"Yes, I'm looking for Nicole Judson," I announced.

"Who are you?"

I prodded Ron. I didn't want to tell her who I was until I saw her face-to-face. She'd never answer the door otherwise. Ron put his mouth right to the intercom. I had to suppress my laughter.

"Uh, ma'am, I'm Detective Armbruster of the Indianapolis Police Department. Myself and this other officer would like to ask Mrs. Judson a few questions if possible." He stood up and looked pleased with himself.

"What's this about?" The woman sounded nervous.

Ron grimaced and turned red. I caught it just before he exploded. He had less patience than I did, if that's possible.

"Mrs. Judson, is that you I'm speaking to?" I intervened. "Please come to the door. I assure you that neither you nor any of your family are in trouble. The quicker you can answer our questions the quicker we'll get out of here. Please."

There was a long pause. "All right, I'll be down in a minute."

"Judas priest!" Ron started again. "These people need an act of fuckin' congress to open the door or what? Goddamn rich people!"

"So you've said before," I whispered. "C'mon, Ron, take some deep breaths."

"I'm fine. I just remember a time when, if you knocked on someone's door and told them it was the police, they answered it, no questions asked. That's the way it should be."

Before I had a chance to reply, the door opened just a crack. An attractive, dark-haired woman peered around it.

"May I see your badges, please?"

I quickly put my hand on Ron's arm and gave him a *just do it and don't bitch* look. Smiling, I held my badge and identification forward so the woman could see it. She immediately became alarmed. This was what I was afraid of.

"Richland County? I thought you said you were local? You don't have jurisdiction here!"

I felt Ron step forward so I stretched my arm out to block him and spoke first.

"Ma'am, Detective Armbruster *is* with the Indianapolis Police. He is merely here with me out of courtesy while I ask you a few questions," I said calmly.

"I can't imagine what you could possibly want to ask me, Sergeant, but I have nothing to say to you." She started to shut the door. I wedged my foot inside before she could close it.

"Mrs. Judson—I'm assuming you *are* Mrs. Judson—there has been another girl murdered at Mary Jane's

Grave, similar to the one you and your friends were accused of. Now, I really hope your conscience has gotten the better of you over the last twenty years and you'll help me. I don't need to remind you that you cannot be tried for aggravated murder again, regardless of what you say."

She looked horrified. "Get your foot out of my door, Sergeant. You assholes up there in Mansfield are the ones who tried me for murder and you expect me to talk now? Forget it!" She looked behind her, then lowered her voice. "I'm a mother now, and I've really put all of that behind me. Now please leave."

"I believe Daniel Griffin had something to do with this current murder, Nicole," I declared, and waited.

I noticed she winced at the mention of Daniel's name. She also started breathing harder as her chest began rising and falling quicker.

"Give me ten minutes and I'll leave," I said softly.

She wiped the sweat that had formed on her forehead. "Ten minutes. I'll open the garage door. We'll talk in there. You have to be gone before my husband gets home."

She shut the door. While Ron and I walked toward the garage door, it opened. After we walked in, it shut behind us. Nicole came out, wearing a black velvet sweat suit and black flip-flops. Her dark hair was pulled back into a braid. She had no makeup on but was very pretty.

"Let's make this quick. My husband doesn't know any of this. Quite frankly, he'd probably have a heart attack if he found out."

It was extremely stupid of her to tell me that. Judging by Ron's smile, he thought the same thing. Now she had to talk to me. If she changed her mind, I would only have to *suggest* that it might benefit us to speak to her husband.

"Mrs. Judson, you just moved here, is that right?" I began with noninvasive questions.

"Yes, that's right. My husband is chief of oncology at St. Anne's Medical Center."

"Do you work?" I pretended to write in my notebook.

"No."

I ignored Ron's *told you so* glance. "Mrs. Judson, when is the last time you were in Mansfield, Ohio?"

She stiffened. "I left the day I graduated from high school and I haven't been back since. My parents moved to Florida that summer so I've had no reason or desire to ever go there again."

"Do you keep in touch with any of your friends, like Meghan Dearth . . . or Daniel Griffin?" I stared dead at her.

She turned red. "Daniel Griffin was *never* my friend, let's get that straight. Secondly, I haven't talked to Meghan since we were in court together. After all of that, my parents wouldn't allow me to be around her."

"Why? According to the jury, you guys did nothing wrong," I said.

She gasped. "I just meant because she was hanging around a guy like Daniel Griffin, that's all!"

"A guy she had sex with and gave blow jobs to in the back of your car in exchange for killing someone. Does that sound about right?" I continued to stare.

Her head swung back and forth between me and Ron, her face now a deep shade of red. She looked like she was about to cry.

"I'm done." Her voice cracked. "Now please leave."

She turned to walk toward the door leading into her house when I calmly made a suggestion.

"Mrs. Judson, Detective Armbruster and I were wondering if it wouldn't benefit us to wait for your husband. Maybe you did tell him some things and he could give us a little insight." I was being tremendously unethical, but God knows I've done worse.

She turned around and shot me a glare that would've melted an iceberg. I stayed cool and composed.

"I know who you are, Sergeant. I've seen you on TV. We'll see what my lawyer and the news stations think about you threatening me," she said arrogantly.

"That's fine. However, by the time all that rolls around you'll still be explaining to your husband why you were tried for murder," I said.

She was shaking as she sat down on one of the two steps that led into the house. Hanging her head in defeat, she sniffled and wipe tears from her eyes before nodding.

"I'll never forget that day as long as I live," she murmured. I quickly reached into my pocket and hit the record button of my tape recorder. "You didn't back talk to Meghan, that's for sure. Everyone always went along with everything she said. God forbid you argued with her. She'd make you an outcast in a heartbeat and turn your life into a living hell. I watched her ruin girls' lives for the rest of their school years even if they really didn't do anything wrong. No one could talk to them—I mean no one. If Meghan caught you talking or being nice to any girl she had made an outcast, you'd be right there with her. I fucking hated Meghan Dearth." She sniffed and wiped her her nose. "When Derek Solis dumped Meghan for Melissa, she went postal. None of us had ever seen Meghan that mad, and we saw her mad plenty. But this was different. She'd never been dumped before. I remember when they broke up she went on this rampage for days, just really reckless behavior. She'd get drunk and drive a hundred miles an hour, hitting mailboxes on purpose, things like that. One night, we were at this party and she was snorting coke like it was going out of style. After that, she found a gun in one of the bedrooms and came out pointing it at everybody, laughing." She inhaled deeply and let it out. "She didn't find out about Melissa until almost a week after they had broken up. That's when she really flipped. I remember her exact words—she screamed them in the middle of the cafeteria. She said 'I can't believe he dumped me for that greasy, cow-shit-eating, horse-dick-sucking, nasty little bitch!' "

"What was that supposed to mean?" I couldn't help but ask.

"I think Melissa lived on a farm."

"Oh."

"So, basically, after that, Meghan came up with the idea to become friends with Melissa. The initial plan was we were going to make her our friend, make her popular, and then totally embarrass her in front of the entire school later on. Meghan said she was going to get everyone to nominate Melissa for Homecoming Court. There's always an assembly where members of the court walk down the aisle with an escort to the stage. Meghan, who was also on the court, would be announcing the other nominees. She said when Melissa got to the stage she would announce there was a mistake in the voting and Melissa only got one vote and she would have to leave, humiliating her. After that she would be shunned by everybody."

I shook my head. I couldn't help thinking what a bitch Meghan Dearth was.

Nicole sighed. "We all went along with it, but when Homecoming came, Meghan said she'd had a change of heart. The rest of us were actually relieved. Meghan went on as normal for the next several months, acting like Melissa was our friend. I remember one day she told me she genuinely liked Melissa and was over it. Until . . . until that night she picked up Daniel." She began to play with her braid. "He was so disgusting. When she told me to pull over and pick him up I thought she had finally lost her mind. She said he was perfect for the job. At the time I didn't know what she meant by that."

I interrupted. "But you didn't ask? Why?"

"Because you didn't question Meghan, that's why. Her father was a judge, the teachers loved her, girls wanted to be her. I felt lucky, at the time, that she was my friend. If only people knew how she really was. She could put on such an act . . ." She scowled at the thought.

"Nicole, how long was this before the murder?"

"Um, I think it was like two or three weeks? I'm not positive. I know that Meghan blew him in the backseat that night and slept with him almost every night after that. I couldn't stand him. Neither could anyone else, but he was with Meghan so we kept our mouths shut. He was so weird and creepy I tried to keep my distance from him."

"How was he weird and creepy?"

"The way he acted mostly. He was always quiet and kind of just stared at you. It used to freak me out. When he did talk, it was always dark shit, like death and evil and that kind of crap. One day he was a pagan, then a Wiccan, then a Satanist, then an agnostic, always something different. I remember what he said to me once, though. He said, 'Death releases your soul.' I didn't bother to ask what it meant."

"All right, Nicole, tell me about the night of the murder."

CHAPTER TWENTY-EIGHT

Her eyes filled with tears again. "We were drinking, and Meghan was the first one to bring up Mary Jane's Grave. Melissa seemed really interested. She'd never been there before. That was when Meghan decided, not suggested, that we go down there. She said matter-of-factly, 'Everybody get in the car. We're going to Mary Jane's Grave.' Meghan drove. Me, Sydney, Alexis, Dillon and Melissa crammed into the backseat. Daniel rode up front with Meghan. They were whispering a lot back and forth during the ride. When we got there, everything seemed fine. We were drinking, laughing and having fun. Meghan seemed in a good mood, which was a rarity." Her chest heaved up and down as she took another breath. "It was when Meghan dared Melissa to kiss Mary Jane's tree that the mood changed. I remember Meghan whispered something to Dillon, and he went over and turned the car stereo up as loud as it would go. Some Stevie Nicks song was playing. Sydney and Alexis were smiling at each other and I felt like the odd one out. Melissa, she was drunk, skipped over to the tree. Daniel was helping her. It was too late when I saw Meghan pick up the rock, a broken piece of tombstone, and hand it to Daniel. Just as Melissa leaned over to kiss the tree, he hit her with it—hard." Nicole started sobbing.

"Take your time, Nicole," I said.

"I'm o-okay. She went down face-first. I remember I was screaming, and Meghan ran over and slapped me across the face, hard enough that it hurt a lot. She told me to shut the fuck up or I was next. Sydney and Alexis gathered more pieces of the tombstones while Melissa lay there. She was mo-moaning, and blood was running down her head. She was trying to get up when Daniel hit her again!" she wailed. "I felt myself gagging and thought I was going to throw up. Dillon slapped me in the back of the head and said, 'Don't puke, dumb ass!' Daniel kept hitting her, but she kept moving. Her arms and hands were flailing out in front of her, and you could hear her gurgling and panicking. It made me so sick."

I could only imagine. Just sitting here and listening to the story, I felt a wave of nausea hit my stomach. What a horrible death Melissa Drake had suffered. She was most likely already dead by this point of Nicole's story. Sometimes it takes the body longer to die than the brain.

I remember once watching a video of an accidental death at a death investigation school. A man into auto-erotic masturbation would half hang himself while he masturbated, always videotaping it. Unfortunately, on this particular occasion the knot slipped and he killed himself. Although he was brain dead, his fists clenched up and his arms began to punch the air for almost a minute. It was a physiological reaction to death and one of the most disturbing things I've ever seen. Melissa Drake probably had similar activity.

Nicole continued, "Meghan was kicking her too, in the head, the stomach, all over! What I couldn't be-lieve was that the others were laughing! They all knew!" she said, her eyes wide. "Finally, Daniel picked up a huge piece of tombstone and smashed her with it. She stopped moving after a few seconds," she cried. "But that wasn't all. Meghan flipped her over and, oh my God, her face! It was all caved in. You couldn't recognize her! Meghan snapped a large branch off the pine tree and pulled Melissa's pants down . . ." Nicole put her hands over her mouth and shut her eyes.

"Go on, Nicole, you're almost done," I said sympathetically.

"She-she put the branch in her, like, you know . . . and she said 'Don't fuck my boyfriend, fuck *this*, bitch!' " Nicole fell apart completely, bending over, grabbing her knees and wailing.

"Jesus, Mary and Joseph," Ron whispered, shaking his head.

I grabbed a few tissues from my purse and walked over to Nicole. I knelt next to her, rubbed her back and handed her the tissues. As soon as she seemed to compose herself, I couldn't help asking a question.

"Nicole, did you tell all of this to the detective you gave your original statement to? Especially the part about Meghan kicking Melissa?"

If she had, I wanted to know why the hell Meghan Dearth's shoes weren't confiscated. They would've had blood evidence all over them.

"No, I never told him about the kicking." She hiccupped. "But even after she was dead, Meghan kept hitting her with the rocks until Dillon told her to stop."

"What happened after?"

"Daniel tossed the pieces of tombstone that they had used in a nearby ravine. I was over by the car crying and they waited for Daniel before walking over to me. They had all been standing in a circle, whispering. I thought they were gonna kill me, too! But Meghan was nice. Scary nice. The rest of them just stood there looking at me with smiles on their faces. Meghan said, 'You know, Nic, things will be different if you ever tell anyone about this. You were here, too! You're now just as guilty. If anyone asks, we all stayed at my house, never left. You got that? God help you if you talk. What happened to that bitch is nothing like what we'll do to you.' What the hell else could I do but agree? They suspected I told that detective something, and they followed me around for weeks. I was terrified! So that's when I said that stuff in court. After that, they left me alone and, like I said before, I left on graduation day and never went back. I heard that Meghan is some bigwig attorney now. How ironic."

"Did you know Melissa's mother killed herself a year after that?"

She bowed her head. "I heard."

I stood looking at Nicole briefly before flipping through the file in my hand. I could tell from the autopsy report that Nicole was telling the truth. Melissa had been sexually assaulted with a pine tree branch.

"Nicole, do you have any idea what happened to Daniel Griffin after that?"

"I don't know, and I don't care, unless he's burning in hell, that is. Sydney and Alexis are somewhere in California, I heard, and Dillon, I heard he's now a homeless bum in Florida." She stood, her eyes red and swollen. "Sergeant, really, I've told you everything. That night will haunt me for the rest of my life, and yes, I deserve it, but please, would you please go now?"

I nodded and walked out as she opened the garage door. Ron had remained surprisingly silent during the interview but unloaded as soon as we got into the car.

"Fucking unbelievable. And you're telling me they got away with that shit? Fucking American justice system was, is and will always be a joke."

"Usually, but this time I might be able to use it to my advantage."

"How's that?"

"These people were only tried for aggravated murder. I've now got them on rape, conspiracy to commit rape and gross abuse of a corpse, not to mention perjury."

"If you can make that fly, I'll stand on my head naked in downtown Indianapolis and sing the theme to *COPS*."

"Be careful, Ron. I'm starting to get a visual. And don't consider backing out on me when I win." I smiled, and cringed at the thought.

"You're over your statute of limitations by six months. Rape is twenty years to the day." He looked smug.

"We'll see about that." I looked even smugger.

He was right, but I had a feeling it was a bluff I could easily pull off if Meghan was as arrogant as I perceived her to be. She was very young when she was prosecuted, so I highly doubted she looked at the autopsy report. She probably thought they had simply missed it, which is why she wasn't charged.

After Ron dropped me off and I started home, I called Michael immediately. I was going to have to back out on my word. My stay in Indianapolis, although brief, was longer than I had anticipated. It would be dark by the time I got home. He insisted on waiting up for me, and I didn't argue. I missed him.

After I grabbed a glass of wine and engaged in much needed physical affection with Michael, we sat down while I played the tape of my interview with Nicole Harstein-Judson. As he had during my interview with Walter Morris, Michael stared at the tape recorder, the lines in his face deepening as Nicole began to describe the murder. After the tape ended, Michael was lightly shaking his head.

"You realize that Melissa Drake suffered horribly when she died, don't you?"

I nodded. I explained to him my intentions regarding the twenty-year-old case. He disagreed completely.

"The state statute of limitations on rape is twenty years. You're over it by about six or seven months."

"Doesn't matter. Section F in the Ohio Revised Code specifically states that as long as the *corpus delicti,* that's the body of evidence and—"

"I know what it is. I did go to law school, remember?" He smiled.

"Oh, right. Anyway, it says as long as the *corpus delicti* remains undiscovered, the statute of limitations doesn't begin until it *is* discovered or brought to the attention of law enforcement. That's how all these priests are getting tried on sex crimes thirty years after the fact."

"But she's already been tried and acquitted. Double jeopardy applies."

"Meghan Dearth was only tried and acquitted for aggravated murder, not rape or gross abuse of a corpse. I can't imagine why those charges weren't added, but it seems that the case was fixed and screwed up from the beginning. Anyway, double jeopardy doesn't apply." I raised my eyebrows with self-satisfaction.

"Says who? The sexual assault was already included in the autopsy, therefore it *was* brought to the attention of law enforcement. Sorry, baby, you're kind of screwed on this one. Of course, there's still the question of why the prosecutors at the time never charged her for that."

I laughed. "I can never get one by you, can I? Actually, yes, Michael, I'm aware it's a bullshit no-can-do charge, but I think I can get Meghan to buy it. As for the original prosecutors, I can't begin to imagine why they didn't put either charge on the indictment. Either they were on the kids' parents' payroll or they were complete dipshits."

I explained my plan to Michael, and how I was fairly confident Meghan Dearth would take the bait. He wasn't so confident and shook his head.

Michael leaned forward. "Let me get this straight. You've got a murder committed a couple of weeks ago that you think is related to one that happened in 1986 . . . or at least you think one of the suspects from 1986, Daniel Griffin, has something to do with the current one, right?" I nodded. "And in finding this out, you come across new evidence that implicates one of the other suspects in the 1986 murder, rape and gross abuse of a corpse—a bull-shit charge, but you think she's going to buy it anyway and cough up a confession. Does that sum it up?"

"Sí. I'm going to tell her there's a warrant issued for her arrest on those charges, mainly to watch her squirm."

"What if she checks into it?" He raised an eyebrow and smirked.

"Then I'm fucked."

"This is a pretty dangerous game you're playing here. You'd better be careful." Michael was smiling broadly now. "And the witch . . . where does she come in?"

"I haven't figured that out yet, but don't think I won't."

"That's my girl." He gave me a squeeze. "There's no doubt in my mind that you'll have this wrapped up by the end of the month."

Michael and I finished our wine before turning in for the night. I had planned on getting an early start for Cincinnati, so I could get home at a decent hour. Michael changed his mind and offered to reschedule his day so he could go with me, but I regretfully de-clined. I didn't need any distractions, which, since he'd been back, Michael had been. In a good way, of course.

I stopped in my office to check through my six-inch stack of business cards. Every time I went to a seminar or dealt with another agency, I kept their cards in case I needed something later from them. I had a slew of detective business cards from Cincinnati PD, but I grabbed one in particular, Detective Simone Vardona.

Simone and I had taught several classes together at the peace officers' training academy in London, Ohio. Last time I spoke with her, she was working vice, going undercover as a prostitute. Simone was the definition of a firecracker. She was one of those people who could make someone feel as small as a mouse, even while she was smiling. I'd also seen her flip side, and she could have the strongest of men cowering in a corner. She was exactly who I wanted standing next to me when I contacted Meghan Dearth.

When I called Simone and filled her in, she said she was looking forward to "verbally crucifying the little bitch."

After I checked in with Naomi and grabbed a cup of coffee to go, I was on my way to Cincinnati and to Meghan Dearth.

CHAPTER TWENTY-NINE

I was meeting Simone at a downtown coffeehouse where we would discuss our strategy on approaching Meghan. I found Simone instantly. Her striking Latina appearance and almost five-foot-ten-inch height made her stand out in a crowd. I've never been one to envy the look of another female, but after being with Simone for less than five minutes, I began to feel like a frump. She startled me with her own opinion.

"God, CeeCee, you blonde bombshell . . . every time I'm around you, I feel like a freakin' plain Jane." She eyed me up and down. "You weigh, what? Ninety pounds? You're not allowed to count your ten pounds of boobs either."

I laughed out loud. "Oh, whatever! I was just wondering if *you* got done sashaying your booty down the catwalk, Miss Supermodel!"

Women; no matter where we are or what we're doing, we always find time to be catty or complimentary, whichever applies at the time.

Simone was quite eager to come face-to-face with Meghan Dearth. Not as eager as I was, though. Simone had been busy while I was driving here. She had already located Meghan's law office and determined that she was working today. Her last name was now Micelli, which happened to be one of the names of the firm.

"She's a partner?" I said, as Simone and I sat sipping cappuccinos.

"Nah, her hubby is, some guy she probably laid as an intern fresh out of law school. From what you've told me about her, I'd say I'm right. I'd heard the name of the firm before—Micelli, Giabaldi and Farrino—so I called the local feds. They've investigated them before but never got anything to stick. The bottom line is they're dirty."

"There's a shocker," I mused.

"I'm anxious to get over there and ruin their day. I love to fuck with lawyers." Simone drained her cup.

The offices of Micelli, Giabaldi and Farrino occupied the first and second floors of the Striker Tower. In the middle of downtown, the Striker Tower was a forty-three-story high rise, which rented space mainly to law and accounting firms.

When we walked in, I immediately headed to the restroom just off the lobby. When I came out and went to the law firm's offices, Simone was already there.

"She's waiting for us and, as you can imagine, didn't sound too thrilled."

"Did you talk to her?"

"No, Jimmy the Greek over there called up to her." Simone pointed to a dark-haired man in a black suit who wore more gold jewelry than any rapper I'd ever seen. "Miss Meghan *Death* is on the second floor with the other big cheeses, probably in the middle of a lunchtime blow job as we speak."

Meghan's office was almost at the end of a long hallway. The partners were down a little bit farther. Her secretary told us to go in her office and when we entered I wasn't the least bit surprised at what I saw. Neither was Simone.

Meghan was seated at her desk surrounded by four other men in black suits and gold jewelry. She had called for reinforcements in an obvious attempt to intimidate us. Nice try, honey, but I've gone up against much worse than this, I thought. I knew Simone had too, and knowing her, she was telling herself, This is gonna be fun!

After Simone introduced herself and then me, she plopped into the chair in front of Meghan's desk and stretched her arms out.

"Really, gentlemen, I know we're special and all, but you shouldn't have put this much effort into giving us a party. Where's the wine and cheese?" She looked around the office while I suppressed a smile.

Meghan remained quiet. She didn't look the same as her high school picture. She used to be pretty. Now it looked as if years of partying, and most likely drug use, had taken its toll; she looked rough. Her brown hair was severely pulled back into a bun, and she wore enough makeup for the entire cast of a Broadway play.

A tall, thin man in his late thirties, who was standing right next to Meghan, spoke first.

"I'm not amused, Detective, and I'm sure your superior officer won't be either when I call him." He glared at Simone, who smiled right back. "Now, Sergeant Gallagher, you can either tell us what this is all about, or you may leave these offices right now."

"Gentlemen, there's really no need to get quite so uptight." I tried to lower their defenses somewhat. "I'm here to ask Meghan a few questions about a crime that occurred in Mansfield in 1986, a crime that she's well aware of."

The tall man, who I now assumed to be Meghan's husband, shot her a look of confusion while her face turned a deep shade of crimson. Like Nicole, Meghan's

husband didn't have a clue. Like Simone, I had the in-
clination that this *was* going to be fun.

"I have no idea what you're talking about, Sergeant.
You've obviously made a mistake, not that I'm surprised
by that, but we are extremely busy here," she said
haughtily.

Simone raised her eyebrow at the "mistake" comment, but I kept smiling. Meghan Dearth, as I suspected,
hadn't changed—except for the worse, if that was possible.

"I'm sure you're busy, Mrs. Micelli, so I won't take up
much of your time." I eyed the other men. "You know,
I'm all about confidentiality, but if you'd like me to discuss this in front of these gentlemen, I don't have a
problem with that." I kept smiling, talking in a disgust-
ingly innocent voice; Simone quietly snickered.

I waited and stared at Meghan, knowing I had just
made her life hell by having to decide whether to air
her dirty laundry in front of her coworkers or only her
husband. The anxiety that washed over her face dissi-
pated within seconds.

She smiled and looked back at her coworkers. "Gentlemen, I remember what this is about and it's nothing.
I'm sorry I bothered you. You can go. There is no problem." She looked back at me. "Sergeant, we'll talk here
in a few minutes. Would you like a cup of coffee?" Her
eyes narrowed into slits as she made a conscious effort
to maintain her smile.

"No, thank you." I continued to lock eyes with hers.

The other suits looked at one another in confusion
before the nod from Meghan's husband assured them
it was okay to leave. Meghan seemed to breathe a sigh
of relief until she saw that Micelli had no intention of
leaving.

"Frank, I'm fine. You can go," she said nervously.

"I'm staying."

Her eyes begged him to leave, but he ignored it. Instead, Frank stood against a wall of law books and crossed his arms. Simone and I were both amused during the exchange. However, I didn't want to be here all day.

"All right, Meghan. May I call you Meghan?" She nodded. "I'd like to get started so we can get out of your hair and let you get back to your extremely busy schedule," I said.

After her last attempt to silently ask her husband to leave failed, Meghan nodded. "Go ahead."

"I'm here because there has been another murder and an attack at Mary Jane's Grave." I watched her face pale considerably. "There were quite a few similarities between this murder and the murder you and your friends were tried for."

Frank Micelli came off the wall. "What the hell are you talking about? What murder?" He looked from me to Meghan.

Meghan picked up a pen and began nervously playing with it. Her hands were trembling. "Frank, please, I'll explain it later. I was a kid, and I was found not guilty because I didn't do anything wrong."

"She's right, Frank," I intervened. "She was found not guilty, but I don't know about the 'didn't do anything wrong' part. I'd say you did plenty wrong, Meghan."

She stood up in a rage. "Sergeant, I was tried and acquitted by a court of law for that crime—a crime I did *not* commit! If you're here to retry that case, your dumb ass should know it's double jeopardy, and you two cunts can just get the fuck out!"

Frank, apparently used to his wife's outbursts judging by his unaffected demeanor, spoke to his wife in an authoritative voice that spread terror across her face. It didn't take a genius to realize he probably beat the shit out of her when they were home. He just looked like the type.

"Sit down, Meghan. You sit there and you listen, and you don't say a fucking word, understand?"

I remained calm. "Meghan, I'm not here to retry a murder case against you. My dumb ass is well aware of double jeopardy. However, I was wondering if you had kept in touch with Daniel Griffin."

Meghan looked at her husband, apparently for approval to answer the question. He nodded.

"I hardly knew him and haven't seen him since the trial."

"You hardly knew him? Huh . . ." I started randomly looking through the Melissa Drake murder file. "You mean the fact that you gave him oral sex and engaged in sexual intercourse with him on a regular basis only deems him an acquaintance? Is that what you're saying?"

Her face grew red again and she answered without approval from Frank. "That is a lie I'm sure you heard from Nicole Harstein. Nicole was always jealous of me and got angry when I didn't want to be friends with her after the trial. She got angry because she had to go back to being the loser that she always was before she met me. As for your innuendoes regarding Daniel Griffin, I don't nor have I ever had sex with someone for my own personal gain. I can only deduce that you asked me that because it's something you, yourself, are familiar with." Her eyes narrowed again and she smiled. "Fucking an FBI agent to get promoted to sergeant is quite a feat."

Before I could explode, Simone piped up, "Is that how you got promoted, CeeCee?" she quipped, trying to calm me down. "Goddamn. I'll have to try that. I don't want to be a detective forever, you know." She leaned over and gave me a high-five.

Simone's ploy worked, since I couldn't help but laugh and shake my head. Meghan's smile faded when she realized Simone got the best of her.

"Are you two bitches finished?" Meghan grumbled.

"Now, Mrs. Micelli, there's no need to be rude," Simone answered.

"Almost." I was ready. "I just have a few more questions, the first of which is: When you took a pine tree branch and brutally raped Melissa Drake with it, was she still alive?" I stayed focused on her.

"Get out now," Meghan sneered through her clenched jaws.

I continued, "The reason I'm asking is, when I issue a warrant for your arrest, I need to verify that she was still technically alive. I know she was dead when you continued to bash her face in with a piece of a tombstone, so that covers the gross abuse of a corpse charge that's also being filed, but what about the rape? Was she breathing?" I stayed calm.

"Frank! Get them out of here!" she screamed.

"Sergeant, no more questions. You need to leave." He stayed composed. "I thought we already determined the application of double jeopardy in this case, and although I'd have to look to be sure, I'm pretty sure the statute of limitations is up."

"She was tried for aggravated murder, not rape. And if you look at the Ohio Revised Code, you'll see that the statute doesn't begin until we are made aware of the crime itself." I omitted the fact was documented in the autopsy. "Look it up, section F. There is solid new evidence that indicates your wife brutally raped a young girl before she helped murder her."

Frank seemed dumbfounded, and I waited for him to ask how this sexual assault could have not been in the autopsy report. Apparently the veteran attorney was so taken aback by his wife's past, it never occurred to him. One point for me. Meghan was standing up with a look of sheer horror and panic on her face. She was still shaking, and now she was sweating. I waited until I got to the door before I launched my last attack, subtle but powerful.

"Oh, Meghan, by the way, you and your friends should have been tried as adults and given the death penalty for what you did. However, I will have a warrant for your arrest by the end of the day for the crimes of rape and gross abuse of a corpse. This will be a warrant that even your daddy can't get you out of. I *will* see you soon." I smirked before walking out the door, but held my breath hoping she wasn't on the phone to the prosecutors to confirm what I said was true.

"Well done, Sergeant," Simone announced when we were in the hallway.

Before we left the building, Simone, always one for surprises, stopped in front of a group of lawyers.

"Excuse me, do any of you have a large mirror I can borrow?" They looked as confused as I was. "The reason I'm asking is before I start my car and blow my own ass off, I'd like to check underneath it for a bomb. No? Okay, I'll guess I'll just use my compact."

She walked away leaving the group of men stunned. By the time I got to our car, I had tears in my eyes from laughing so hard. Simone was fumbling around inside her purse, looking for her keys, when my laughter stopped dead.

CHAPTER THIRTY

I happened to look at the front of the building just as Frank Micelli came barreling through the doors in a state of panic. He was headed right for us in a dead run. Only when I heard what he was yelling did I realize who he was after.

"Meghan! Noooooo!" he was screaming.

Out of the corner of my eye, I caught a glimpse of the gun barrel pointed toward Simone. Meghan was less than ten feet from her, holding a small revolver. Meghan's eyes showed the depth of how mentally disturbed she truly was.

"Simone! Get down! Gun!" I screamed as I reached for my own weapon.

Simone had just enough time to drop before Meghan fired the first shot. Missing her head by mere centimeters, the bullet shattered the driver's side window. By then, I was returning fire. Squatting behind the tire for cover, I fired two shots at Meghan, both hitting her directly in the chest, causing her to jerk backward while still holding the gun. When I heard another shot and saw a bullet strike Meghan square in the forehead, I realized Simone had gotten to her own gun.

The gun dropped from Meghan's hand as she fell backward, hitting the pavement with a slight thud. Every nerve in my body on red alert, I swung the barrel of my gun directly toward Frank Micelli, who was now screaming at the sight of his wife's dead body.

"Show me your hands!" He didn't comply until I repeated myself. Hands out to his sides, he started walking toward Meghan's body.

"Don't fucking move! Stay right where you are!" Simone was now up, taking small steps toward him with her gun pointed out in front of her.

People all around us were screaming and yelling, and I could already hear the wail of oncoming sirens. It was difficult to get control at that point since Frank was screaming and the entire law firm full of thugs had emptied out into the parking lot. I thought Simone and I were about to have a major problem when I saw three Cincinnati Police cruisers scream into the parking lot. Feeling only a slight sense of relief, I checked on Simone.

"Are you hit?" I called out.

"Nope, A-okay. You?" She was holding her badge up over her head with her free hand, alerting the oncoming uniformed officers that she was on duty.

"I'm fine."

Frank was still standing with his hands out to his sides when the uniformed officers came running to our aid.

"Check him for weapons and detain him," Simone ordered.

The officers led Frank to one of the marked police cars, where they patted him down and put him in the backseat. Other officers had arrived by then and were keeping the lawyers at bay while trying to cordon off the area. Simone looked as shaken as I felt.

No matter how many shootings an officer gets into, it's never easy. I felt the familiar pounding of my heart

while my adrenaline pumped through my body, causing me to noticeably shake. As I started to settle down,
the dizziness and nausea kicked in. I walked over to a
curb and sat on it, taking long, deep breaths while I
wiped the sweat from my brow. Having been through
this several times before, I was familiar with the physiological effects that occur following a critical incident
like this.

Simone, looking pale, walked over and sat next to me
on the curb. We sat and stared at Meghan's body for several minutes.

"Thanks, Sarge. I owe you one," she said flatly.

"Always a pleasure." I set my gun next to me.

"Homicide is on their way, along with every brass ass
and administrative dickhead in the department."

I felt myself cringe. The impact of where I was finally
hit me. Of all the places to get into a shooting, Cincinnati had to be the worst. After the riots several years earlier in which a white police officer shot an unarmed
black man, cops in Cincinnati get put through hell the
minute they lay their hands on someone. I could only
imagine the rain of shit that this incident would bring.
As if reading my thoughts, Simone raised the issue.

"CeeCee," she whispered, "we'll be fine. The security
cameras caught it all. If she was black, *and* a female,
she could've walked out of there pointing a rocket
launcher at us and we'd have gone to prison for life if
we fired back," she said cynically.

"Jesus, Simone! I went in there under false pretenses!
I'm screwed because there was no warrant!" I shuddered at the thought.

"As far as I'm concerned we were in there inquiring
as to the whereabouts of that Daniel fellow. That's a legitimate interview for a current homicide investigation.

If her husband says anything, I'll simply say he was mistaken, under duress after finding out about his wife's past. You told her you'd get a warrant for her arrest if she knew where Daniel is and wasn't telling—a legitimate Obstructing Justice warrant. No worries, I got your back, sister."

Her attempt at consolation wasn't exactly making me feel better. Meghan was a female attorney, which would be bad enough. Looking around at the uniformed officers and men in suits walking around the scene, I realized how much I wanted my own people here. I asked Simone to get me a cell phone. I needed to call Naomi.

I didn't tell her much, only that I had been involved in a fatal shooting and was okay. She was going to notify the chief and sheriff before calling me back. Before she hung up, I asked her to call Michael.

"Naomi, tell him I'm fine and he does *not* need to come down here. I'll lose it if I see him," I pleaded.

"I'll try my best, but you know how he is."

Naomi called me back within five minutes. The sheriff had called one of his contacts at Mansfield Lahm Airport. They would take a private plane down and be here within an hour. Michael, as expected, said he would be flying down as well and hung up on her before she could protest. Simone, overhearing my conversation, told me she would have two marked units ready to pick them up at the airport. I relayed this to Naomi, then remembered something.

"Naomi, make sure you bring me a union attorney."

She was quiet for a minute. "You've never asked for the union before. Is something wrong down there, CeeCee?"

"Other than the fact I'm in Cincinnati, no."

"I understand completely. I'll take care of it. Before you hang up, I need to talk to whoever's in charge of the scene down there."

I handed Simone the phone and she took it over to the lieutenant of the homicide division. I had noticed when I was speaking to Naomi, Simone was on another cell phone briefly, whispering into it and looking around to make sure no one heard her.

I let out a long sigh and put my head in my hands. I couldn't believe I'd just shot and killed Meghan Dearth. It was surreal. Nevertheless, my main concern continued to be the city police watchdog groups. They had so much power down here I shuddered at the thought of what lay ahead of me. I never had to worry about this sort of thing in Mansfield. Groups like the ACLU weren't as strong, and they never overrode the credibility of law enforcement when it came to shootings in the line of duty. Even the ACLU rarely questioned an officer's actions in Mansfield. But, again, I was in Cincinnati, and I was scared.

Simone, seeing my anguish, leaned over and began whispering in another attempt to cheer me up. Believe it or not, it worked.

"CeeCee, take a deep breath and relax." She looked around and then leaned back over. "Phone calls are already being made as we speak. This will be cleared by the end of the week guaranteed, no grand jury, no watchdog groups, no prosecution. Trust me."

I looked at her, my eyes wide. "How the hell could you possibly guarantee that?"

"I really didn't want to tell you this but, what the hell. You know after I went through my divorce I kind of played the field. Anyhoo, to make a long story short, a couple times a month—by no means on a regular basis—I, uh . . . I, well, I've been sleeping with the mayor. That was him on the phone."

My mouth fell open, and I just stared at her. Although thrilled, I was surprised at Simone. It seemed out of character for her.

"You're sleeping with the mayor of Cincinnati?"

"Yup. Keep your voice down. Look, it's not like I'm lying on my back to rise up the ranks. We met at a fund-raiser and kind of hit it off, and I like the guy. The fact that he's married makes things that much easier, no strings attached." She smiled. "It also helps in something like this. God forbid his wife finds out about us."

"You threatened the mayor?" I was in awe.

"No, no, of course not. I didn't need to. He was more than willing to have this cleared by the end of the week. I told him I'd make it worth it." She winked.

I groaned. "No offense, Simone, but I hope you are the best lay that man has ever had."

"No doubt about it, dear."

Knowing full well the power of sex, I felt my fears begin to dissipate. The mayor would have to do what Simone said. She literally had him by his short hairs. I called Eric and explained what had happened. Then I talked to the girls.

I saw the first news helicopter flying over the parking lot about ten minutes before Naomi, the sheriff, the chief and my union attorney arrived. There were four more after that. Since I was involved, the press would have a field day. Fortunately, they always portrayed me in a positive light.

My superiors were a sight for sore eyes. Each was overly concerned about my emotional well-being. I spoke with my attorney at length, while the others talked with the upper echelons of the Cincinnati Police Department, including the chief of police. Once my attorney had the full story, I gave my statement to the lieutenant of the homicide division. They had the entire incident on the security video, so it wasn't like my statement meant anything. All they had to do was watch it to see that neither I nor Simone had done anything wrong.

The lieutenant was very kind, and I knew immediately he wasn't going to make an issue of the shooting. He told me about the statement Frank Micelli had given the other detectives. Interestingly, Frank never mentioned the threatened warrant regarding a sexual assault. He just told them we were interviewing her about a homicide investigation he hadn't been aware of. Whew.

It seems after Simone and I had left Meghan's office, Meghan went over the edge. She was screaming that she wasn't going to jail and all kinds of crazy things. Frank said she walked out of her office. He thought maybe she was going to the restroom to take a breather until he saw her walk past the doorway carrying something in her hand. He ran down to his own office, opened his top drawer and saw that she had taken his gun. That's when he went chasing after her.

Frank also confessed that Meghan had been having mental problems for the past two years. She had been in and out of psychiatric hospitals, made several suicide attempts and was so medicated on antidepressants he was amazed she could even function.

"After Mr. Micelli calmed down, he actually seemed a little relieved," the lieutenant informed me, and then he told me something else. "Sergeant, I'm just putting you on notice that the news stations have obtained a copy of the tape, so expect to be all over the five o'clock news. Considering this involves you, don't be surprised if it goes national by morning."

I nodded and turned around to join Naomi and the others. Instead, I ran smack into Michael. He led me by the arm off to the side, his face panic-stricken.

"You're okay." He was looking at me up and down as if he expected to see a bullet hole somewhere.

"Honey, I'm fine. You didn't need to come down here." I felt myself on the verge of tears at the sight of him.

He pulled me close and held me tight. I would be lying if I said I wasn't ecstatic that he was there. He always made me feel safe.

I took the next several minutes and explained what happened, including my fears of Cincinnati. Michael was trying to tell me I had nothing to worry about when Simone came over. I introduced them.

"So, this is the reason you were promoted?" she said, mocking Meghan's words. Michael looked confused.

"Yes," I said to Simone, and then to Michael, "I'll explain later."

"We're supposed to be at the department first thing in the morning to give formal statements," she said. "It's probably best that you stay here for the night. The hotel room will be on the Cincy PD."

At that point, I was thoroughly exhausted. I wanted to leave, but first I had to clear it with the detectives in charge. Since I would be staying the night here, they said that would be fine.

Michael and I walked into our hotel room just as the ten o'clock news began. As the lieutenant had promised, the video of the shooting was the first piece aired. The announcer gave a brief history of my past before the video:

"For the third time in less than three years, decorated

veteran Sergeant Detective CeeCee Gallagher of the Richland Metropolitan Police Department had to take a life to protect her own and the life of a fellow officer. This time, however, the incident occurred here in Cincinnati . . ."

I watched it in a daze. On video, the shooting happened quickly—not like I remembered it. It was only a few seconds from the time Meghan raised the gun to the time we were ordering Frank to show his hands.

Michael turned pale when he watched the video. Sitting on the bed, he put his hand over his mouth. When it was over, he looked ill.

"If you hadn't looked over, she would have gotten you both."

"Shoulda, coulda, woulda. Michael, she didn't. Please, I don't want to dwell on it. It's over. I just want to give my statement in the morning and go home."

I spent the next forty-five minutes talking to my parents, assuring them I was okay, before falling asleep on the bed, fully clothed.

I woke up an hour before I was supposed to be at the police department. I had nothing with me, clothes or otherwise, so I did my best to look presentable. Michael waited in the lobby while I gave my statement, which took the better part of an hour. As I was leaving, I heard Simone call my name from behind me. I turned around, and she gave me a quick squeeze.

"I'll call you and let you know when it's been officially cleared. No worries, girlfriend." Her usually glowing look turned serious. "Listen . . . I'm really grateful to you. I watched that video and I about pissed my pants. If you hadn't said anything, she'd have killed me. Thank you, CeeCee."

With a promise to Simone to keep in touch more frequently, I left Cincinnati and headed home. Michael drove, and as soon as we crossed the Richland County line, I breathed a sigh of relief.

Per our union contract, I was automatically granted ten days off, with pay, as stress leave since I was involved in a shooting.

Five days after the incident, Simone called to inform me that we had been officially cleared and the case had been closed. There were no complaints or outcries from any of the watchdog groups either. The mayor had seen to that. My own department had cleared me from any wrongdoing within twenty-four hours.

The days I was off I more than once found myself almost relishing the fact that I'd shot and killed Meghan Dearth. As much as I hated to admit it, she did nothing but prove she was guilty and save the taxpayers the expense of a trial. I don't care how deranged she was at the time of the shooting, she was perfectly sane when she killed Melissa Drake. As far as I was concerned, she got the punishment she deserved.

On my first day back to work, I was more than anxious to dive into the cases at Mary Jane's Grave. I had been fielding phone calls in my office for an hour when the Communications Center called me.

"Sergeant Gallagher? We heard what happened in Cincy and we're glad you're okay," the male voice said.

"Thank you, I appreciate that." Most of the calls I'd gotten since I arrived had been like this.

"There's another reason I called. I've been waiting for you to get back because I found that information you were looking for."

"What information is that?"

"Daniel Griffin. We've located him." I held my breath. "He was using a different name, but we tracked him through his Social Security number. He was living at the Koogle Road apartments here until recently."

"When did he move?"

"The day after your shooting. He left a forwarding address with the apartment manager so the guy could mail his deposit to him, though."

"Where did he move to?" I asked, feeling my pulse quicken.

"Savannah, Georgia."

CHAPTER THIRTY-ONE

I closed my eyes and let out a not-so-quiet groan. I had been crossing my fingers that Daniel Griffin would make things easy for me and still be in the area. At least he was dumb enough to leave his new address.

"Sergeant? Do you want the forwarding address?"

"Go ahead with it, and give me the number for the local police down there."

I called the Savannah Police Department and requested they check the address discreetly for anything matching Daniel Griffin's name or Social Security number. I was waiting for them to call me back when Naomi walked into my office, holding a bouquet of roses.

"These are for you." She set them on my desk.

"Who are they from?" I looked for a card.

"I have no idea, there's no card. Maybe they're from Michael since it's your first day back."

"No, he would have sent a card, but I guess I can check."

I set them aside just as my phone rang. After obtaining the information I was waiting for, I hung up and looked at Naomi.

"What?" she inquired.

"I think I'm taking another road trip."

I quickly explained the phone call before Naomi flew

off the handle. I also gave the strong circumstantial evidence that pointed to Daniel Griffin.

"Naomi, look at the facts. The skinned dog was almost identical to the one Daniel was convicted of killing. He was in Mansfield during the murder and the attack, and he left the day after the news broadcast of the Meghan Dearth shooting. That leads me to believe that he thought I was onto to him and getting close, so he took off."

"But what's the point? I mean, why would he kill again after all these years?"

"How do you know he ever stopped? According to his NCIC check, he'd only been back in Mansfield for six weeks. He'd been in Virginia Beach before that. You don't think that's a coincidence, do you? Maybe he's been killing this entire time and just hasn't been caught yet."

"Still, what are you going to do down there if you find him?"

"There's no if. He's been found. Savannah PD just confirmed he's living at the forwarding address. I feel strongly enough that once I get the opportunity to interrogate him, I'll get him to confess. If all else fails, maybe there's enough for a search warrant to search his new residence."

Naomi looked hesitant. She was contemplating my request, but also weighing my last experience against another one. Eventually, she let out a loud sigh.

"All right, you can go, but I'm going with you this time."

"Fine by me." I could use the company.

"I'll go ahead and make the flight and hotel reservations, you get a hold of Savannah again and make arrangements."

"That sounds great but I'm not *flying* anywhere," I boldly announced.

Naomi looked irritated. "Oh, c'mon CeeCee! You

need to get over that, for crying out loud. That's like a thirteen- to fourteen-hour drive!"

"Just look at it this way, it'll give us plenty of time to catch up, and the scenery is beautiful on I-77."

I wasn't going to budge and Naomi knew it. I hated to fly and only did it if it was absolutely necessary. The last time I had been on a plane was after the Carl James Malone case when Michael took me to Jamaica. I was so drunk by the time the plane landed, Michael almost had to carry me. Finally, Naomi shook her head and grumbled that she would drive.

"Just meet me here about five in the morning. That'll put us in Georgia around dinner time so we can eat, get our hotel rooms and relax before we get with Savannah PD the next day," I said.

"Five it is."

After Naomi left, I began to mull over the best way to tell Michael about my impending trip to Georgia. Then I looked again at the flowers Naomi had brought in. They had to be from Michael. I couldn't imagine who else would have sent them. I called his cell phone, miraculously reached him and asked him.

"Sorry, Cee, I didn't send them. Are you sure it wasn't Eric trying to cause a problem again?"

"I don't think so. We're done. There's no going back, so he wouldn't even try." I thought for a minute. "Michael, I know you're probably gonna flip but I have to go to Savannah, Georgia, tomorrow. I think I've found a solid suspect."

He groaned. "Why is it every time you find a suspect you have to go out of town? My nerves can't take this."

"I know, I'm sorry, but I have to. Naomi said she'd go with me." I sighed. "How about if we talk about this when I get home? Are you going to be on time?"

"Should be."

After I hung up with Michael I again stared at the roses.

I decided to make my day a brief one so I could go home and pack my things for the trip. I was completely packed and had take-out dinner ready for Michael when he came home. He still wasn't thrilled that I was leaving.

"Every time my phone rings when you're gone, I cringe. This time I'll expect a phone call that you *had* been taken hostage before eventually killing the suspect and saving Naomi."

"Very funny."

"I want you to check in with me at the very minimum twice a day."

I went to bed early. Since most of the day would be spent driving, I didn't take too much care in my appearance when I got ready to leave. I merely whipped my hair up into a ponytail and threw on casual, comfortable clothes. When I met her at the department, Naomi was dressed the same. According to her, Coop had his own concerns about our trip.

"He said every time we're together on something like this it worries him."

"That sounds familiar. He and Michael must've had a powwow. I'll keep my eye out for a car following us the entire way down. It'll probably be those two."

After stopping for a light breakfast, Naomi and I were on our way to Georgia. As promised, she drove. Once we were on the interstate, she wanted me to refresh her memory regarding all the facts of the case.

"Essentially, we have our current murder, which produced diddly-squat of evidence. We find out later there was a murder twenty years ago that also involved a young girl, Melissa Drake. One of the suspects, a psychopathic devil-worshipper, likes to skin animals. Lo and behold, we find a skinned dog that has distinct similarities to one of the psycho's earlier projects. The other suspect, a sociopath and narcissistic bitch, is no longer in the picture as she was killed by yours truly. The psycho, Daniel Griffin, was in the area until the day after the news broadcast of the Meghan Dearth shooting and had only been here for several weeks before the current murder. I am now on my way, with my glorious captain, to interview this psycho and beat him into a confession. Any questions?"

Naomi laughed. "Yes. Where does the witch fit in?"

"Ah, the witch: I forgot to add the part about the numerous tales of the supernatural from various witnesses during the murders. We have in no particular order: a crying baby, smell of smoke, loss of cell phone service, rocks hurling through the air by themselves, a bleeding tree, curses and last but not least, an old woman in white." I proceeded to bellow out my best witch cackle.

Naomi laughed again. "Copy that. What's with all the history, though? I think at one point you thought it might have something to do with this current murder."

"I did up until Daniel Griffin fell into my lap. There are a lot of unanswered questions to Mary Jane Hendrickson's death, no doubt about it." The tone in my voice turned more serious. "She allegedly had a baby that there is no death record of, and her age at death was changed for unknown reasons. I followed her ancestors down to Maryanne Hendrickson, who eyewitness accounts say had a child. That's where I hit a dead end. There's no record of a child born to her anywhere. There's also no mention of fathers anywhere. And supposedly this is all connected to Ceely Rose, a murderess who wiped out her family with arsenic and was survived by a brother that no one talked about."

"Whew."

"No kidding. When this is all said and done, I'd like to try to look into that more, on my own time of course."

"Of course."

After driving for six straight hours, Naomi gave up the driver's seat. She slept off and on for a little while. Then we stopped just outside of High Point, North Carolina, to grab lunch. I checked in with Michael, mainly to assure him we hadn't been kidnapped by terrorists or shot by a highway sniper. We pulled into our hotel parking lot in Savannah a little over three hours later.

"Thank God," Naomi muttered after I nudged her to let her know we had reached our destination. "To think this could've been a lovely three-hour flight, with a drink in my hand no less. I can't believe I let you talk me into driving, CeeCee."

"Actually, it took us about an hour or so less than I thought. C'mon, let's get settled into our rooms, chill out for a while, and go grab a drink. There's a pub over there by the lobby."

We did just that, having two drinks at the pub before calling it a night. We were meeting the detective lieutenant at the Savannah Police Department first thing in the morning, so we went to bed early.

We had somewhat of an audience waiting for us when we walked through the doors of the police department. Detective Lieutenant John Cahill introduced himself first, surrounded by twenty to thirty other officers, some in uniform, some in plainclothes.

"We don't normally have a welcoming party, Sergeant, but some of the guys here wanted to meet you and your captain. They've seen y'all both on TV about those high-profile murder cases. Most of 'em have read your book, Sergeant. Consider yourselves a little like celebrities around here." He extended his hand with a wide grin. "We're more than happy to help y'all."

Naomi and I spent the next half an hour meeting and

greeting. Some of them had even brought my book in for me to sign. A couple took pictures. Naomi and I kept giving each other secret glances that said *can you believe this?* We've had other law enforcement show enthusiasm in meeting us, but nothing like here in Savannah. They were some of the kindest people we had ever met. Even the chief of police came out to meet us.

Finally, Lt. Cahill clapped his hands loudly and said in his slow, Southern drawl, "All right, fellas. We gotta get goin' now. I'm sure Captain Cooper and Sergeant Gallagher appreciate y'all fawnin' all over 'em but we got work to do."

We followed Lt. Cahill down several brightly lit corridors and through two large double doors. Walking into the first office to our right, Lt. Cahill asked us to have a seat.

"Can I git y'all some coffee or tea?"

Naomi and I declined, taking our seats in front of an old steel desk completely cluttered with papers, notes, trinkets and several ashtrays.

"Well, now . . . I know y'all are anxious to get going. I've had an unmarked car sittin' on this fella's trailer since ya called yesterday, and there hasn't been any movement. His car's still there, so he hasn't left. I figure I'll have some uniformed officers park down the road in case things get outta hand. For the most part, we can jist keep it quiet and go up and knock on the door. Sound okay?"

"That's fine, Lieutenant," I replied. "How far is it to Daniel Griffin's trailer from here?"

" 'Bout twenty-five minutes. Before we leave, I wanted to show you this." He shuffled through the piles of paperwork on his desk and handed me a thin green file. "I checked with the owner of the trailer that Daniel Griffin is renting to see if he could give me any information. Apparently, he rented the trailer under the name Roger Jacox. I decided to run the name through NCIC and that was what it hit on." He nodded at the file I was holding.

I opened it and looked, not surprised in the least. According to the National Crime Information Center, Roger Jacox was wanted for questioning in the disappearance of two women in Virginia three years ago. I handed the file to Naomi, who shook her head when she read it.

"I guess you were right on the money, CeeCee."

"Maybe. Nothing's concrete yet."

I handed the file back to Lt. Cahill, who suggested we get started.

CHAPTER THIRTY-TWO

Naomi and I rode with him since we hadn't a clue where we were going. We were out of Savannah quickly and began to travel down desolate back roads. I admired the scenery and remembered how much I loved the South. The Spanish moss hanging from the thick, overgrown trees that lined the roads was beautiful.

We turned onto a narrow dirt lane, which had thick crabgrass running up the middle and went toward the small blue, run-down trailer that sat at the end of it. A small black hatchback car with Ohio license plates was parked in front of it.

"Here we are, ladies . . . Southern paradise."

We hadn't even stopped before I could see the front door to the trailer was slightly ajar.

"Looks like he might be expecting us," I mumbled as I got out of the car.

Lt. Cahill nodded toward the back of the trailer and started walking that way in case there was a back door that Daniel could try to escape through. Naomi stepped off to the side, out of sight, while I approached the door with my gun drawn. I could see partially inside the trailer through the crack in the door, and it looked completely empty.

I knocked on the door hard enough that it swung open while I shouted, "Daniel Griffin? Police!"

Now with a full view of the inside, I could see what little contents were in the trailer, none of which was Daniel Griffin. There was only one large room with a soiled, bare mattress off to the side and a small kitchenette against the farthest wall. However, the contents troubled me.

Before I went in, I told Naomi it was clear. While she yelled out to Lt. Cahill, I walked directly to the old mattress and the papers that lay next to it. There were Mansfield newspapers focusing on Meghan Dearth's death, her obituary and stories of the murders. Next to them were the remnants of melted black candles and freehand sketches of the pine tree at Mary Jane's Grave. Daniel Griffin was plainly gone, and I didn't think he would be coming back.

"I guess he knew we were coming," Naomi said softly from behind me, looking over the papers as well. "I'll call the prosecutor's and have a warrant issued immediately."

"Wait, Naomi." I continued to look over the scene in front of me. "This is too obvious."

"What do you mean?"

Lt. Cahill came in behind me. "I mean exactly what I said. If Daniel Griffin knew we were coming, why would he leave this shit? He wouldn't. This is all laid out too perfectly, I'm afraid. I agree that you need to issue the warrant—we still have to question him—but something doesn't seem right here."

"You might be right, Sergeant," Cahill said. "That car out there came back stolen. Wasn't entered as of yesterday when we ran a check on it, but it was today. Whoever took it only took it within the last twenty-four hours or so. According to our information, Daniel Griffin, or

Roger Jacox, has been here for over two weeks now, and he was driving a silver pickup truck."

"Who's the owner of the stolen vehicle?" I asked.

"The owner lives in Mansfield. I think they said Kagle or Koogle Road."

Naomi and I looked at each other. This didn't make sense. Daniel Griffin drove his own truck down here and somehow got back to Mansfield to steal a car? Maybe it was possible, but the odds were very slim. If Daniel wanted a different vehicle, he would've stolen one here in Georgia, or in a surrounding state. If he thought we were looking for him, stealing a car from his former apartment complex in Ohio would do nothing but make it easier for the cops to find him. I was mystified.

Naomi was already on the phone with Coop, sending him over to the apartments to re-interview the owner of the stolen car, specifically to see if there was any connection to Daniel Griffin. I had already checked to see if Daniel had any living family members, but it appeared there were none. Then I directed my attention to Lt. Cahill.

"I need to find some direct evidence to the murders. This stuff is great and it's probably pointing us in the right direction, but as of right now it's just circumstantial." I gestured to the papers and drawings. "Do you guys have a crime scene investigation unit or lab that I can use to process this trailer?"

"I'll get 'em out here in about thirty minutes," Lt. Cahill said as he dialed his phone.

At the very least, I could get Daniel's fingerprints and DNA on file in case we needed them for a possible match. Of course, there was nothing found at any of the crime scenes to match them to, but if there were any further crimes at the grave, we could be certain.

After Lt. Cahill called his crime lab, the Evidence Collection Unit, he called his Communications Center to put other local agencies on the alert for Daniel Griffin and his silver truck. There wasn't a warrant issued yet, but he could still be stopped and held for a reasonable amount of time for questioning.

I couldn't help feeling uneasy about our findings. Unfortunately, I had found out the hard way in the past that when things appear simple, they are usually anything but.

I stood by while the Savannah Police processed the trailer and car for evidence. When they were almost finished, I called Michael. He agreed with me.

"Definitely not your norm, Cee. This killer has been a step ahead of law enforcement the entire time. Daniel Griffin didn't go through the trouble of covering up all of these murders, twenty years apart no less, to allow himself to get caught by leaving such blatant items for you to see. I'd say you need to find him. And quickly."

"Why?"

Before Michael could answer, I heard someone calling his name in the background. He hung up with a promise of calling me back as soon as he could.

By the time we were getting ready to leave, Naomi had heard back from Coop, who had spoken with the owner of the stolen vehicle.

She looked dismayed. "Nothing. The gal who owned the car said she parked it there at ten P.M. before going in her apartment. When she went to leave for work at six A.M. it was gone."

I tried to figure out the drive time. "So that would mean the car was most likely taken before three A.M., since Savannah had an undercover car watching this place by three P.M., and the car was here. Did the girl sound on the up and up?"

Naomi nodded. "Single mother, full-time job, no

record. Coop said he had no reason to believe she wasn't telling the truth. And before you ask, she doesn't know Daniel Griffin. She lives two buildings behind his former one."

I sighed. "I feel like this trip was a waste of time."

"We're covering all potential suspects in a murder case. Nothing can ever be considered wasted." She paused. "I know you didn't want me to do this now, but, considering what we have, I called the prosecutor's office and they're getting a warrant issued for Daniel Griffin."

"No, you're right. Everything's pointing to him, and we need to get him picked up. I just can't shake this feeling I have about those newspapers and crap in there. It's just too perfect."

Naomi was silent for a few moments. "Look, there's nothing more we can do here. Savannah will forward all the evidence to our lab. Let's go check out of our hotel and get the hell out of here. They'll let us know if they find him."

I was in total agreement. It had been only two days but I missed Michael terribly. We went back to the police department with Lt. Cahill and wrapped things up, mainly for their paperwork. Then we gave them our sincere gratitude and said our good-byes.

As the sun began to set, Naomi and I set forth on our long trip home with a strong feeling of disappointment, not knowing what awaited us there.

CHAPTER THIRTY-THREE

We arrived in Mansfield in the early morning hours. Knowing Michael was sleeping soundly in our bed made me particularly eager to get home quickly. I had told him I might be another day or so, so he was quite surprised when I crawled into bed and wrapped my arms around him. With his eyes still closed, he pulled me tightly to his chest.

"You're home, baby. I missed you." His voice was groggy with sleep.

"Hey, how did you know I wasn't a burglar?" I whispered.

"A burglar doesn't smell this good." He nuzzled his face against my neck and promptly fell back asleep.

My own sleep came shortly after, ending late the next morning when I jerked myself awake, as I often did when I was scared I would oversleep. Michael had already left for work. I was in no hurry to get to the office since Naomi already told me I could come in when I wanted. I got there around lunchtime. I found Naomi in her office with Coop, giving him the details of our trip.

"Afternoon, CeeCee. You get any sleep?" Naomi asked.

"I slept well. I can't say you look like you got much sleep, though. Is everything all right?"

She smiled bashfully. "It's fine, and no, I didn't sleep,

thanks to this one here." She nodded at Coop. "Two days without me and I was pretty much sexually assaulted when I walked through the door."

"Hey, I'm only human," Coop mused. "Naomi was telling me what you guys found in the trailer. Sounds like he's the one."

"Most likely. Have we heard anything from Savannah yet, Naomi?"

She shook her head. "No, they said they'd call as soon as they had something. What's on your agenda for today?"

"I'm going to write up everything from Savannah. That should take the rest of my day. I'd like to run down to the grave again and look around. I want to see how accurate, and recent, Daniel's drawings of the tree are. There have been changes to it over the years, according to the photographs I've seen. People trying to set it on fire and chop it down, for one. I can't really tell from the pictures I have if he drew those twenty years ago or recently."

"Let me know when you leave. I'll go with you," Naomi said before answering her ringing phone.

Writing up our trip to Savannah did, in fact, take up the rest of my day. It was early evening by the time I was attaching the paperwork to each of the files. As I grabbed my purse and car keys, I saw Naomi walk past my door.

"I'm going to run down to the grave now. You still want to go?" I called to her.

She poked her head into my doorway. "Okay, let's make it quick, though. Coop and I have dinner reservations."

It was near dusk as we turned onto the dirt road that led back to the grave. There was still some daylight, but it had a creepy orange glow. The dense trees lining the road made it seem like we were driving through a tunnel.

"No matter how many times I come back here, I'm always freaked out," Naomi said.

I simply nodded. It wasn't the darkness of the road or the grave itself, it was the feeling people got there. It was hard to describe, a combination of eeriness, foreboding and sadness would come close.

Pulling to the gate, I saw that most of the leaves from the trees had fallen. A kaleidoscope of orange, red and brown covered the graves. With the sun setting, it actually proved quite beautiful.

I grabbed the copies of the drawings we'd found in Daniel's camper and walked to the pine tree, Naomi in tow. I held one of the drawings up to make a comparison.

"What do you think?" Naomi was leaning over my shoulder trying to get a glimpse.

"I think this drawing was definitely recent. See the white marks from where those kids from the robbery tried to chop it down? See how detailed they are in the picture?" I pointed to the small, wispy lines in the drawing. "This was drawn within the last couple of years at least. Those weren't there twenty years ago."

"So what does that mean?"

"It confirms Daniel Griffin has been here in the last several years, but it doesn't give us enough to say exactly when."

She took the drawing from me to examine it closer. "It's better than nothi—"

Naomi was interrupted by a loud shriek that came from the woods to our right. My first thought was that it was a crow, but when I heard the familiar snapping of twigs and crunching of leaves, I didn't know what to think.

"Did you hear that?" Naomi whispered.

"I heard it," I whispered back, removing my gun from my holster.

I started toward the noise. It was getting darker, and it was hard for me to see anything. I walked slowly and carefully, mostly so I wouldn't trip and fall over a broken tombstone with my gun in hand. The area where the noise came from was completely darkened by shadows and the setting sun. When another twig snapped, I stopped. I was hoping whoever was in the woods wasn't looking at me, so I could walk up on him quietly. I was still a good twenty yards away when Naomi yelled from behind me.

"Police officers! Don't move!"

The sound of running began and didn't stop until it faded into the dense woods. I was furious at Naomi. If there was the slight chance I could've gotten close enough to the person I would've at least given a good chase. Now I was too far away and the person was gone.

"Goddamn it, Naomi! Why'd you do that? Now I can't catch him!" I put my gun back in its holster. "What? You think he was just gonna stand still with his arms in the air because you yelled police?"

"Well I had to do *something*, CeeCee! Besides, it was probably a deer anyway," she said, though she sounded unconvinced as she scanned the woods.

"I doubt it. I think Mr. Griffin has found his way back to Mary Jane's Grave. We need to search these woods, front to back and side to side, which is going to take a very large group of officers." I looked up at the old, abandoned house before turning to walk back to the SUV.

I had taken no more than five steps when the vehicle blared to life. Its headlights came on and the radio roared: " . . . *There is magic all around you, if I do say so myself . . .* "

I was now jogging toward the car to shut off the deafening music. But as quickly as it came on, it stopped again. I opened the driver's side door and looked at my keys, which still hung in the ignition, turned to off, and tried to find a rational explanation.

"What the hell?" Naomi said nervously from behind me.

"I don't know. Could've been a power surge or problem with the electrical system." I mumbled.

"Do cars have those? Power surges, I mean? Doesn't the damn thing have to be on first?" Naomi almost seemed panicked.

"Naomi, relax, for Christ's sake! I'm sure there's a rational explanation, but I really don't want to discuss it right now. Let's just get the fuck out of here."

She didn't argue and seemed more than happy to get into the passenger seat. I didn't realize I had been holding my breath until the tires of my car rolled onto asphalt and off the dirt road. As hard as I was trying to think of an explanation for what happened, I wasn't having much luck in finding one. Naomi interrupted my thoughts.

"Fitting, wasn't it?"

"What was?"

"The song . . . about magic and all. Funny, it was a Stevie Nicks song. Remember back when there was the rumor that she was a witch?"

"Kind of, it was about as true as the Mary Jane-was-a-witch story. No truth to it whatsoever." I turned into the department parking lot to drop off Naomi at her car.

"I just thought it was kind of weird is all." She opened her door and got out. "I'll get with the sheriff in the morning about searching the woods and let you know. See you tomorrow."

I thought the entire incident was strange too, but I

was doing my best not to admit it. I was more concerned about who, or what, was in the woods. I didn't think the sheriff was going to go for a full-scale search that would require numerous hours of overtime. Not that he wouldn't agree with it, it's just that he has to answer to the county commissioners, the ones in charge of the money.

Michael was waiting for me with take-out Chinese food on the table. I was famished. I hadn't realized how little I had eaten today. During dinner, I told Michael about my car at the grave. He seemed a little amused.

"Maybe the woman in white started it. Did you see her in the driver's seat?" He wiped his smiling mouth with a napkin.

"I certainly didn't see her or hear her offer to be my chauffer for the night, Michael, and I'm being serious. The headlights and radio really did come on by themselves. Ask Naomi."

He pushed his plate forward. "Really, CeeCee, there's a ton of reasons that could've happened. I'm not a mechanic, but it was probably something with the car's computer system. If you're that worried about it, take it to your department's body shop and have them check it out."

"I'm not *that* worried about it. It was just strange, that's all." I began clearing the table.

"I'll get this. Why don't you go open a bottle of wine?" Michael took over.

He joined me in the living room, grabbing the glass of pinot noir that I had waiting for him. I was already on my second round.

"The only thing I can tell you is you probably need to up your search for Daniel Griffin. I would say it was a good chance he was in the woods tonight, which concerns me. No matter how many times I say it, you need to be more careful."

I had a thought. "How would he know we were coming, Michael? I mean, I just decided to go down there this morning. Also, he's coming in from the woods somewhere, not the road. Those woods are thick, unless he was coming from the campground area."

"Most likely he is, but it's my guess that he didn't know you were coming and you surprised him. He was probably there planning his next murder." Michael drained his glass and set it on the table. "C'mon, it's late and we need to get some sleep."

I hardly slept and was ready for work an hour early. I had anticipated a long, boring day ahead, catching up on all my other cases that I'd completely ignored for the last month, but I couldn't have been more wrong.

When I arrived at the department, every detective we had was running around like mad. I had obviously missed something. I caught Coop in his office.

"What the hell's going on?"

He was grabbing a camera and other items off his desk. "The Detroit and Chicago boys went at it hard last night. They shot up each other's houses and I think the body count is up to five right now, including two little kids who got caught in the crossfire."

"Do we have any of them in custody?" I asked, already knowing how hard it was to track down a member of the Detroit or Chicago gangs. They changed their identities daily. Most of them could only be identified by their fingerprints.

"Believe it or not, we've got all but two. The uniforms did a hell of a job catching them. Supposedly, one of the triggermen is holed up over at a house in Johns Park. That's where we're all headed. SWAT's been called out too." Coop brushed past me in the doorway.

"You wanna come with me?"

"Of course."

Ignoring my cases for one more day certainly wasn't going to hurt. Not to mention, I wanted this guy behind bars. He was ultimately responsible for the deaths of two children, accidental or not.

I soon watched the awesome scene unfold in Johns Park without a hitch. The bad guy was caught, and no cops got hurt. All in a day's work.

Naomi was still out at the murder scenes when I got back to my office. I started pulling all my old cases and began arranging them by priority. I put a couple of them off to the side, armed robberies and shootings probably committed by our suspects in the gang murders.

I was getting ready to leave for lunch when Naomi came back. She looked haggard.

"Can you believe this shit? I've been out there since three o'clock this morning. Bastards. Those little kids were only two and five years old."

"Hope Daddy thinks his crack was worth it." I shook my head. "You want to go eat? I'm starved."

"Absolutely, any minute my stomach is going to go into seizures. Let me grab my purse and lock up my office." She dashed out the door while I gathered my own things.

Ten minutes later Naomi still hadn't come back. What the hell is she doing? I thought. I was about to go down to her office when she appeared in my doorway, a look of distress on her face.

"What's wrong? I thought we were going to lunch?"

She walked in and sat down. "Savannah PD just called me. They've found Daniel Griffin."

My heart skipped. "They did? Where? Can we talk to him?"

"He's dead, CeeCee. A hunter found his body about a hundred yards behind his trailer, in the woods."

I groaned and sat down. "Let me guess, he killed himself?"

"That's the kicker. He was strangled. And according to Lt. Cahill, he's been dead for at least two days. So far, there's no evidence, but they'll let us know if they find any."

"Two days! Then that wasn't him in the woods last night."

"CeeCee, don't jump to conclusions. Like I said, that could've been a deer."

"Oh, c'mon, Naomi, you know better than that. This means he wasn't the killer, which puts me back to square one." I put my face in my hands and sighed. "Who the hell is it?"

"Let's go eat. You'll think better with a full stomach."

I barely ate a thing. I was so dumbfounded by the death of Daniel Griffin I could barely think at all. Naomi dropped me off at the department after lunch; she had to go meet with the coroner. I sat at my desk, opened the Melissa Drake murder file and stared at the photograph of Daniel Griffin. With no more leads, I'd be forced to inactivate the case and send it to the cold case squad, a black mark for any detective. I began crumpling up Daniel's picture out of sheer frustration, when my phone rang.

"Sergeant Gallagher."

"Sergeant? This is Karen from the Holmes County Records department. I'm sorry it's taken this long for me to get back with you, but we've been busy." She gave a slight hesitant laugh. "You inquired about any marriage and/or birth certificates involving a Madeline or a Maryanne Hendrickson?"

"That's right." I wasn't holding any high hopes.

"We couldn't believe it, but we found both a marriage and a birth certificate for Maryanne Hendrickson and her child. The marriage license was from 1936." Her voice was full of pride, as if she'd just located Noah's Ark.

"Well? What was her husband's name?" I asked impatiently.

"His last name was Drake. Maryanne Hendrickson's husband was Nathaniel Drake. They had a son in 1945. His name was Martin."

CHAPTER THIRTY-FOUR

I was stunned. Melissa Drake, who had been murdered almost twenty years ago, was a direct descendant of Mary Jane Hendrickson. Melissa's father, Martin, was Maryanne's son. How could this be? I wondered, before realizing I had wondered out loud.

"I'm sorry? Sergeant, did you hear me?"

"Yes, ma'am, I did, and thank you so much. Is there any way you could make me copies and fax them here?"

"Of course, I'll have them there in five minutes."

After hanging up the phone, I stood and began pacing anxiously in my office. None of this made any sense. Ceely Rose is the key? I felt like I was starting a thousand-piece jigsaw puzzle with no picture on the box to go by.

I grabbed the file off my desk and flipped through to the page of follow-ups. Martin Drake and his son, Nicholas, had left town after his wife committed suicide. I hadn't put too much effort into tracking them down, but I certainly would now. I had a feeling they could answer a lot of my questions, including who the killer was.

I took every photograph I had relating to Mary Jane Hendrickson and Ceely Rose and laid them out on the floor in chronological order.

Ceely Rose was first when she murdered her family. Exactly one year to the day after that, Mary Jane Hendrickson died, her age being altered. Within twenty days after Mary Jane's death, Ceely's brother, Randall, and his friends James Mengert, Albert Tucker and Gerald Moffett died, all within five days of one another. Mary Jane's daughter, Madeline, survived and had a daughter of her own, Maryanne. Maryanne married Nathaniel Drake and they had a son, Martin, who had a daughter, Melissa, who was ultimately murdered at her great-great-grandmother's grave some ninety years later. I was right about the history having some connection to the murders, but that was all I had. What about Danielle Horton and Kari Sutter? And the dog? Where did they figure in?

"What am I missing?" I asked my empty office.

"I don't know. You need me to look?" Naomi said from behind me. She looked at the collage of photos. "What are you doing with these?"

"I'll tell you in a minute. Have a seat. I have to make a phone call first." I called the Communications Center. "Find me a current address on Martin and Nicholas Drake, ASAP."

I gave them all the information they would need for the search and hung up. Naomi looked confused.

"Melissa's father and brother? What are you looking for them for?"

When I told her, she looked as shocked as I was. She reached over and picked up the Melissa Drake file.

"You were right, CeeCee. You were right all along about looking into the history of the grave. I've got to be honest with you, at first I thought you were pretty much wasting your time but now . . ." She pulled out the photograph of Melissa Drake. "Now it makes some sense, not a lot, but the connection is definitely there." She looked at the photograph and set it down. "What do you think Martin and Nicholas Drake know? Why are you trying to find them?"

"I think they could tell me what this is all about, Naomi. I think they know everything about what's happened at the grave, but they're keeping their mouths shut for some unknown reason. It's that reason I want to understand." I took a deep breath. "I think they could tell me who the killer is."

"If they're alive. I mean, Martin Drake's got to be in his early sixties and Nicholas . . ." I could see Naomi doing the math in her head. "Nicholas would be thirty-six, thirty-seven? Who knows? Maybe they committed suicide or died of cancer."

"That's a cheery, positive outlook." I threw her a look of disgust. "I'm waiting for Communications to find them for me."

My phone rang and I was surprised to hear the Communications Center on the other end. They were never known for speediness, so I was grateful. They gave me the information I had requested. Then I asked for something else.

"Find their driver's license photos and fax them to my office, would you?"

Naomi was tapping her fingers on my desk impatiently. "Well?"

"They're alive and well and in Ocala, Florida. Start packing."

She put her hands up. "Whoa. Call Ocala first and let them confirm that they're living at that address. And if we go, don't even think about driving. I am not spending the next eighteen hours in a car."

"That's fine. You'll just have to carry my drunken ass off the plane." I picked up the phone and called the number Communications had given me for the Ocala Police Department.

They said it would be a couple of hours before they could get a car to the address. Naomi told me to let her know immediately when I heard from them. Then she returned to her office.

Too anxious and wired to sit around and wait, I decided to take a drive. I heard my fax machine turn on just as I started to leave. Seeing the driver's license photographs I requested, I set my car keys down and looked at them. They had the same emerald green eyes that Melissa had. I put the photos with the others and headed out.

I drove around, gathering my thoughts and trying to put pieces together until I unknowingly found myself driving past the Pleasant Valley Cemetery. I quickly hit my brakes and turned into the small gravel clearing.

I got out of my car and walked back to the graves of Randall Rose and his friends. I looked at the dates again, reading them out loud.

I took a step back and looked at the four graves. There were no other graves in the row and these were almost hidden in the back of the cemetery. *Hidden?* It was as if they were being punished for doing something wrong, but what? Whatever it was, it was enough to banish them and separate them from their family's final resting places.

"What did all of you do?" I asked boldly.

"Who are you?" said a deep, low voice from behind me.

I spun around, almost tripping over my own feet, to face a large man, who appeared to be in his late fifties. He wore blue jeans, a dirty Carhart jacket and a blue ball cap, and had almost a week's worth of black and gray facial hair. He was as wide as he was tall—something about him reminded me of a bull—and he stared at me with dark, accusing eyes. I looked to the parking lot and saw the dual-wheel, megasize pickup truck he had driven. I hadn't even heard him pull up.

"I said, who are you?" he asked again.

"Just a visitor." I eyed him suspiciously. "Who are *you*?"

"A concerned citizen." His eyes narrowed as he looked at me. "You always in the habit of talking to hundred-year-old tombstones? What's your business here, ma'am?"

I was getting a tad uncomfortable. I was in the middle of the Appalachian foothills with no cell phone signal and no police radio. No one even knew I was here. If this man really wanted to give me a hard time, I might be in a significant amount of trouble, especially since he looked angry.

I tried to appear unfazed. "Excuse me, sir, but you might want to tell me who *you* are before I start answering questions for you. This cemetery is a public place and I have every right to be here."

His face furrowed as he took a step toward me. "You don't have a right to—"

I switched gears, took out my badge and held it out for him to see. He just looked confused.

"Sergeant Gallagher with Richland Metro, sir, and it would be in your best interest to stop walking toward me." I put my badge away and took a deep breath. "Now, since we've begun the *who-are-you* game, you can tell me who you are and why you're so interested in what I'm doing. What is your name?"

"I'm Luke Mengert." He nodded toward James Mengert's grave. "My family is buried here, my great-grandfather James included, as you can very well see. The only time anyone comes here, outside of family, is to tear up the place. That's why I was asking." His face was still intense.

I was a little taken aback by his identity. He was

obviously not threatened by me in the least, and he was clearly protective of the graves. Which led me to one conclusion: he might know something.

"Tell me, Mr. Mengert, what do you know about your great-grandfather's death?" I pointed back at the grave. "And all the others, if you know."

"James Mengert drowned." He looked angry again. "As for the others, it's the same story. Why are you asking?"

"I just think it's odd that they all died five days apart, don't you?"

I hit a nerve. I saw a flash of surprise come over his face, but it was just a flash. Then the anger came back, much worse.

"Why are you asking, Sergeant?"

"Mr. Mengert, I'm investigating several deaths that have occurred at the cemetery at the end of Tucker Road. You know, Mary Jane's Grave?" I walked over to Randall Rose's grave. "My investigation has led me to Randall Rose's sister, Ceely, which ultimately led me here. These four men did something back then, and I believe it was something very bad. Do you know what I'm talking about?"

A sinister smirk came to Luke Mengert's face. His stare sent a wave of chills through my body. I had to fend off the visible shudder that went with them.

"You seem like a smart woman, Sergeant. I hope you're smart enough to know when to back off and leave things be, if you know what's good for you."

"I'm sorry, are you threatening me?" I asked stoically.

"I don't need to threaten you. The fact is you may have already done yourself in." He grew calmer, which only alarmed me more. "I'm going to leave now, and I suggest you take your bitch-ass and do the same. There's nothing for you here. Nothing but trouble, that is."

Normally, if someone talked to me like that I'd have

them in handcuffs within seconds. However, Luke Mengert would be able to snap my neck with two fingers and there was nothing I could do about it. With no backup, I knew it was in my best interest to heed his warning and leave. I made a mental note to deal with him later, no doubt about it.

"All right, Mr. Mengert, I'll leave." I smiled. "Don't worry, though. I'll be in touch with you again. Count on it."

I found myself holding my breath as I walked past him, expecting him to clobber me at any second. Overwhelmed with relief once I was safe inside my car, I had to suppress the urge to flip him the bird as I pulled out of the parking lot, where he stood watching me leave.

I drove away, passing Mengert Road no less, and turned into a long driveway about half a mile from the cemetery. The drive was cloaked in woods so it covered me well as I turned my car off and waited for Luke Mengert. I hoped he hadn't gone the opposite direction.

It was fifteen minutes before Luke's truck drove by. I quickly nosed my car to the edge of the driveway and looked down the road to see where he had gone.

I saw his brake lights at once and all of my nerves lit up like the Fourth of July. I was sure he had seen me and was turning around. However, he turned into the next driveway, which had a mailbox with *Mengert* painted on it. I let out a nervous giggle, then backed up again and got out of my car.

A medium-sized section of woods separated the driveway I was parked in from Luke's house. I could only pray the home owner whose drive I was blocking didn't come home and raise a stink about my car being there.

I made my way through the woods until I got a clear view of Luke Mengert's property. He lived in a two-story brick home with a medium-sized barn behind it that bordered a fenced-in field with horses. I saw Luke's truck parked already, but I didn't see him. Seconds later the side door flew open with such force it slammed against the house with a loud *crack!*

Luke Mengert was carrying something in his hands. It looked like a shoe box. He was on a mission. He headed directly into the barn, where he stayed for a few minutes, before coming back out, still holding the box. Now he had a small plastic bottle as well. He walked to the side of the barn and put the box down. He squirted the contents of the bottle—which I had now assumed to be lighter fluid—on the box, set it on fire and stood there while it turned to a pile of ashes.

I saw the distress on his face and the heaving of his chest as he stomped on the ash a few minutes later, then stood and looked down on it. I was dying to know what he had burned. My thoughts were short-lived. I noticed Luke was no longer looking down at the pile of ashes anymore. He was now staring directly at me. I knew damn well he couldn't see into the woods, but a wave of horror went through me nonetheless.

"Oh, shit!" I muttered. I slowly started to back up. The last thing I needed was another confrontation with him.

I ran back to my car and drove away in the opposite direction. Nervously laughing to myself, I called the Communications Center and asked them to find me all information on Luke Mengert. I had memorized his license plate, so it would be much easier for them to find. Next, I tried to call Naomi to see if we'd heard back from the Ocala Police Department. I only got her voice mail. My last call was to Michael.

"I'm on my way home. Naomi hasn't called, has she?"

"Hello to you too, baby," he quipped. "My day was fine. How's yours going?"

"I'm sorry. I didn't mean to be so short." I looked over

at the road names so I could keep track of where I was. "It's just that I've had quite an interesting day, and I can't get hold of Naomi."

"You can tell me about it when you get here. How long will you be?"

I slowed my car down to read the name of the road I was next to, then I hesitantly turned onto it.

"Actually, Michael, I might be a little later than I thought."

Once I had turned onto Tucker Road, I headed toward Mary Jane's Grave for what would be the very last time.

Chapter Thirty-five

Earlier in the day, I had looked over the photographs taken of the grave and the abandoned house. Something about them kept gnawing at me, and I was determined to find out why. Luke Mengert was my motivation. He had some part, whether miniscule or large, in this.

It was near dusk as I made my way down the now too familiar tunnel of trees to the grave. The usual feelings of dread and apprehension came as soon as my tires rolled onto the gravel. Before I parked at the gate, I picked up my phone to try to call Naomi again. There was no signal, not that I was surprised. The incident of my car radio and headlights blaring to life came to mind. I noted that it was probably in my best interest not to write off spooks entirely, assuming my lack of belief might potentially piss them off, if they existed. Standing beside Mary Jane's Grave, alone under a darkening sky, was not the place I wanted to be proven wrong.

Since I hadn't planned on coming here, I didn't have my heavy-duty flashlight with me, only a small penlight that might illuminate the stem of a leaf if I was lucky. As the sun went down, it became cold. I began shivering and breaking out in gooseflesh, which I hoped was from the cold, so I decided it would be best to grab my jacket out of the backseat. Once I was satisfied that I had all I needed, including my car keys, I started for the tree.

I had barely walked through the gate when I stopped dead in my tracks. It was the smell, a rancid, overwhelming smell of something being burned. It was a smell I was familiar with, the smell of a body, or bodies, being burned.

I had been on the scene of several fires where people had been trapped inside their homes and had burned to death. It was a distinct and indescribable smell.

I realized that I was surrounded by smoke. Where it had come from or why it was there I couldn't determine since I couldn't see. But as fast it came on me, the smoke was gone, dissipating upward toward the trees. It was only then that I became aware of the jackhammer that used to be my heart, pushing out of my chest. Despite the cold, I felt the sweat run down my face. My breath came in short puffs from my dry mouth. What should have been my cue to sprint to my car and leave turned out to be one more reason to go on.

As unnerved as I was, I walked forward, determined to find the answers and scratch the itch that had been bothering me. Suddenly the cemetery itself screamed out the sounds of a baby crying. I tried to pinpoint the source but it was coming from everywhere: the trees, the ground, the sky and the graves themselves.

I was beginning to lose my composure when a strange wind ripped through a small part of the cemetery, whirling leaves and sticks in an odd, circular pattern. With the sound of the baby still tearing at my ears, I forced myself to walk toward the wind. Once I took a step, it stopped. So did the crying. But it was replaced by the faint sound of a woman weeping. Standing no more than five feet from the pine tree, I blinked my eyes as I watched an old woman wearing a white dress appear at the base of the tree. She was the one weeping. For a split second I couldn't move, or breathe for that matter. I was succumbing to the grip of sheer horror. It took every ounce of energy I had to break free from my frozen stance and try to walk to my car, the hair on my neck standing upright. I kept looking at the woman out of the corner of my eye as I passed, convinced she was going to run over and behead me or worse, but like the other phenomena, she faded away.

I had more than enough. My legs felt like pure rubber when I ran to my car. Having bona fide chest pains, I was certain this little horror show was going to throw me into cardiac arrest. I began fumbling around in my pockets for my car keys. I prayed out loud I hadn't dropped them somewhere. That's when I was hit in the back of the head with a small rock.

More rocks and sticks followed, pelting me all over. I was too busy covering my face to see where they were coming from. My terror was slowly being replaced with anger.

"Stop!" I screamed to the empty graveyard.

Shockingly enough, the rocks and sticks stopped coming. I stood there, looking out over the cemetery, and gasped for air while I wiped the sweat off my brow. Just then I heard a faint sound coming from the far side of the cemetery, just inside the woods. It was a short, quiet cough.

It took me only a split second to identify the sound and another split second to pull myself together and throw my fear out the window. I started a record-breaking sprint toward the woods and the sound. If I was right, more sounds would follow. As I neared the edge, I heard the running start. Not a deer, not a coyote or a rabbit, but a person running fast and hard. I noticed the small trail that ran alongside of me and decided to use it, knowing I would have better footing and a better chance of keeping up.

Only when my face hit the ground did I become aware that I had tripped. And only when I saw what I had tripped over did everything come together. It was a black wire, a wire that had clearly gone unnoticed when the officers checked the cemetary the night we used Danielle Horton as bait.

The person running had gained some distance when I fell, but that was okay. Once I saw the wire, I knew exactly where he was going. The *itch* I had all day came partly from the photograph of the abandoned house. Specifically, the thin, almost invisible wire that ran from the house to the outside door of the storm cellar several feet away from the tattered front porch.

The house was supposed to have been abandoned, and unmodernized. No electric lines, phone or cable had ever been connected. Looking at the wire in the photographs earlier had piqued my curiosity, but stumped me nonetheless. I hadn't paid attention. Although my instincts were on, and something about the photograph had bothered me, I had failed to understand what it was. Now I understood completely.

Making my way uphill through the woods to the house, I was cautious. I no longer heard the person running and, for all I knew, he could be waiting behind a tree ready to clean my clock. When I finally came out into the large yard I had a clear view of the house, though it was almost completely dark.

I heard a loud rattling sound from behind the house and made my way around, much slower now, gun in hand and ready to fire. I was taking deep breaths as I rounded the corner. In back, I saw every window and door boarded up. I couldn't figure out how the person—I guess it would be safe to say the killer—got inside.

Maybe that wasn't what I'd heard. Then something inside the house suddenly was knocked over. I kicked at the boards over the door until they gave way.

It was totally dark inside the house. My penlight provided minimal help. I tried to control my breathing as I let my eyes adjust. I thought the sound had come from the back left corner of the first floor, near the beginning of the stairwell.

I slowly sidestepped, and half stumbled, toward the corner. There was debris all over the floor, what I assumed to be boards, drywall and other parts of the disintegrating house, but it was too dark to see. The closer I got to the corner, the stronger the smell of decaying flesh got.

We weren't missing any bodies, at least to my knowledge, so I was apprehensive at finding the source of the smell. But I found it when I accidentally walked into a small curtain that hung low from the ceiling. Except it wasn't a curtain.

I reached up to push the cold, clammy, gel-like material away from my face and became even more startled when I grabbed a handful of hair instead, dog hair to be exact. I had walked into the skin of the dog we had found at the grave, and it was beyond rotten. I let out a slight yelp before my stomach began convulsing.

I impulsively turned toward the door, gagging and spitting, trying to control my heaving. I only wanted to get outside and into the fresh air as quickly as possible. A difficult feat since I had to blindly make my way through the field of items that covered the ground. I was almost to the door when I was hit from behind in the lower back with such force it knocked me down and sent my gun flying. For a brief moment, I thought my back was broken. Only when I was struck again, in the back of my legs, was I able to react.

I turned around to face my attacker. A large, dark figure stood before me, but I couldn't see who he was. When I saw him begin to lift what looked like a long, thick tree branch, I reacted.

Among all the debris, my hand found a board. Not a deadly weapon, but it would be enough to stop the threat. I sat up, ignoring the screaming pain that tore through my back, and swung the board at the man's knees. He let out a loud grunt and fell sideways onto the floor next to me. By then, I was doing my best to stand up over him. He was doing his best as well, trying to get back up. I made it first and swung the board again, harder, against the side of his head like I was trying for a home run. Groaning, the man fell backward and hit the floor with a loud *thud*.

I furiously looked around for my gun, which I found lodged between two pieces of paneling not far from where I had fallen. My penlight, still on, lay directly below the dog skin. I grabbed it and made my way back to the man, holding the light directly in his face. I almost fell back again in shock when I realized I was looking down at Martin Drake.

He was unconscious, but still breathing. I turned him over on his side, took my handcuffs off my belt and put them on him, sliding one of the cuffs through the belt loop on his jeans so it would be harder for him to move.

I stood up and winced at the searing pain that throbbed in my back and legs. I needed to call for help, but being able to do it was another story. I didn't know if I was in any condition to hike back through the woods to my car. Right now, I wasn't sure if I could make it through the front door. And there was something worse to worry about: Nicholas Drake. I assumed he was with his father, very close by. I wasn't able to see much of Martin Drake, but I could see enough of him to know that he would never have been able to run through the woods as quickly, and with such maneuverability, as the man I had been chasing.

As I walked through the front door, I decided my first priority would be to get to my car and radio for help, then look for Nicholas later. Evidently, that just wasn't meant to be.

As soon as I stepped out of the door, a shot rang out and flew past and missed my head by mere centimeters. The bullet hit the old, rotting door frame and exploded, sending wood fragments and small splinters flying all over me. Thankfully, I closed my eyes fast enough, but I had to brush the wood chips away from my eyelids before I could open my eyes to see where the shot had come from.

A tall figure stood by the entrance to the storm cellar. Strangely, he was still pointing his gun at me, but he didn't fire it. I raised mine, taking slow steps toward him.

"Nicholas Drake! Police officer! Drop your weapon!"

We were in a standoff, a good, old-fashioned draw down. He was breathing hard, and the tip of his gun was bobbing up and down from the tremors in his hand.

"You killed my father!" he cried, his voice cracking.

"He's not dead, Nicholas. Drop the gun!"

He remained defiant, raising his chin a bit, now gripping the gun with both hands to keep it still.

"You're not gonna shoot me!"

"Maybe she won't, but I will," said a familiar voice from my right.

Taking my eyes off Nicholas for a brief moment, I saw Michael standing about ten feet away, his gun raised and ready.

"Drop the gun, Nicholas," another calm, familiar voice commanded.

Coop and Naomi stood to my left, also with their weapons raised and pointed at Nicholas. I wasn't in a position to ask any of them how they came to be here. I assumed I'd find out later. Right now, my attention was on Nicholas, who was surrounded with nowhere to go. Off in the distance, I heard the sounds of sirens. The cavalry was coming.

I was about to order Nicholas again to put down his gun, but knowing he was cornered with no way out, he quickly put the gun to his temple.

"Nicholas, don't—" was all I could say before he pulled the trigger.

CHAPTER THIRTY-SIX

The force of the shot bowled him over to his left. He landed beside the storm cellar doors, which were sprayed with brain matter and blood. Nicholas Drake, just like his mother, had committed suicide—right before our eyes.

"Jesus!" Naomi yelled, running over to him.

I turned my back to Nicholas's lifeless body and took a long, deep breath. Michael was at my side in a flash. He put his arms around me and squeezed, which caused me to scream in pain.

"Cee? What's wrong? Are you hurt?" He let go and looked at me with deep concern.

I nodded, turned around and lifted up the back of my shirt. I didn't need to see my lower back to know it was probably black already from bruising.

"Oh my God! What the hell happened?"

"My legs got it, too." I put my gun in its holster. "Martin Drake is inside and cuffed . . . probably needs an ambulance to look at his head. I whacked him a good one after he hit me with a board."

Michael looked confused as he turned to the door of the house. He sat me down and he went inside. Coop was directly behind him with his flashlight. When I heard moaning coming from inside a few minutes later, I knew Martin Drake was conscious—and hurting.

Naomi stood with me while the other police officers, the crime lab and coroner arrived to take Martin Drake to jail and his son to the morgue. When Martin first saw Nicholas's body, he screamed in grief.

"Oh, God! Not my son! Please, not my son!" he sobbed and fell to his knees.

The uniformed officers and EMTs had to hold him up and walk him to the ambulance.

As wrong as it sounds, I felt my eyes brimming with tears at Martin's grief. They were both brutal murderers, but Martin Drake had now lost his entire family.

"You don't think he killed his own daughter, do you?" Naomi asked quietly.

"No." I watched as Martin was lifted into the ambulance. "Daniel Griffin and Meghan Dearth killed Melissa Drake . . . but I do think that's what prompted this, their killing spree, I mean. I think it was revenge for Melissa's murder."

Coop and Michael joined us. Michael made an honest attempt to lure me to the ambulance so my back and legs could be checked out but I was more than aware of what broken bones felt like and already knew I didn't have any. Of course I would be sore as hell until the bruising went away.

"Why did they wait twenty years?" Coop asked. "And they were all relatives of Mary Jane, including Melissa, who was killed at her grave. How do you explain that?"

"There are a lot of loose ends that need to be tied up. I'm hoping I find some answers when we search this place top to bottom, starting with the storm cellar. I predict we're going to find a large cache of high-tech audio and video equipment down there. By the way, how'd you guys figure out to come here?"

Naomi explained that the Ocala Police Department had called shortly after I left the department.

"I tried to call you, but I guess you weren't getting a signal wherever you were."

She must have called about the same time I was standing in the Pleasant Valley Cemetery with Luke Mengert. The southern part of the county had only small pockets of cell phone signals, and I guess the cemetery wasn't one of them.

"Their apartment was empty," she continued. "They hadn't lived there for over a year but still had a lease on it. Ocala talked to the management company of the apartment complex, and Martin had written another mailing address on the initial application." She looked at Coop apprehensively, as if she was afraid to say what was next. "Hold your breath, CeeCee. The other address was Martin's father's house outside Bellville."

"Nathaniel Drake? Don't tell me he's still alive."

"Yes, sort of, I guess. Only he doesn't go by Nathaniel Drake anymore. He changed his name over fifteen years ago." She paused. "He changed his name to Walter Morris."

I was dumbfounded. I had been inside Nathaniel Drake's house twice and never would have figured it out. He had warned me, though, by God. He knew what his son and grandson were doing.

Naomi went on. "I sent uniforms to Nath—Walter's house to find Martin and Nicholas." She looked over as the coroner began to put Nicholas in a body bag. "Walter, at first, denied knowing them, but I guess with a certain amount of pressure, he ceded. He actually told them everything. He said it was time, that over a hundred years was enough. He told the uniforms that Martin and Nicholas were at the grave . . . and Maryanne's house."

I still didn't get any of this. I didn't understand what Walter meant by a hundred years was enough. I was still reeling from the shock of his true identity as Naomi continued.

"I was so excited, I called your house when I couldn't get you on your cell. I figured you'd already be home by then. When Michael told me you had gone down to the grave, I knew you'd be in trouble." She shook her head.

"Of course, I had to come along after Naomi told me what was going on," Michael interjected.

I thanked all of them for coming to my aid, then told them about my run-in with Luke Mengert and my supposed supernatural experiences at Mary Jane's Grave when I first arrived.

"I'd have to remove ten pounds of shit from my underwear if I'd seen a chick like that sitting by the tree," Coop joked.

We all laughed. "I think a lot of those wires will explain that. You know, I should be ecstatic that we caught these guys, but I'm not." I sighed. "I feel like there's still so many pieces missing . . . like Luke. I know he has *something* to do with this, but what?"

There wasn't time for an answer because Bob from the crime lab, who had been processing the entire scene with the others, called out to us. They were standing next to the storm cellar and had opened both of the old, wooden white doors. We all walked over and peered down the cement steps that were now lit up by floodlights the lab had erected.

"What is it, Bob?" Naomi asked.

"I think you all better go down there and take a look. If I hadn't seen it with my own eyes, I'd never have believed it."

CHAPTER THIRTY-SEVEN

Since Bob had done such an outstanding job of grabbing our attention, Coop and I bumped into each other trying to be the first down the steps. I won.

My thoughts of the four of us being cramped together down there were erased as I came down the last step and looked around. The cellar was not really a cellar at all. I'm sure it had been long ago, but now it was more of a small warehouse. Someone had taken a great amount of time and effort to hollow out more ground, widening the cellar and cementing its walls.

I was right about one thing: the high-tech equipment. Nevertheless, I never could have imagined such a large quantity of equipment that occupied the space and lined the walls. Most of it looked like audio and video equipment whose capabilities I couldn't even begin to fathom. Standing before me were the phenomena of Mary Jane's Grave. The two other entities were above ground, although one wouldn't be for long, and one was on his way to prison.

Michael let out a low whistle. "I'd say this stuff is worth a couple hundred grand."

"If it isn't stolen." Coop walked toward the middle of the cellar to a large, black machine that resembled an old film projector.

"What's that?" Naomi joined him.

Coop looked around it, fumbling with switches and pushing buttons. It was quite a sophisticated-looking piece of equipment, one I'd never seen before. Coop hit a large silver switch on the right side of it, and the machine produced a quiet, whirring sound. I gasped loudly when something on the other side of the room caught my eye. It was the old woman in white, sitting on the floor between two speakers.

"What the hell!" Bob yelled from halfway down the steps, a point from which he could clearly see the image.

Coop laughed. "It's a hologram machine. I didn't know they could make these but, evidently so. There's your ghost, CeeCee."

I walked toward the apparition. "I wonder who she is."

"Nobody," Michael said. "They can design anything they want to on a computer and then download it into the machine. It has its own memory stick."

I stood in front of the image and waved my hand back and forth through it, causing it to waver a bit, like a blip in a television screen.

"They couldn't have gotten it up here, though. I saw this a few minutes before I chased Nicholas from the grave."

"I'm sure they have more than one," Naomi pointed out. "I don't know what half of this stuff does, but I'm seeing several pieces of matching equipment."

"I'd like to ask Martin how the hell he knew I was coming tonight," I said.

"He probably didn't. I think they were setting up for a possible weekend attack and you showed up so they went with it," Coop surmised.

Michael pointed to the hundreds of cables that went

up into a corner and disappeared. He said they were probably buried down the hill to the grave. If we dug, we'd most likely find some of this equipment at several locations in the cemetery. He walked over to a wall of video monitors and began flipping switches. We all sucked in our breaths as one by one the monitors came to life, showing different angles of the cemetery. We stood and watched one monitor in night vision that showed other crime lab members and uniformed officers searching for more evidence around the pine tree.

"How are they getting their power?" I wondered softly, my eyes still glued to the videos.

"I'm sure they illegally tapped into the farm down the road and drew it from them. It's not that hard, kind of like when people steal cable TV from their neighbors," Coop answered.

I noticed a silver folding chair sitting in front of the monitors. Martin Drake must have sat here and ran the equipment, watching, while Nicholas was at the grave. I picked up a black plastic piece about a foot long with wires running into it. It reminded me of a power surge outlet protector, but this had buttons that were lit up in red on top.

"I'll bet that runs everything with the touch of a button." Michael guessed. "Martin sat here and didn't have to so much as break a sweat."

He reached over and turned up the volume on the main monitor we were watching and pushed one of the buttons on the black operating bar. The sound of the crying baby blared through the cemetery, causing all the officers and lab personnel to visually jump. We couldn't help laughing. Michael turned it off.

"What about my car the day Naomi and I were here? I wonder how they did that." I ran my finger along a long, silver object that resembled a microphone.

"A lot of that we're going to have to ask Martin about," Naomi answered. "If he'll talk, that is." She paused and grimaced. "What's that door?"

I turned to see what she was talking about. We had missed it because it was on the same wall as the steps we'd come down: An old, brown, wooden door right next to the steps.

"Bob?" I called up the stairs. "Did you see this door down here?"

He appeared at the top. "Yup, nothing in it but an old dress and chest with old shit in it. You're free to dig around. It's already been processed."

I looked over at Coop, who merely shrugged and went back to playing with the equipment. I opened the door to the small closet. There was enough light in the cellar to illuminate its entire contents. When I saw the old white dress draped across the wooden red chest, I silently cursed Bob. I walked back over to the steps and called him down. He looked confused until I pointed to the dress.

"Remember how you *forgot* to tell me a piece of material was found in Kari Sutter's hand? I think you may want to process the dress, since I'm sure the material came from it." I sounded annoyed.

Bob's face turned red as he darted up the stairs to grab a plastic evidence bag. He was quiet as he gently put the dress in the bag and carried it back up. I looked at Naomi and shook my head.

I kneeled down in front of the chest and opened it. It was empty, except for an old, faded piece of blue material, a tarnished silver baby spoon, and two yellowed pieces of paper in large, glass picture frames. I took both out and saw they were letters. I yelped out loud when I saw who had written them.

"This is it!"

"What?" Naomi kneeled next to me, looking puzzled.

"These letters were written by Mary Jane and Madeline Hendrickson. Look at the dates, the one written by Mary Jane is dated a week before she died, and Madeline's was written two months after." I pointed to the tops of each frame.

"They look like the Declaration of Independence, for crying out loud. Can we actually read these?" She held one, extending her arm straight out and bringing it back in as if looking though a magnifying glass.

"I sure as hell am going to try." I stood and walked back into the cellar, taking a seat in Martin's director's chair.

It was going to be difficult. The writing was antiquated, and the paper was old. I had Mary Jane's letter to her sister, Sophia Secrist, dated February 23, 1898. I couldn't help wondering why she had written her a letter when they lived so close to each other.

The beginning of the letter talked about nothing in particular. One part that caught my attention was a reference to her child, named Ezra, at the beginning. She said he had begun to crawl.

It was the middle and the end of the letter that caught my attention. I read it out loud to Naomi.

"... I came upon that wretched woman's brother yest'day. He smiled at me as I carried Ezra through the market place. As I've so said, many a time befor, evil surrounds that woman, and now her brother. Her presence is one with Satan himself. Is believing in my gift a sacrifice for others? Being a kindly neighbor I only delivered the remedy for the poison ivy she came upon in the woods, the plant that caused her legs to swell and itch. The brother carries his own evil now, evil that shows through his eyes into my

*own. I fear for myself and my children as the gift tells
me they shall come soon. I have written our cousin
Seth and shall be sending Ezra and Madeline along
in ahead weeks so they may remain safe and in
God's hands. I my self shall remain to tend to the
crops and such, befor traveling to them later. I will
write to you and Samuel once I've arrived.*

    Your sister,
    Mary Jane"

"That's kind of creepy," Naomi commented. "Who's
coming for her?"

"I don't know, but maybe Madeline can tell us."

I began to read Madeline's letter out loud, but stopped
as soon as I realized its contents. Then I began again, in
silence. Madeline's letter was also to Sophia, her aunt,
dated June 12, 1898.

    Dearest Sophia,

    *I write to you with a heavy heart, knowing I shall
join you and Samuel soon. It comforts my soul more
to pen you my memory than to tell you in person.
The time is now for the secret to be told.*

    *Mother came to me last night in my slumber and
told me its time. She told me of the gift blessed to us
from our Lord and how it caused her blasphemous
demise. You have stayed patient, wanting to know
about that night, and now you shall. The grief you
shall feel will overwhelm your soul, as it has done
mine until Mother came to me.*

    *That night was bitter cold. Mother and Ezra had
just arrived in the carriage after their trip to Doctor
Nolling's when they came. And with those fore men
came evil, led by the devil. They carried their lanterns
bright as they tore Mother and Ezra from the carriage.*

I watched from the study window. Mr. Randall Rose declared death to Mother and Ezra, for causing the woman to murder her family one year past. Mother tried to tell him it was only remedy for the poison ivy, but he wouldn't listen. He damned her for giving the almight Ceely Rose the arsenic she used to murder her family. Mr. Randall Rose branded Mother a witch. He said only witches had arsenic, and Mother had given it to Ceely. The others, Albert Tucker, Gerald Moffet, and James Mengert, stood silently with the evil spreading through their smiles. I was scared, scared like I've never been befor.

Randall Rose threw Mother to the ground and dragged her by her hair to the large pine that stands in front of our home. He made her neel down and watched as the others threw Ezra back and forth befor using one of the old gravestones to murder him by crushing his small head with it. Oh how Mother screamed. It was as if my soul had been ripped out of my body as I watched them beat her and force their manhood on her, making her have relations with each one of them. I remember throwing up on my dress as this took place. Mother kept screaming as they hung the rope off a large branch. The men stood befor her and declared her again a witch. Mother grew silent and I thought her to be dead. As I heard the words she spoke then, I felt a chill in the room where I stood watching. She spoke in Latin, but I understood. She said:

"The evil bestowed upon you shall forever be upon this ground. Five sunsets shall separate each one of you from your master, Satan, and your deaths shall include pain and suffering felt from the gates in Heaven to the depths of Hell. I bestow suf-

fering upon your relations from the winter, summer, to the spring, and fall.

I curse each one of you, I curse you all."

The fear on the men's faces will forever be burned into my mind. Randall Rose told Mother to Dye Witch! befor he pulled on the rope which embraced her neck. Mother dyed swiftly. As Mother hanged lifeless from the tree, James Mengert poured kerocene on Mother's body. Randall tried to set her on fire, but only her hands began to burn. I felt as if I might faint into blackness when I saw Randall Rose look up to the window where I stood.

It was too late to hide. Befor I could escape his wrath he had me by my own hair, dragging me to the woods behind the house. He forced relations on me several times befor he stopped. I felt he was going to kill me like Mother, but Gerald Moffett called out to him. He said they needed to bury Mother and Ezra's body's befor visitors came calling. When Randall forgot about me, I ran as fast as I could to your house. I hadn't known you and Samuel were traveling so I hid in the barn, smelling the smoke from the fire they had set that burned our house down. I waited until I no longer heard their voices. I couldn't tell you when you came home, it was too difficult. You, like the newspaper, believed me that Mother had taken ill. They never even questioned the whereabouts of dear Ezra. Mother kept saying she needed to register his birth since he was born at home with the midwife but never did.

Now, as the evil seed planted in my womb by Randall Rose grows each day, I feel you must know the truth. Mother told me of the gift last night. I am fearful of it, althou I know I shouldn't be. The men all died, each five days apart as Mother promised. She said the families of the men shall be forever tormented. I told her of the threats told to us by the families of the men, and the promises of money. They know not of my baby. The secret of their sons shall be kept forever, as not to embarrass them all. She told me the suffering will go on as long as the secret remains. I know she doesn't understand Aunt Sophia, our need for money; she is in another place.

Alas, as I write to you from cousin Mary's I pray to our Lord you won't suffer over this much. I shall see you soon but we shall never talk of this again. The men buried Mother and Ezra benethe the tree from which she hung. I shall never go there.

Your niece,
Madeline Hendrickson

Tears welled up in my eyes and I realized I was looking at the first, and maybe only, record of little Ezra's death. I felt such an overwhelming sense of grief I couldn't even speak.

"What does it say?" Naomi snapped. Seeing my tears, she quieted down. "What is it, CeeCee?"

I saw Michael, also looking concerned. He walked over to me with Coop at his side. I didn't even know where to begin.

I wiped at my eyes. "It all makes perfect sense now." I took a deep breath. "To sum it up, Mary Jane Hendrickson and her baby were brutally murdered by Randall Rose, Albert Tucker, Gerald Moffett and James Mengert. Randall believed that Mary Jane was a witch and gave Ceely Rose the poison she used to murder her family. In actuality, she only gave her an herbal remedy to treat poison ivy." I asked Naomi if she had a tissue. She produced one from her pants pocket and I wiped my nose with it. "This woman was forced to watch her baby being beat to death with a tombstone. After they killed her baby, they beat her and repeatedly raped her before hanging her and setting her on fire. And if that wasn't enough, Randall took Madeline, who had to just sit and watch her mother and brother get murdered, and raped her, getting her pregnant in the process."

"So the story is true!" Coop was amazed. "Why the secret?"

"The families of the men didn't want to be disgraced. Mary Jane allegedly cursed them and they died just like she promised. I don't know what to think of that, so maybe they were scared and ashamed. They threatened Madeline and bribed her with money to keep quiet about the whole thing." I thought back to earlier in the evening. "I would guess that Luke Mengert had a similar letter implicating James Mengert. I'll bet that was what he burned. Obviously, these people take this curse seriously."

"No offense, but wouldn't you?" Naomi asked. "I mean, the men did die five days apart, as promised. That'd be enough to scare me."

"That I don't have an explanation for. They died in legitimate accidents is all I can say and maybe they caused their own fate. If you're walking along a ledge after someone told you for a fact you would fall, you just might fall. I'm amazed. These men were brutal killers and the goddamn township names roads after their families. Here we stand, on Tucker Road."

"Madeline Hendrickson and Randall Rose were Martin Drake's grandmother and grandfather," Michael said. "And Melissa Drake died right on top of her great-great-grandmother. That's an explanation I would love to hear." He paused. "You realize that all the Hendrickson women died in March, don't you? Not to mention the whole M thing . . . Mary Jane, Madeline, Maryanne, Melissa." He emphasized the M in each name. "The piece of dress found in Kari Sutter's hand is symbolic of all their deaths."

"Forever the profiler, aren't you, sweetheart?" I winked at him.

"What about the dog?" Naomi asked.

"I think that was done to lead us to Daniel and throw us off track. Martin and Nathaniel certainly had faith in law enforcement. They assumed we'd go back and look into Melissa's murder." I had a thought. "Now that I think about it, I think they did that so we would *lead* them to Daniel and Meghan." I stood up from the chair. "They killed Daniel and left the evidence at the camper. They would've killed Meghan, but I beat them to it."

Bob interrupted me when he called down, "Just to let you know, we found the fire poker and blowtorch in the house with the dog skin!"

"Lovely," I grumbled. "Let's get out of here. I want to get to the station and take a crack at Martin."

Michael and Coop had to help me down the hill to my car, which Michael drove. When we quietly drove out of the tunnel of trees and onto the asphalt, I whispered something.

"What'd you say, hon?" Michael asked.

"I said I will never come back here again. All I can think about is how that poor woman and her children suffered," I said softly.

Michael didn't respond; he merely drove me to the department in silence.

Chapter Thirty-eight

Martin Drake had a mild concussion and a good gash on his head, but he didn't require any stitches. The corrections officers had him waiting for me when I arrived in the interrogation room. After I got all the legalities out of the way, I was a little surprised when Martin said he wanted to confess everything. I leaned back in my chair, crossed my arms and quietly waited until he began. His eyes began to fill with tears, and he stared down at the table as he spoke.

"You have no idea what it's like, Sergeant, to lose a child. Melissa was my baby girl and what they did to her . . ." He stopped and took a deep, breath. "That's not important now. What's important is it'll all stop and hopefully she can rest."

"Who? Melissa?" I asked.

"Mary Jane," he said confidently. "You see, Sergeant, for a century my family's been tormented over her murder. Those men were savages, and they killed my great-grandmother and uncle. For years, I've had to stand by and watch as her name was run through the mud with witch this, and witch that, while Ceely Rose was an icon. It wasn't right." He coughed lightly. "And then they took my Melissa. That was when I knew Mary Jane was giving me a sign that it wouldn't stop until I did something."

"But you waited twenty years, Martin? Why?"

"Believe it or not, I tried to make it go away, but when I came up here about a year and a half ago to visit my father, I saw nothing had changed. I saw the bottles and the broken tombstones. I knew it was time. This had gone on long enough, and these kids needed a lesson. Nicholas and I moved up here with my father a year ago and began to plan. He's an MIT grad, you know, Nicholas is." He looked up, remembering Nicholas, and put his head back down. "Nicholas did the most. He was a genius with special effects and stuff like that. It was so easy." He drifted off into space.

"Martin." I tapped my pen, snapping him out of his trance. "Did Melissa ever know about your family?"

"Of course not!" he barked. "Do you think she would've gone down there if she did? My own wife didn't even know. Our family history was hidden in shame and secrecy, for something that we didn't even do." He looked at me and gave a small smirk. "By the way, did you like your flowers, Sergeant?"

"I'm sorry?"

"The roses I sent you. Did you like them? They were my way of saying thank you for saving me the headache of having to take care of that little bitch Meghan Dearth."

"I can't say I'm that flattered, Martin. One question I have is why didn't you kill Danielle Horton?"

"She was too fat." He laughed. "Once we knocked her out, we were having too hard of a time setting everything up. Plus, there were too many of her friends around, so we decided just to send a message."

"And the dog skin? I'm assuming you did that so I would lead you to Daniel, right?"

"Very good, Sergeant. I'm sorry about your swim in the lake a while back, but Nicholas thought you were going to see him. I only told him to follow you and see what you were up to." He laughed again. "But it was his idea to chase you down the road that night. He thought if we scared you enough, you'd back off the history lesson . . . and us. Apparently, we underestimated you."

"Apparently."

I thought back to the night I was pushed into the lake, and when I was followed after being at the grave. Both Martin and Nicholas had well passed the brink of insanity long ago. Looking into Martin's eyes told me that much. I remembered the interview I'd had with Gary Fenner.

"Martin, there was a fatal car accident about fifteen years ago, a group of boys after they left the grave. Did you have anything to do with that?"

He looked confused and shook his head. I remembered Gary's description of the woman in white he'd seen. It differed from everyone else's. In addition, Gary claimed she was holding a baby.

"Martin, do you know what color Mary Jane's hair was?"

"I don't know. Any pictures of her were destroyed. I know my grandmother's and mother's hair was red."

I couldn't help getting a chill. I would chalk that incident up to the short list of the unexplainable. Things I refused to think about, questions that had no answers.

"Martin, Madeline and Mary Jane both refer to '*the gift*' in their letters. What was it?"

Martin shut his eyes. "The gift, Sergeant, is not something you or anyone else could possibly understand. It was very powerful."

"Is it supposed to be like ESP or make them a clairvoyant? Something like that?" I thought he was being slightly dramatic.

"More powerful than those put together. As you're

very aware, Sergeant, it was the gift that killed those men five days apart. What on this earth or in any human being is capable of that?"

"I'll tell you what's capable of that, it's called drowning, choking and farm accidents to name a few," I said sarcastically.

He laughed and stared at me with pure evil in his eyes. "You know with your intelligence what is mythical and what's coincidence. Their deaths were no coincidence, Sergeant. She told them they would die five days apart, and they did!"

"Human beings are notorious for subconsciously determining their own fate. These men, each hearing a curse placed upon them ensuring their deaths within five days of each other, became overly cautious, nervous and absentminded. After the death of one, the others became basket cases on the fifth day. What would be a normal walk along the edge of the pond became an intense challenge not to fall. Focusing all energies on the edge, he fell in and drowned, same with the others. It *was* coincidence, Martin, and if you would've seen that, maybe you wouldn't have been driven to kill."

He smiled. "If only you knew how wrong you really are. You read the letters; you read how Mary Jane visited Madeline two months *after* her murder. It was the gift that made it possible."

I slammed my hands on the table. "Listen to yourself, Martin!" I knew it was pointless to reason with someone who had reached the level of insanity that he had, but I couldn't help it. "Madeline had just watched her baby brother get tossed back and forth like a football before getting his head caved in by a tombstone. After that, she watched her mother get beaten, raped, hung and set on fire before being dragged to the woods and raped, herself. To top that off, the sick bastard got her pregnant.

Now, if you think that any normal sixteen-year-old girl, whether now or back in 1898, wouldn't be half out of her mind or, most likely, totally and completely delusional, you are sadly mistaken! Martin, Madeline probably went over the edge the night that happened. Understandably, but she was crazy just the same! Why can't you see that?"

He remained smiling. "If thinking that makes you feel better, Sergeant, so be it."

"A few more questions . . . Whose white dress is on the chest in the closet?"

"It was Mary Jane's favorite dress. My grandmother kept it."

"How did you guys get my car to turn on by itself the day Captain Cooper and I were in the cemetery?"

"Nicholas did that, don't ask me how. But I have to tell you, Sergeant, how we laughed at you two, your faces when that car blared on!"

"I can't say I'm amused."

I talked to Martin for more than an hour before finally getting his full confession on tape. His voice was filled with such intensity, I felt myself sympathizing with him, an emotion I wasn't accustomed to when it came to murderers. I formally charged Martin with the murder of Kari Sutter, and I also charged him with attempted murder in the attack on Danielle Horton.

By the time we were finished and I called for the corrections officers to take him away, I was exhausted. My back and legs were throbbing, despite the four aspirin I had taken earlier.

Michael was in my office, waiting to take me home. After several calls from the sheriff and the chief offering their congratulations on the arrest, I welcomed the thought of sleep. Michael had to help me up to our bedroom and out of my clothes. I lay on our bed drifting in and out of sleep while he prepared several ice packs to place under my back and legs. My pain replaced by fatigue, I did my best to stay awake until Michael returned. Reaching out to touch his face was the last thing I remembered before drifting into a deep sleep.

I slept in the next morning and didn't make it to work until early afternoon. I had already gotten the okay from Naomi. The only thing I did in my office was check my messages. I had another issue on my mind that I needed to deal with: Walter Morris, also known as Nathaniel Drake. I had to know, and needed to hear from his own mouth, if he had any knowledge of what Martin and Nicholas had been doing, and specifically, did he do anything to stop it. It was almost as if he was waiting for me when I pulled into his driveway. He was sitting in a lawn chair on the front porch.

"I knew you'd come," he said somberly. "After they were here yesterday, I knew it was only a matter of time. What questions do you need answered, Sergeant?"

Walter stared straight ahead, sitting up with both hands clenched on the handle of his cane. He was cold, distant and unfriendly, not the Walter I remembered.

"Did you know? Did you know what they were doing, Walter?" My words were almost inaudible.

"I suspected. Oh, yes, did I suspect . . . but I didn't dare ask. By the time they got here, young lady, they were both already out of their minds with the sickness. Runs in the family, you know. My wife, Maryanne, and her mother were as fruity as they come. Not that you could blame them, considering what they'd been through and all. No matter what, I loved my Maryanne." He leaned forward and set his cane at his feet. "Madeline treated Maryanne like the devil himself. Even when Maryanne was just a little thing, a toddler, Madeline would refer to her as '*the bastard.*' When I met and married Maryanne it was the same thing. I remember the first time I met Madeline. She said, 'I'll pray to our Lord for you, sir. I'll pray that he forgives you for loving a bastard.' That cunt. I know she had been through something awful, but Maryanne never asked for that. Quite frankly, I hope Madeline Hendrickson is burning in hell for what she did to my wife."

"I understand," I said, and had another thought. "Maryanne was dead for a week before she was found. Where were *you*?"

He winced slightly. "Away for three weeks . . . job opportunity came up. Not that we needed the money, but I wanted to get away for a while. We were having some husband and wife problems and I think Maryanne's mental issues were really getting the best of her—I couldn't take it. I'll never forgive myself for that."

"Why the name change, Walter?"

He sighed. "I wanted a fresh start. No one 'round here knew me anyway—I always kept to myself—so when Maryanne died, I moved out here to this farm. The money those families paid them to keep quiet was phenomenal. Maryanne and I never had to work, and I had the money when she died." A tear streamed down his cheek.

"Walter? Is there anything I can get you before I leave?"

"No. It's all over, and that's what's important. Now I can at least have some peace." He held out his hand. "Sergeant, believe it or not, I truly thank you."

I disregarded his hand and leaned over to kiss his cheek. I drove away thinking I might become a weekly visitor. However, that would never happen. The next morning, Walter Morris died. He had found his peace.

That day, saddened by the news of Walter Morris's death, I requested the exhumation of Mary Jane Hendrickson and her son. They had been murdered. Even more than one hundred years later, they were still victims and their bodies needed to be processed. It would take a week or so for the judge to sign the request and get everything together. As I was leaving for the day, Naomi walked into my office with some interesting information.

"You know we've been checking into Martin's and Nicholas's backgrounds, right?" I nodded. "It seems that Nicholas attended Massachusetts Institute of Technology and was a certified genius. As you probably guessed, most of the equipment in the cellar was stolen. Nicholas would give himself fake identities, get jobs in computer software companies or stores where the equipment was sold. He'd work there one day, steal all he needed and vanish without a trace. By the way, Savannah Police filed their own murder charges against Martin, for Daniel Griffin's death. Of course, it's just a formality. Ohio will never hand him over. He'll get the death penalty here."

"If he's proved competent to stand trial," I added.

"True."

I said my good-byes to Naomi for the day and went home to start dinner before Michael arrived. Sitting on our sofa afterward, Michael tried to persuade me to play hooky the next day.

"I can't, Michael. I have entirely too much to do."

He frowned. "What? Everything's done with the case. What more could you possibly have to do?"

I smiled. "I have a lot to do, darling. I have a wedding to plan."

CHAPTER THIRTY-NINE

I didn't keep my word about never returning to Mary Jane's Grave. My intentions were good, but I couldn't resist. I knew it wasn't necessary for me to be at the exhumation of Mary Jane and Ezra, but I had to see.

Usually, a court-ordered exhumation requires the body is placed back in the grave within forty-eight hours. In this case, the judge gave seventy-two hours because Mary Jane and her son would not be going back under the tree. Amazingly, as the story got out to the media, residents throughout the county called for a proper burial of the two and contributed thousands of dollars. A new headstone was purchased, one that would include all residents of the cemetery, including Mary Jane and Ezra. She would be placed next to her sister, Sophia.

Curiosity being as it was, researchers and anthropologists from all over the state converged on the cemetery that morning at seven A.M. None had ever opened a grave more than fifty years old, with the exception of one anthropologist from Kent State University who had helped unearth mummies in Jordan.

Before the dig began, the police chaplain spoke a few words in memory of Mary Jane and her son. Afterward, a backhoe moved in to clear the first foot or so of dirt. Even if Randall and the others hadn't buried Mary Jane and Ezra very deep back then, the bodies surely would've sunk farther into the earth by now. Several of the researchers told everyone not to get their hopes up. Since neither Mary Jane nor her son was buried in a casket, chances were, nothing would be found, not even bone.

The rest of the digging was done with shovels so as not to disturb any remains. Two to three feet down the ground becomes nothing but thick clay, hard to dig through.

It was late afternoon before any remains were retrieved. One of the researchers dug up a piece of yellow bone about the size of a twelve-inch ruler. After that, it was like a gold mine. Numerous teeth were found, which caused everyone to give one another high fives. Teeth retain DNA much longer than other bone, so these could be tested against DNA taken from Martin Drake. The last piece found was a small yellow, cuplike piece of bone, about half the size of someone's palm. Some of the anthropologists speculated it was more than likely part of Ezra's skull, but it was too early to be sure.

The dig was successful. A normal person wouldn't think so; all the remains, small pieces of yellow bone, could easily fit into a shoe box. There wasn't enough to find out how they died, but there was plenty to confirm who they were and give them a proper burial. Since murder has no statute of limitations, the homicide of Mary Jane Hendrickson and Ezra Hendrickson had to be written up as a legitimate, solved murder case with no arrests due to the suspects' deaths. The historical aspect of the case had people fascinated everywhere.

Martin Drake was found incompetent to stand trial. He was remanded to the Ohio State Psychiatric Hospital in Massillon indefinitely. He was now the sole survivor of the Hendrickson family.

More than one hundred people attended the funeral of Mary Jane Hendrickson and Ezra. The flowers, balloons and teddy bears laid at their tombstones were phenomenal. News stations broadcast most of it.

If there was a small problem of people trespassing at the grave before the murder case, the problem now grew into epic proportions. Every weekend hundreds of curious tourists, teenagers and ghost watchers rained down on the cemetery. Half the manpower of the police department was used consistently to run everyone out. The township erected steel gates with padlocks where the dirt road began back to the cemetery. Family members complained it was unlawful because they weren't able to gain access to deceased relatives, and they filed a lawsuit. The court ruled the cemetery must be accessible to the public from dusk till dawn, so the township got creative.

They met with the historical society from Malabar Farm that put on weekend "Ghost Haunts" that led groups to the Ceely Rose house. They were thrilled to add Mary Jane's Grave to the tour so they could tell the real story. In doing this, the township got a percentage of the admission fees. There were designated nights and times for the haunts that the township agreed to allow the tours into the cemetery. This basically satisfied the curiosity of the public. They could now visit both the Ceely Rose house and Mary Jane's Grave lawfully. Of course, there were still the few stragglers who went down to the grave once in a while, but it wasn't any different than before the murders.

Several weeks after the burial of Mary Jane and Ezra, I was served court papers naming me as the primary defendant in a federal lawsuit filed by the family of

Meghan Dearth. They also named the Cincinnati Police Department, Simone Vardona and the Richland Metropolitan Police Department. The case was thrown out in the first pretrial hearing.

A month after the case was officially closed, I was standing in the entrance of the Hidden Hollow Camp lodge. The lodge stood on one of the highest hills in the county and overlooked all the others. The view was breathtaking. Mary Jane's Grave sat at the foot of it, deep in the woods. I was deep in thought when I felt a small hand grab mine. I looked down and saw Sean, looking ever the gentleman in his little tuxedo. He looked terrified.

"Sean, honey, what's wrong?"

"What if I make you fall down when I'm walking with you?" The strain on his face intensified.

I laughed. "Honey, if I fall, it'll be my own doing, not from you." I squeezed his hand as the music began. "Are you ready?"

He nodded. Sean and I made the slow, short walk into the lodge and down the makeshift aisle created for my and Michael's wedding. Since we were having only our family and closest friends attend, the audience was small but intimate.

Michael looked wonderful, and my bridesmaids, Selena and Isabelle, were beautiful. I felt my own tears coming as I saw Michael's watery eyes when we said our vows. A few months ago I thought this day would never come.

I saw Vanessa only once after the ordeal she put us through. Trying to be civil to her was one of the most difficult feats I have ever attempted in my life, so I wasn't. Michael wasn't home, so I had no choice but to take Sean out to her car after one of his weekend visits. Once he was inside we had a very short exchange of words.

She glared. "Getting all ready to marry my husband, are you?"

I smiled at her. "Yes, as a matter of fact I am. Oh, and Vanessa? Don't hold your breath waiting for an invitation in the mail." I couldn't help adding "Bitch."

She started to respond but intelligently decided against it and got into her car fuming instead. Michael decided after that he would make every effort to be there when she arrived to pick up Sean. I agreed that would be best.

When the minister declared us Mr. and Mrs. Michael Hagerman, Michael lifted me off the ground and we kissed. It was a short one; we couldn't help laughing in conjunction with the kids' loud giggles.

Later on in the evening, Michael and I had our first moment alone. He was still beaming.

"I still can't believe you're finally my wife. I swear, as God is my witness, I never, ever thought this would happen."

"Oh ye of little faith. Things always work out. I love you."

We shared the kiss that was interrupted during the ceremony. After Michael went back to our guests, who had just finished dinner, I stepped outside onto the patio to get some fresh air.

I shivered at the brisk, cold air that met my skin, skin that wasn't covered much by my strapless dress. I walked over to a small cement wall that encased the patio to prevent anyone from falling off the edge down the steep hill.

I looked down at the mass of woods below and thought back to Mary Jane Hendrickson. She was buried down there, peacefully now, with her son. Her murder was one of the most humbling cases I have ever worked in my career.

"Sleep well, you two," I whispered into the cold, dark night.

As I turned to walk back inside, a faraway sound caught my attention. I looked back down to the woods and, for a brief moment, I thought I could hear a baby crying in the distance.

I'm sure it was only my imagination.

Turn the page for an advance look at Stacy Dittrich's
next thrilling novel.

CeeCee Gallagher will return in . . .

THE BODY MAFIA

Coming in Spring 2010

PROLOGUE

Zamboanga City, Philippines

"Two hundred fifty thousand U.S. dollars, my friend . . . as promised," the man said as he handed the American a large yellow envelope.

The American slowly opened the envelope, pulled out the crisp, clean bills, and flipped through half of the stack like a deck of playing cards. He was making a conscious effort to keep the bills hidden from view.

An intimidating man—the American, thought the Filipino as he eyed him up and down. Standing well over six feet tall and wearing a shiny black suit that most likely cost him thousands of dollars, the American never spoke during their meetings. After the quarterly packages were delivered to the hospital by those who worked for him, the American would meet the Filipino to collect his money in the crowded marketplace. With no more than a nod and the slightest glimpse of a smile, the American would be on his way. The noise of blaring motor scooters, cars and street merchants would make it difficult to engage in a lengthy conversation even if the Filipino insisted. But today things would be different. Today the American would have to speak. The Filipino's boss wanted a definitive answer from the American and his employers.

Satisfied he had accurately counted the money, the American turned to walk away.

"Sir, one moment, sir," the Filipino began in his broken English.

The American, not accustomed to such a display of words, turned and faced him with a look of unconcealed curiosity. Remaining silent, the American's nod signaled the Filipino to continue, his look of curiosity changing to disdain.

The Filipino was nervous. He knew who the man was and where he had come from; he'd heard the stories from his boss. This man, his employers and their colleagues were some of the FBI's most highly touted priorities, but even they couldn't touch them. His mouth dry, the Filipino did his best to swallow before speaking.

"Sir, he want more and he want them quickly. He say he double money if packages come sooner. Here's list." The Filipino held out a small piece of paper and noticed his hand was trembling. "He want answer from you before you get on plane."

The American looked intently at the list before focusing back on the Filipino. The man's eyes narrowed to mere slits before the tiniest hint of a smirk formed at the corners of his mouth. The Filipino, worried the man would see his heart beating through his shirt or the sweat that had formed on his brow, did his best to smile. The man's answer came sooner than expected.

"Tell him . . . we'd be happy to."

CHAPTER ONE

"Are you ready for this one, CeeCee?"

My good friend and fellow detective Jeff Cooper stuck his head into the doorway of my office. Coop wore his trademark grin, and his blue eyes were sparkling. Married to the boss, Captain Naomi Cooper, Coop was our division comedian. We were all detectives in the major crimes division of the Richland Metropolitan Police Department in Mansfield, Ohio. I, Sergeant CeeCee Gallagher, was working diligently on a rape case when Coop interrupted.

"If it's the one about the retarded guy in the pool, you already told it to me yesterday," I said.

"No, it's not a joke." He walked into my office and sat down in one of the chairs facing my desk.

"Spit it out. I'm busy on the Taylor rape case."

"You might as well put it aside. You and I are headed down to Bunker Hill Road. A lady was driving south toward State Route ninety-seven, and a buzzard dropped a hand on her car."

I stopped shuffling papers and looked at him. "A what?"

"A hand."

I quickly caught on. "Coop, I don't have time for this."

"I told you, CeeCee, it's not a joke. The lady was driving and said she saw a couple of buzzards on the road chewing on something. She thought maybe it was a dead possum. When she got close enough, it scared the birds off the road, and one of them kept its 'chew toy' in its little claws when it flew up. Or are they called talons? Apparently, the damn thing couldn't hold it very well, because he dropped it right on this woman's windshield and, yes, it was a human hand. Needless to say, she freaked out and wound up smashing into a tree."

"Is she okay?" I asked, knowing I'd have done the same thing.

"Yup, physically, but you can imagine how you'd feel if you just left a shitty day at work and then had a hand dropped on your car."

"Since you haven't mentioned it, I'm assuming the mystery of where the hand came from is still going on?" I couldn't imagine a living person who recently had their hand cut off would leave it lying around for the damn buzzards.

"The uniforms are walking the woods right now looking for either a body or other parts. We've already called the hospitals to see if someone came in missing a lefty, maybe from an industrial accident or a car mechanic, who knows? But none of them have." He ran his fingers through his thick dark hair.

The "uniforms" Coop referred to were the uniformed patrolmen who drove marked cruisers and worked out on the road. In the southern part of Richland County, the woods around the area where this occurred were very dense. I was sure there had to be at least fifteen to twenty uniforms down there. I started shoving files into my briefcase while Coop waited impatiently, tapping a pen on my desk.

"You should ask your dad about the time someone found an entire arm in the middle of the road. I guess some motorcycle guy was drunk off his ass and wrecked. Tore his arm clean off. He got back on the bike and drove away like that."

"I don't need to ask. Uncle Max probably took a picture of it, and I've *probably* seen it already." I grabbed my keys, ready to leave.

My father, Mitch Gallagher, and his brothers Max and Mike were old-timers with the department—all lieutenants. Each supervised a different shift of road patrol; my father was in charge of the night shift. I wasn't joking about the picture. My uncles, with their morbid sense of humor, had albums full of homicide pictures and body parts that they passed around to my cousins and me during family functions. Needless to say, growing up surrounded by cops made for a less than normal childhood. My father's other brother, Matt, was shot on duty in the late 1970s and had to retire early. He lives in North Carolina.

"Yeah, I'm sure you have. God knows I've seen Max's album plenty. Don't remember an arm in the road, though. Of course, he probably has ten to fifteen different albums of that shit."

I laughed and shook my head as I walked out of my office behind Coop, heading to his car. After I had gotten into the passenger seat, I looked at my watch.

"Damn," I muttered.

"What?" Coop started the car and began pulling out of the parking lot.

"I need to call Michael and tell him I'm going to be late." I pulled my cell phone out of my briefcase.

My husband, Michael Hagerman, was a supervising agent with the FBI in Cleveland. We didn't have any children together, but my two daughters from my previous marriage, six-year-old Isabelle and thirteen-year-old

Selina, would be getting home from school soon. Michael needed to be there to get them off the bus. My ex-husband, Eric, and I share custody of the girls.

"I'm still up here in Cleveland, Cee. There's no way I'll get home in time."

"All right, I guess I'll have to call Eric and see if he can do it. How come you're still up there?"

"I'm up to my ass in this case I've been working. I don't know when I'll be home." He sighed into the phone. "I wouldn't wait up if I were you."

I imagined Michael was rubbing his temple with his free hand, which he sometimes did when he was stressed. The thought of not seeing him that night upset me. I loved him more than I could ever explain, and even regular workdays seemed too long until we saw each other. I imagined his handsome face, which put most famous actors to shame. His thick brown hair, bright green eyes, and dark complexion made even the most masculine of men take a second look. Not to mention his tall, muscular body. I, myself, was no slouch. I modeled in New York right out of high school and still maintained my tall athletic body and long blonde hair. My large chest and green eyes still turned quite a few heads, but I had just as much insecurity as anybody else. To be with a man like Michael upped my daily self-maintenance to an entirely new level. He says I'm nuts, and I say, "Not all of us were born perfect, buddy."

After I finished talking to Michael, I called Eric's house and spoke to his live-in girlfriend, Jordan, who is also a uniformed officer with the department. It was her day off, so she had no problem picking up the girls and keeping them at her house until I got home. Crisis solved.

"What's Michael working on?" Coop asked as he drove toward Bunker Hill Road.

"I haven't a clue. Normally, he talks about his cases,

but not this one. It's some secret-squirrel, hush-hush investigation. If he doesn't discuss it, I don't bother to ask."

"Oh."

It was another twenty minutes before we pulled into the scene of the crashed car and cut-off hand. By then, most everyone had finished with their duties and was getting ready to leave. I saw our crime laboratory van parked by the wrecked car and thought that would be as good a place to start as any. Bob English, one of the laboratory technicians, was loading evidence bags into the back.

"Whatcha got for me, Bob?" I peered inside the van.

"Hey, CeeCee! Not a lot, but what I do have is freakin' weird. Here, look at this." He pulled out a plastic box and opened the blue lid, exposing the hand.

"Oh my God!" I turned my head away and, for entertainment purposes, made a loud gagging sound.

The hand looked like a Halloween prop—except for the smell. Most of it had been chewed away by the buzzards and probably other animals. Some flesh was still attached, but the protruding metacarpals were the most evident. It was large enough that I took a wild guess and assumed the hand was from a male. The pinky finger was the only digit in decent shape.

"Are you going to be able to print the pinky, Bob?" I held the box up and looked underneath to see if I could see through the plastic.

"I should be able to."

"If you get anything back on it, let me know ASAP. Where's the woman who was driving the car?"

"A uniformed sergeant took her home. She was upset as hell, no surprise."

"I needed to talk to her." I was starting to get angry.

"Relax, CeeCee," Coop interrupted. "I talked to her on

the phone, which is how I knew what happened. I told her when she settles down we'll be over to talk to her more extensively."

"How do we know she isn't some whack job who cut off her husband's hand and drove around with it? Maybe he's in pieces somewhere else."

"We don't, and the uniforms found nothing, but if you want to start walking the woods looking for her husband's severed penis, be my guest," he joked.

"I do believe I'll pass on that offer."

Once Coop and I got all the necessary information and took photographs of our own, there was little else for us to do until the fingerprint came back from the lab. Or someone showed up wanting his hand back.

We got the results of the fingerprints back the next day. The pinky print matched forty-two-year-old Daniel Huber, address unknown. When Coop and I tracked down family members, it was learned that none of them had spoken to Daniel in years. Daniel battled a drug addiction that included stealing from his parents. The family finally had given up on him and he became homeless. And now, handless.

It was while Coop and I were sitting in his office pondering our next course of action that our captain, Naomi Cooper, came in. A beautiful woman by most standards, Naomi had transformed her severe business-woman look over the years. Now, with her dark-blonde hair falling loosely to her shoulders and exchanging dark suits for the khaki pants and light blue blouse that she wore, Coop's eyes lit up.

"Hey, sweetheart, come over here and give daddy some sugar." Coop puckered his lips.

Naomi blushed and smiled. "Later—at home—knucklehead."

"Thank you, Naomi," I said. "If I had to look at his lips for one more second, I believe I might have fainted."

She giggled. "Actually, I just popped in to see what the deal was on the hand. If it amounts to anything, I'll assign your open cases to the other detectives."

I explained to Naomi where we were with the case. She agreed that unless we found the rest of Daniel Huber, there wasn't much more we could do.

It was two o'clock in the morning two days later when Coop called. Michael was still awake, working in his home office, and answered the phone. It took more than several shakes from him to rouse me from the coma I was in. I was only half awake when he handed me the phone.

"Yeah, it's Gallagher," I whispered, my voice hoarse and scratchy.

"CeeCee, it's Coop. Sorry to call so late, but we found the rest of Daniel Huber."

"I'm assuming, since you're calling me this late, that he is no longer among the living?"

"You assume right. There's another piece of him missing, too."

"His other hand?" I looked over at the alarm clock on my nightstand.

"Nope . . . we think it's his liver."

I sat straight up, now wide-awake. "His liver!"

"Right. Just meet me behind the E&B Market on Fourth Street. That's where he was found, about half an hour ago, by the garbagemen. I'll fill you in on the details when you get there."

He hung up. I got up and dressed, while Michael sat on the bed and watched silently. It was unusual for him not to ask me a million questions when I got called out like this.

"You're awfully quiet," I said. "They found the rest of the guy who lost his hand." I had given him details of the case earlier. "It looks like he also had his liver removed. Can you believe that?"

"I heard." He stared at the floor.

"Michael? What's the matter with you?" I stopped putting my shoe on and looked at him.

He looked at me with a halfhearted smile. "Nothing, I'm just tired is all."

"Then instead of staying up all night like you have been, why don't you try to get a good night's sleep?"

"Can't." He stood. "I've got too much work to do."

He walked over and kissed my cheek, then went downstairs to his office. I merely shook my head. Michael was highly intelligent. He was one of those people whose mind never shut down, not for a minute. When he was really involved with something, it was hard to focus his attention elsewhere. I'd learned to live with it, but I had yet to see him as involved as he was now. I didn't bother to say good-bye when I left. He probably wouldn't have heard me anyway.

The E&B Market was on the north side of the city, in the worst neighborhood. "The Hot Zone" or "THZ," we called it. It's where the Detroit and Chicago drug dealers fought their battles. It's also where we wouldn't be able to find one cooperative witness. In that particular part of town, no one dared be caught speaking to the police. In the past it's proved fatal. Coop had beaten me there and was talking to one of the garbagemen when I arrived.

The entire area behind the market had been cordoned off with yellow crime-scene tape, with the county coroner and the crime lab inside the perimeter. The crime lab had erected mobile lights to illuminate the scene. I could see several lab techs hard at work. Some were taking photographs, another was on his hands and knees, and one was carrying evidence bags to the van. One uniformed officer stood just inside the tape. He would be keeping the crime-scene log, documenting every person who went in and out of the area.

Standing outside the tape was a group of uniformed officers, mainly rookies, hoping to get a quick glimpse of blood and gore. There was always a group like this at every homicide scene. We kindly referred to the group as the "pigpen." One rarely saw senior officers in the pigpen. They had seen enough murders and dead bodies in their careers that they began driving in the opposite direction as soon as a homicide call was put out. I felt their pain.

As each year of my career passed, with each homicide, I consistently found myself saying, This is it, this is the last one. After this I'm transferring to the traffic division. But I kept plugging away in major crimes. Once, after I had investigated a serial child murderer, I went so far as to fill out a transfer form and give it to Naomi. She wadded it up right in front of me, threw it in the garbage and told me to get back to work.

Walking into the crime scene, I gave the officer in charge of the log my name and rank. The body was a good twenty-five feet away from the entrance. The closer I got, the more I felt my stomach flip. I don't care how many homicides a cop has gone to; if he's human, he'll always react.

Daniel Huber was lying on his back, his face looking directly up at the sky, his eyes were open, and he was completely naked. What drew my attention was the part of his body that was opened up—his right side. Of course, there was also the stump at the end of his left arm where his hand used to be. Whoever filleted him almost cut him in half. What I noticed immediately was the lack of blood. Not a drop. A cut like his would have bled out a sizeable amount, but the ground was dry. I waited until Coop was finished talking to the garbage-man before I waved him over.

"Certainly not the prettiest I've seen." I nodded at the body. "Explain to me how, out of that mess, you could tell his liver was missing."

"One of the first uniforms on the scene completed a year of nursing school before she decided to go to the police academy. Carla Reynolds. Have you heard of her?"

I shook my head.

"Anyway, she told me her opinion when they called, and the coroner confirmed it. He doesn't know if anything else is missing, but he said definitely the liver."

"Witnesses?" I looked around at citizens who had gathered in the alley outside the tape.

"Please. Here in THZ? You know better than that. I've got uniforms knocking on doors trying to get statements, but the majority of people won't even open the door." The lines in his face deepened. "Basically, the garbage truck pulled up behind the building, and there was the body. They didn't pass anyone or see any cars. This is going to be one of those 'most difficult' cases, I think."

"I think you're right, Coop."

The next several hours were spent knocking on doors, taking statements, talking to the officers who were first on the scene—including Carla Reynolds—and taking photographs for our own file. Once the autopsy was performed on Daniel Huber, we would know more. Unfortunately, that would take several days, if not a week. The crime lab didn't recover much, cigarette butts next to the body that could've come from anyone and several of the full garbage bags to name the most important.

Daniel Huber, according to the coroner, had been

dead for at least four days. An important bit of information the coroner told me was that whoever removed the liver had pretty decent medical experience. They had to, or they'd risk damaging the organ. The downside is that we were dealing with a secondary crime scene, merely a "body dump." The site of the actual murder was still unknown, hence the lack of blood.

Once finished at the crime scene, I went home and slept for a couple of hours. Michael was already gone, and the girls stayed at Eric's, since they were supposed to go there today anyway. I had a slight theory about Daniel Huber's murder when I got to the office the next morning, and I relayed it to Coop.

"Do you think it's possible that someone has a family member dying and is desperate for an organ donor? So desperate that he or she would take one from a homeless person?"

"I guess it's possible," Coop said. "But that doesn't explain the hand. It's not like a left hand is a hot commodity on the donor list."

"I know, but I think we should still try to obtain a list of local people on the waiting list for organs. There can't be *that* many, and we'll have to check out their family members. The coroner said the killer absolutely had to have medical experience. This would narrow down the list considerably."

"You could be right." He thought for a moment. "How 'bout this? You type up all the statements and get the file in order, and I'll start making phone calls to get a hold of the list?"

"Works for me." I knew Coop hated paperwork.

It took me two hours to get the file in order. I went home afterward, deciding I had done enough for the day. Not to mention, I missed Michael horribly. As luck would have it, he was home. Predictably, he was in his office working his "mystery case." I stood in the doorway for several minutes before he even noticed I was there. He looked up from his file with sheer surprise.

"Oh! Hi, honey." He got up from his desk and started my way. "I'm sorry, I didn't even know you were there." He kissed my cheek.

"I can see that." I gave him a tight squeeze. "Still working the secret case, are you?"

"Yeah. Cee, honey, I know I've been distracted, and I'm sorry. Hopefully, this will all be over soon."

"I hope so, too. Why don't you join me for a glass of wine while I watch the news? I'll make dinner in a little bit. You could use the break. Please?" I stuck out my bottom lip like a small child.

He grinned broadly. "Okay, you suckered me into it, even though you know how much I hate the news."

Michael brought in two glasses of wine just as I was getting comfortable on the couch, and turned on the television. The newscaster was repeating a news clip that made Michael stop dead in his tracks.

"*Cleveland businessman Niccolo Filaci was brutally murdered in his South Euclid home just over an hour ago. Details are sketchy as police are still on the scene. Co-owner of several construction companies in the area, Mr. Filaci has long been suspected of having ties to the mafia. An anonymous source at the FBI would not confirm or deny the allegations.*"

I looked at Michael and saw his face had gone completely white. He had just set the glasses of wine down on the coffee table when his office phone started ringing loudly. I wanted some answers.

"Michael, you need to tell me what's going on," I demanded, standing up.

"Let me get my phone." He waved me off and headed back toward his office.

I followed him, and stopped, as he closed the door in my face. Pressing my ear against the door, I tried to listen to his conversation to no avail. It was completely muffled. I was starting to worry. His reaction to the newscast answered at least one of my questions. When he finally opened the door, I confirmed what I already knew.

"You're investigating the mafia, aren't you?"

He leaned against the doorframe, crossed his arms and quietly answered, "Yes, I am."

"Please, Michael, tell me what's going on. I saw your face during the broadcast. I'm worried. Who is Niccolo Filaci?"

He reached out and gently stroked a piece of my hair. "I'm sorry, Cee, but I can't."

"What do you mean you can't?" I was floored. "Michael! We've never kept secrets from each other. You *have* to tell me what's going on!"

He took me by my hand and led me to the small loveseat beside the window in his office. After we both sat down, he pulled me to his chest and embraced me.

"Look, I know something like this is difficult for you. God knows you flip out if you're not in on everything, but please trust me, Cee. It's nothing to worry about. When the time is right, I'll talk to you about it."

I was a little angry and pulled away. "What? Don't you trust me? I mean, my God, you act like I'm gonna go post what you tell me on the department bulletin board!"

"That's not it. You just don't understand. Please trust *me*. Have I ever lied to you?"

"No."

"All right, then . . . let's go have that glass of wine."

"It's done."

The large man with thinning gray hair sat behind his impressive cherry desk, leaning back in his chair and folding his hands. The news that his employee just announced was well received. Niccolo had gotten what he deserved. How dare a Filaci try to cut in on his money!

"Did he suffer?" the man behind the desk asked.

"Greatly, sir."

"Did you give him the message?"

"Word for word."

The man behind the desk clapped his hands and let out a loud whoop. He would reward this particular employee with a large bonus. Now that his cash flow was greater than ever, he could afford to. He further suppressed his excitement as his employee took a seat in a chair by the wall. He is certainly an intimidating fellow, the man behind the desk thought. He could only imagine the fear that had run through Niccolo Filaci's body at the last moment—the moment he knew he was going to die.

"Well done, Frank. Well done. Now, on to further business." The man behind the desk sat up straight in his chair. "You said earlier you told the Philippines we were okay with the new order?"

The man nodded.

"Good. Now, what about the agent? He's bringing entirely too much heat."

The man in the chair smiled. "Don't worry. I'm working on it."

GREGG LOOMIS

Author of *The Sinai Secret*

It was a gala evening to celebrate the find of the century—previously unknown Gospels containing startling revelations. But before the parchments could be revealed, shots rang out in the British Museum and the Gospels—along with Lang Reilly's friend—were taken. An ancient and mysterious organization will gladly kill anyone who comes close to the parchments, but Lang can't be intimidated. The more his life is threatened, the more determined he is to find the truth behind...

THE COPTIC SECRET

"Dan Brown fans will find *The Julian Secret* a delight."
—I Love a Mystery

ISBN 13: 978-0-8439-6274-1

COLLEEN THOMPSON

"[Thompson] more than holds her own in territory blazed by Tami Hoag and Tess Gerritsen."

—*Publishers Weekly*

In Deep Water

Ruby Monroe knows she's way out of her depth the minute she lays eyes on Sam McCoy. She's been warned to steer clear of this neighbor, the sexy bad boy with a criminal past. But with her four-year-old daughter missing, her home incinerated and her own life threatened by a tattooed gunman, where else can she turn? Drowning in the flood of emotion unleashed by their mind-blowing encounters, Ruby is horrified to learn an unidentified body has been dredged up, the local sheriff is somehow involved, and Sam hasn't told her all he knows. Has she put her trust in the wrong man and jeopardized her very survival by uncovering the secrets…

BENEATH BONE LAKE

ISBN 13: 978-0-8439-6243-7

ED GORMAN

NEW YORK TIMES BESTSELLING AUTHOR

It started as a burglary. That would have been bad enough. But when the masked intruder forced Dr. Olson at gunpoint to open his safe, the doctor knew he was really in trouble. In the safe were two DVDs, private movies he had made of those girls he had kidnapped... and killed. Suddenly the burglary became blackmail. But blackmailing a serial killer can be a dangerous game. Especially when he's as smart—and good with a scalpel—as Dr. Olson.

THE MIDNIGHT ROOM

"One of our best and most underappreciated thriller writers." —*Booklist*

ISBN 13: 978-0-8439-6108-9

☐ **YES!**

Sign me up for the Leisure Thriller Book Club and send my FREE BOOKS! If I choose to stay in the club, I will pay only $4.25* each month, a savings of $3.74!

NAME: _____

ADDRESS: _____

TELEPHONE: _____

EMAIL: _____

☐ I want to pay by credit card.

☐ **VISA**   ☐ **MasterCard**   ☐ **DISCOVER**

ACCOUNT #: _____

EXPIRATION DATE: _____

SIGNATURE: _____

Mail this page along with $2.00 shipping and handling to:
Leisure Thriller Book Club
PO Box 6640
Wayne, PA 19087
Or fax (must include credit card information) to:
610-995-9274

You can also sign up online at **www.dorchesterpub.com**.
*Plus $2.00 for shipping. Offer open to residents of the U.S. and Canada only.
Canadian residents please call 1-800-481-9191 for pricing information.
If under 18, a parent or guardian must sign. Terms, prices and conditions subject to change. Subscription subject to acceptance. Dorchester Publishing reserves the right to reject any order or cancel any subscription.